FISHY BUSINESS

IN THE SAME SERIES

FISHY BUSINESS

THE FIFTH GUPPY ANTHOLOGY

22 TALES OF MURDER AND MAYHEM BY THE RISING STARS OF MYSTERY!

EDITED BY LINDA M. RODRIGUEZ

WILDSIDE PRESS

CONTENTS

ACKNOWLEDGEMENTS

The stories in Fishy Business were much improved by the sharp eyes and good judgement of editor Linda Rodriguez.

Dark Sister: Poems is Rodriguez's 10th book. *Plotting the Character-Driven Novel*, based on her popular workshop, and *The World Is One Place: Native American Poets Visit the Middle East*, an anthology she co-edited, were published in 2017. *Every Family Doubt*, her fourth mystery featuring Cherokee detective, Skeet Bannion, and *Revising the Character-Driven Novel* will be published in 2019. Her three earlier Skeet novels—*Every Hidden Fear, Every Broken Trust, Every Last Secret*—and earlier books of poetry—*Skin Hunger* and *Heart's Migration*—have received critical recognition and awards, such as St. Martin's Press/Malice Domestic Best First Novel, International Latino Book Award, Latina Book Club Best Book of 2014, Midwest Voices & Visions, Elvira Cordero Cisneros Award, Thorpe Menn Award, and Ragdale and Macondo fellowships. Her short story, "The Good Neighbor," published in *Kansas City Noir*, has been optioned for film.

Rodriguez is past chair of the AWP Indigenous Writer's Caucus, past president of Border Crimes chapter of Sisters in Crime, founding board member of Latino Writers Collective and The Writers Place, and a member of International Thriller Writers, Native Writers Circle of the Americas, Wordcraft Circle of Native American Writers and Storytellers, and Kansas City Cherokee Community. Visit her at lindarodriguezwrites. blogspot.com.

INTRODUCTION

Fishy Business, the fifth Sisters in Crime Guppy Chapter's short story anthology, features twenty-two member-written caper related stories. Each story was required to have one or more crimes perpetrated by the main character(s) in full view of the reader. Selections were made by a non-Guppy three judge panel who reviewed the blindly submitted tales. The anthology's authors range from award winning short story writers to individuals for whom this is their first publication credit.

The Guppy Chapter originally was created in 1995 by several unpublished members of the Sisters in Crime internet chapter who formed a land-mail group to share ideas and support each other's writing attempts. By 1996, they sought national recognition as the Great Unpublished (Guppies). During the next few years, the Guppies were chartered as a SinC chapter, grew its membership to become the largest Sisters in Crime chapter, became wholly internet based, and expanded its supportive efforts to include a list serv, classes, and *First Draft*, an educational newsletter. It also officially changed its name from the Great Unpublished to the Guppy Chapter of Sisters in Crime to reflect that almost half of its members are published.

The over seven hundred and fifty Guppies who are "lured by mystery, hooked on writing!" join me in hoping you enjoy *Fishy Business*.

Debra H. Goldstein
Guppy Chapter President

THE WANNABE

LIDA BUSHLOPER

Isaac loitered in the lobby of the great hotel, mindful of security cameras and hotel staff. His first goal was to be unnoticeable. His second goal was to keep a surreptitious eye on the doors to the huge conference room as the wannabes trickled out from the cattle call taking place inside. The sign on an easel, "Auditions Today—Models, Actresses, Singers," just outside the closed doors was the lure for his personal quarry. He watched the door bang open and shut as young, innocent hopefuls came and went. Every day, dozens of naïve wannabes hitchhiked, bused, drove, or crawled their way to Los Angeles, determined to break into show business.

Many of the young ladies emerging from the room were Isaac's type—young, dewy-faced, blond. But he had other, even more important, criteria. The most important was that she had to be alone—no mothers, no boyfriends, or anybody else to keep her out of trouble, or to comfort her about her inevitably disappointing experience. Then, she had to be upset, and thus vulnerable to his come-on. Isaac knew what they themselves would soon find out, that the so-called "auditions" were mostly an excuse to sell acting lessons, head shots and makeovers. The self-styled agents were shills and the services the most expensive to be had.

Isaac was patient. But it never really took long. Soon enough the perfect candidate stormed out of the conference room and hurried toward the glass exit doors of the hotel. Isaac got there ahead of her and held the door open in counterfeit gallantry. Once out on the sidewalk, away from prying security cameras, he felt a bit safer. He made a pretense of noticing her face and doing a double take.

"Hey, whatever it is can't be that bad. You look pretty upset. Are you okay?"

Grateful for any kind word, the girl, who looked to be about twenty, peered up into Isaac's face with red rimmed eyes.

"It's nothing but a con game in there. They just kept pushing me and pushing me, trying to get me to sign up for a bunch of crap I don't need.

I don't need acting lessons. I was the lead in every high school play. All I need is an agent and I know I can make it. But they insisted I needed 'polish' and bullshit like that."

Isaac wasn't used to such language coming out of the mouths of the girls he selected. He preferred purity and innocence. But he was realistic enough to know that that might be scarce these days. It didn't stop him from playing his part perfectly.

"You're an actress? And you need an agent? Well, that's lucky. *I'm* an agent. I was waiting to meet a client, but he didn't show up." Isaac whipped out his fake business card and handed it to the girl.

"Lester Benjamin. Do you have your résumé? Any head shots?" The girl looked at his card tentatively, as though she wasn't ready to believe her luck could turn so quickly. Shyly, she drew her portfolio out of her tote bag and handed it over to Isaac. He made a show of looking at her pictures and scanning her flimsy credits.

"Well, it's obvious those auditions in there are a scam. If it were legitimate, from what I see, they would have snapped you up in a second." He glanced at her to make sure she was taking the bait. "It's true, you're not quite ready for the big time, but I've been in this business for years, and I know star quality when I see it." Another glance told him she was all but hooked. "Your stage work is exceptional, but you need more experience in front of a camera, and you do need some new head shots..." With satisfaction, he watched her face droop.

"There's no way I can pay for that," she whined. "I've found a waitress job, but my money's almost gone." Isaac gazed at the sidewalk as though deep in thought, then appeared to come to a decision.

"Look, I know I'm taking a risk here. I wouldn't do this for just anyone. But I have a feeling in my gut that you're special and that someday you're going places. If I give you a few pointers, help steer you in the right direction—and, hey, let's be honest—maybe pull a few strings with some of my contacts—well, I think we can get you over this slump." She was getting there. He could see her suspicion and resistance melting. Almost.

"I just told you. I don't have any money to pay an agent right now. I can't believe you're gonna do any of that for free. And if you think for one minute I'm..." He stopped her with an upraised palm.

"Whoa, whoa, I can't believe that you thought that I..." He gave a snort of disgust. "Look, if that's what you think of me, there's no way we can work together."

"No, no," she hurried to back off. "I didn't mean anything. I just don't see what you can possibly get out of this."

"Are you kidding? Listen, part of my job is spotting talent. I think you have the makings of a truly great actress. And once you hit it big, all the other big names will be after me to sign them up, too. Believe me, Lester Benjamin doesn't do any favors. I can assure you, I'm only in this for myself." That selfish sentiment always seemed to reassure them, although Isaac could never quite understand why. She was mollified now, and desperate hopefulness had returned to her face.

"But what do I do? I've been running around to every open casting call I could find. Nobody seems to want me. I'm out of money, and I can't hang on any longer." The tears welled up in her eyes again.

"Look, I've got some photo equipment at my place. I can take some new head shots. You can pay me back when you get your first job."

"But I'm a nobody," she protested. Isaac patted her shoulder.

"Not for long, I assure you. Not for long." And the hook was firmly set. He whipped out his fake engagement calendar. *One of these days*, he thought, *I'm gonna have to get one of those Blackbird things*. But for now, the old-fashioned date book was enough to fool these rubes. None of these idiots seemed to notice how behind the times he was. He pondered the pages, just as if there were important stuff recorded there.

"You know, I had a cancellation tomorrow morning. If it's okay with you, we'd better grab a slot when we still can. I'm pretty booked up the rest of the month." Once again he saw a cloud pass over her face.

"What's wrong?" He kept the annoyance out of his voice.

"Darn. I'm scheduled to work tomorrow morning." She looked downcast, then raised her chin in determination. "But this is more important. I'll call in sick. I wouldn't dare tell them the truth. I might lose my job, or worse, they'd just laugh at me."

"Hey," he said, "you're thinking smarter already. No point in letting those idiots know what you're up to, at least not until you hit the big time. I bet they won't be laughing at you then, right?" She smiled at the thought.

Isaac got her name (Kate Spenser) and phone number. He arranged to pick her up the next day on Hollywood Boulevard, then drove home, happy with the morning's work. Isaac prided himself on being the best at what he did. Yet, he was always amazed at how eager these stupid kids were to believe what he was dishing out. Their yearning made them easy prey, whether for him or for all the sharks who just wanted their money. One small thing niggled at the back of his mind. The girl, though he was certain he had never met her before, seemed vaguely familiar. But he shook it off. All his choices were the same type and therefore bore some resemblance to each other. That must be it.

* * * *

When he cruised by the appointed spot the next morning at 10:00, the girl jumped into the passenger side of his car, clutched her canvas bag against her chest, and slunk down in the seat until her head was below window level. She looked like she was auditioning for Scarlett O'Hara, with her huge picture hat and lace gloves.

"What the heck are you doing?" he asked. He was more amused than alarmed.

"I was scheduled to work, but I called in sick. I don't dare take a chance that anyone might see me. I might get fired. I hope we get to your place in a hurry." Isaac couldn't believe his good luck. She was taking all the precautions for him. That had certainly never happened before.

It wasn't long before they pulled into his one-car, stone-walled garage. The house was on a road that wound up into the Hollywood Hills. The basement, like the garage, had been dug out of the hill itself and was walled with stones. It was underground, surrounded by solid earth, and about as soundproof as you could get. He led her up the outside stairs from the garage into the house, across the living room, into the kitchen at the back. From there, an indoor staircase led down into the basement. She followed him down willingly enough. He crossed the room to a small refrigerator.

"I'll get us some ice and some drinks. What would you like? Soda? Iced tea? Or something stronger?" It was one more move to induce her to let her guard down. He couldn't afford for her to get spooked at this delicate stage. She giggled.

"It's 10:30 in the morning, silly. Iced tea sounds great."

"Don't touch any of the equipment. It's a pretty expensive set-up." Another colossal lie. It was all cheap crap he used just for show. But she wouldn't know the difference.

Besides, she was pawing through the rack of costumes, and looking over the props and stage makeup Isaac had assembled for what he hoped was a more authentic setting. Turning to her with the drinks in his hand, he said, "Well, let's get started. Pick out anything you'd like to wear for the pictures."

"Oh, I brought some of my favorite stuff. I hope that's okay."

"Whatever floats your boat," he said. He saw her flinch at his tone and softened his delivery. "It's just that I have another appointment later and we need to get started." She nodded in assent.

"I'm going to use this little digital camera first, just to get an idea of how you come across." Isaac was no techie, but he had taken pains to learn how to download the digital pictures into a computer and print high quality pictures. "We'll switch to the studio equipment later. Or maybe next time, after we see how this goes." She was perfectly relaxed now, certain he was legitimate and that they were at the start of a real working relationship. She might even be so idiotic as to think secretly that *she* was using *him*. But from now on, what she thought didn't matter. It was almost time. Isaac's groin was already throbbing and tingling. He felt his heart starting to pound in delicious anticipation of what was coming. But he had to keep his emotions in check just a few minutes longer. The whipping post, the chains, the shackles, the other tools to satisfy his appetites were hidden behind the white screen, just behind her. He would take a few actual photos of her posing in front of that screen. It would give him an extra thrill when he relived the experience over and over—until he felt it was safe to do it again.

"Okay, Kate, let's see how you pose." He waited while she dragged a ridiculous pink feather boa out of her tote bag and draped it dramatically around her shoulders. He began snapping flash pictures as she flipped it this way and that way around her neck, face and hips. He always took flash pictures and lots of 'em. He wanted only the best to choose from when he made up his special, private scrapbook later on. He also hoped it would prove a bit disorienting to his subjects.

"Okay, that's enough to start with, now let's…" Before he had a chance to stop her, she darted over and stood behind him.

"How do I look?" she said eagerly, leaning over his shoulder to look into the tiny viewfinder. Caught off guard, he had no choice but to hold the camera up so she could see.

In the next instant, he was fighting for breath, the boa with the hidden garrote wound unbearably tight around his throat. In the few seconds before losing consciousness, instinct caused him to dig furiously at his neck and throat, leaving deep gouges as he struggled to loosen the suffocating wire. His mind, usually so in control, spun wildly with confusion. Then he blacked out. He didn't stay out for long, but when he woke, the utter confusion of his situation was even worse.

He realized he was hog-tied with some thin, brown twine that rubbed his skin raw as he struggled against it. And struggling got him nowhere. The knots just seemed to get even tighter. He tried to call out, but duct tape over his mouth kept his efforts to the level of muffled squeals. Then the girl appeared in front of him, and he became truly afraid. Gone was the pretty young ingénue wannabe. Instead he faced a serious, calm, intelligent woman, whose eyes were filled with cold hate.

"There were a few things I left off my résumé. I grew up on a farm. I'm a junior amateur rodeo champion. I can rope and tie a fighting calf in record time. You, on the other hand, weren't fighting at all." Isaac mumbled something from behind the duct tape.

"I suppose you'd like to know what's going on, hmmm?" she said in a teasing tone. She took a heavy square of paper out of her bag and held it in front of his face. When his eyes focused, he saw himself. The photo was grainy, but it was unmistakably him.

"Recognize yourself? My sister took this with her cell phone. You probably didn't notice. She was so excited, she told me almost minute by minute how her grand plan to break into show business was going. Of course, you used a different name with her. But you weren't that hard to find. She told me in detail how you met. Perhaps you remember my sister?" She whipped out another photo and dangled it in front of his face. His girls may have all been the same type, but he remembered every one distinctly, thanks to his private, secret photo albums. He knew she had been one of his. Now, with the little bit of brain that was still thinking intelligently, Kate's familiarity made sense. Kate (if that was her real name, which he now doubted) saw the tacit admission in his face.

"I'm the one that answered the phone when they called to tell my family about the body they found. You were more careful after that, weren't you? They haven't found any more bodies, but I know there must be more. I wonder if they'll ever find *your* body. It doesn't matter. Nobody knows who or where I am. Just one more face in a crowd. No one will remember seeing us together, not at the hotel, not in your car. Just the way you wanted it, right? Well, me, too. Trace evidence? Even if they find mine, among all the rest that must be down here, who would they trace it to? No, I'm not worried."

His eyes were pleading with her now. He was clearly terrified. He wanted at least to ask her what she planned to do. She gave a little smile. She seemed to be reading his thoughts.

"I know what you did to my sister before you killed her. The autopsy of her body told us everything." She picked up a small folding knife, opened the blade and slowly raised it to his eye. He cringed back in terror.

"Hell," she said, disgusted. "I'm not like you. I don't even have the guts to hurt you a little before I put you out of my misery. I'm just here for my sister. And to make sure you never hurt anyone else ever again." She folded the knife and put it back into her bag.

"Well, now that you know why I'm here, I may as well get on with it." She picked up the boa again and placed it loosely around his neck. He twisted desperately against the bonds that held him. Sweat poured into his eyes, making them burn. His shrill mewling grew more frantic as he felt the boa tighten slowly. Suddenly it loosened and he felt a wild wave of hope.

"Oh, before I finish," she said, "I thought you might like to know you were right about one thing at least, whether you knew it or not." He questioned her with his eyes. She whispered softly into his ear.

"I do have the makings of a truly great actress."

Lida Bushloper writes short mysteries, essays, and poetry. Her work has appeared in *The Lyric*, *The Formalist*, *Light*, *Kings River Life*, *Mysterical-e*, and *Flash Bang Mysteries*. Her essay "My World Champion Sister" is included in the anthology, *In Celebration of Sisters*. Visit her at www.lidabushloper.com.

NOVA, CAPERS, AND A SCHMEAR OF CREAM CHEESE

DEBRA H. GOLDSTEIN

Kenny Kaplan slammed his newspaper, with the advertisement face-up, onto the Sunhaven Retirement Home breakfast table. "It's a schmear. I tell you, a real schmear. There's no way the deli can be selling the whole thing for three dollars and ninety-nine cents."

When Rose extricated the newspaper from his age-spotted hand and held it close to her face while she skimmed the advertisement, Kenny realized his wife must have once again left her readers on the Agatha Christie book on her nightstand.

"It seems like a reasonable price to me."

"Maybe twenty years ago. Today, you can't get a bagel with Nova, onions, capers and a schmear of cream cheese for under six dollars. He's either substituting lox for the Nova he's advertising or faking it on the capers."

"Well, he did just take over running the deli. Maybe it's one of those one day special loss things to get people to try him?" Rose put the paper back on the table and tasted the scrambled eggs on her plate. "If you want to talk about something that's a scam, try your eggs. Powdered again."

Holding on to her rye toast, she pushed her plate toward the middle of the table. "Aren't you going to eat something? You know what Dr. Johnson said about keeping your blood pressure under control and making sure you eat when you take that medicine. I don't think he'd be very happy with you this morning."

Kenny took a bite of his eggs, but his gaze was again focused on the newspaper. "I was in the business for fifty years. You don't use Nova as a loss leader. He'd be losing his shirt. No, something's fishy with this business."

"I don't get it. Lox smox. It's all salmon, so what are you so upset about?"

He reached over and covered her almost translucent hand with his own mitt. "It may all be salmon, but it's not the same. Smoked salmon is the generic term for any salmon cured with cold or hot smoke. In the trade, when we call it lox, we're saying it was cured in a salt-sugar brine or rub while Nova is cured and cold-smoked. Nova costs more. A top of the line deli serves a product made from the salmon belly." Kenny touched his thumb and forefinger together and kissed his fingertips. "That's true perfection. Your customers not only know it, they'll pay for it."

He drummed his fingers on the advertisement. "I wouldn't expect him to use the belly cut, but at this price, there's no way he's using Nova either."

"So?"

"He's advertising Nova. That's simply not right. I'll bet he's cutting corners on his lox and his capers."

"Now you're telling me he's pulling a caper with the capers?"

"Probably."

"How?"

"Capers are the edible flower buds of the *Capparis spinosa*."

Rose leaned across the table. "I love when you talk dirty."

The vein in the middle of Kenny's forehead became more prominent. "Rose, they're the buds on a bush which, while it can be cultivated, doesn't grow everywhere. For capers, the buds are picked before they open into a flower bloom and then they're brined or dried. You've seen them in dishes like chicken piccata or with fish. Because they must be picked by hand, they're expensive."

"Is that another reason you think he's not delivering what he claims in this ad?"

"That's right. I'm betting instead of capers, he's substituting pickled nasturtium seeds."

"Wait a minute. Even I know nasturtiums grow anywhere. They've got a whole area of them in the flower garden out back."

Kenny rolled his eyes. "Well then, if we get bored enough, we probably can figure out a way to make our own fake capers. Right now, I want to figure out what this guy thinks he's pulling over the eyes of my former customers."

"Why don't we go find out?" She pointed to her cold eggs. "Even if he's selling fake deli products, they can't be as bad as this morning's breakfast."

He looked at her and smiled. Rose might think he was smiling at her, but he already was planning how he was going to take the young guy down. He'd spent fifty years of his life in that deli. It bore his name. One of the reasons he'd sold out to the young one was his promise to maintain the integrity behind the name. No siree, Bob! No one was going to cheapen the name of Kaplan's Deli while he was alive.

Kenny reached for his walker. Rose, leaning on her cane, waited for him. "Rose, do you want to drive or should I?"

* * * *

As Rose pulled into the handicapped space, Kenny stared at the front of the deli. The awning and signage still read "Kaplan's Deli." The new owner hadn't removed any of the mouth-watering pictures of corned beef sandwiches, seven-layer cake, or Brown's cream soda posted in the windows. It was Kenny's belief that for customers waiting to get in, these unpriced images got the juices flowing and had a subliminal impact on what they eventually ordered. The only jarring addition to the entrance was the bagel and Nova picture, the same one that was in the ad, pasted on the front door with its $3.99 price tag.

Seeing it reignited Kenny's smoldering anger, but he held himself in check as the new owner welcomed Rose and him to Kaplan's. After seating them, the young man handed each a menu. "I'm sure I don't have to tell you what's on the menu. Nothing's changed."

"Except the prices," Rose said. She smiled demurely at the quickly retreating owner. "What are you going to have?"

"The bagel with Nova, cream cheese, capers, onions and tomato. I should test my theory before I say anything. What about you? Don't you need to read the menu?"

"I know it by heart. I'll have the cheese blintzes with a dab of sour cream."

After they placed their orders with the waitress assigned to their table, Kenny looked around the room. Almost every table was full. He listened to the rude patter of the waiters and waitresses and was glad to hear they still gave better than they got. Being insulted was one of the things that made people come back to neighborhood deli restaurants like Kaplan's and the now-defunct Stage and Carnegie's in the city. It was as much a part of the atmosphere as the pickles on the table and the oversized sandwiches and portions the waiters and waitresses hustled from the kitchen.

He missed this world. Everyone told him it was time to retire and move to Florida, away from the snow and the work necessary to run a successful deli, but until the heart attack, he hadn't given in. Even then, he'd insisted on staying in the neighborhood. Looking at his walker leaning on the wall next to the booth, he knew the question wasn't how he was going to regain control of his business, only how he was going to con the owner into honoring his commitment. "Hand me my walker, please."

Rose did as she was asked. She clicked its arms into place and steadied it while he got his balance.

"I'll be back in a moment." Better not tell her what he was going to do. She'd only get mad. Luckily, the men's room and the door to the kitchen were in the same direction.

He placed the walker in front of him and stepped through it like he'd been taught. His progress was slow, but that was okay. It gave him time to think through his plan for when he reached the kitchen. Obviously, he wasn't going to kill or kidnap the owner, but Kenny had a scheme to get him on the right path. He pushed open the kitchen door and was almost knocked from his feet by a bustling waiter exiting the parallel door.

As fast as the action in the kitchen was, there wasn't room for his walker. He parked it against a wall. Using the counters and appliances, he maneuvered down the line toward the stockroom, exchanging pleasantries with the few staff members from his time who still worked there.

Out of the corner of his eye, he saw another young one, probably the floor manager because he wore a button-down shirt, move to cut him off, but one of the old timers prevented him from reaching Kenny. Kenny couldn't hear what was said, but the manager turned and left the kitchen, ignoring Kenny.

Still, Kenny knew the time before the manager notified the owner of his presence was limited. He hurried into the stockroom and flicked its light on. Quickly, he peered at the shelves until he found the one with condiments. He scanned its contents—pickles, olives, and finally capers. They were the real thing. He looked above and below the jars of capers, but there were no knockoffs anywhere. Hearing someone turn the doorknob, he reached for the light switch, but stopped himself. Whether it was the new guy or a worker, Kenny knew acting like he owned the moment would let him bluster his way through any confrontation and out of the storeroom.

The door didn't open. A voice outside the door was loud, but got softer. Kenny glanced upwards and said a prayer to whomever had interceded in the moment. Shutting off the light, he made his way from the room toward the walk-in refrigerator and freezer. The weight of the door to the refrigerator was heavier than he remembered, but there was no problem remembering where the fish was kept. He was impressed. Everything was as neatly labeled as when he'd been in charge. It was easy to find the lox: Nova and regular sat side by side distinctly identified.

Kenny was confused. Nothing was out of order in the kitchen or storeroom. The only thing to do now was to go back to the table and taste what he was served to see if regular lox was substituted for the Nova. As he reclaimed his walker, he scratched his head. Why would anyone deliberately want to lose money?

He was still pondering this question when he pushed the kitchen door open. Suddenly, there was a shout and the entire room burst into singing "Happy Birthday."

Kenny looked around, bewildered. When the song ended, Rose came up to him and took his arm. "Happy birthday, Kenny." She led him back to their table on which sat a cupcake with a lit candle and a lox platter.

"What?"

"Blow out the candle, Dad," the new owner said. "You haven't been here since the day you turned the keys over to me. Mom and I figured you'd be infuriated when you saw the price in the ad and would feel obligated to put me in my place by hook or by crook."

"But?"

"But, this is still Kaplan's. Considering who taught me, do you think I'd lower your standards?"

Kenny hung his head.

Rose tucked her hand under his chin and raised his face up. "You remember what Agatha Christie said about there being no fool like an old fool in the opening of *The Mysterious Affair at Styles*?"

"Yes, but as I look at the price my younger wife and son concocted to put on this sandwich to get me here, I'm also reminded of Christie's comment in *Murder at the Vicarage*."

"What's that, dear?"

Kenny placed the Nova on his bagel and with a flourish added a schmear of cream cheese, as well as the onions and capers. "She noted how the young think the old are fools, but the old know the young are the fools."

He savored his first bite. For $3.99, he might take an extra sandwich home with him.

Judge Debra H. Goldstein's new Sarah Blair cozy mystery series will be published by Kensington Press in 2019. She also is the author of *Should Have Played Poker: a Carrie Martin and the Mah Jongg Players Mystery* and the 2012 IPPY Award winning *Maze in Blue*. Her short story, "The Night They Burned Ms. Dixie's Place," *Alfred Hitchcock's Mystery Magazine* (May/June 2017) is an Agatha and Anthony Award Short Story Nominee. In addition to being the Sisters in Crime Guppy President, Debra serves on the national Sisters in Crime board and is Vice-President of the Southeast Region of Mystery Writers of America. Visit her at www.debrahgoldstein.com.

WINDFALL

RITA A. POPP

Trina's VW Beetle rattled down the quarter mile of dusty lane between pecan trees so old their branches met overhead. In a *canopy*, a word Trina guessed she learned from Miss Harmon back when the retired teacher fostered little girls out here in the country.

The adobe ranch house, the color of desert earth, looked unchanged: weathered but respectable. Trina parked the Bug by a white car marked Clark Estate Sales as a middle-aged woman came out to greet her.

"Miss Valdez? Right on time. The house is jam-packed, so watch your step. I'm Jean Clark."

Exhaustion showed on the estate agent's lined, dry face as she ran a hand through graying hair in need of more than a finger combing. She didn't offer Trina a seat in the front room; there wasn't one to be had. Mounds of bedding and throw rugs covered the sofa and chairs. A mish-mash of dinnerware, silverware, candles in their holders, cacti in ter-racotta pots, and old-fashioned figurines covered a line of trestle tables. Boxes of toys sat in front of the fireplace.

Trina felt sad to see Miss Harmon's things in a jumble. "All this is going to be sold?"

"As I explained on the phone, Miss Harmon willed the house, her ten acres, and the bulk of her possessions to the local homeless shelter. It's a modest windfall for that organization. Miss Harmon had no family, so no one is objecting to small bequests to former foster children. How long did you live here, if I may ask?"

"From when I was six. I got adopted when I was almost ten. Miss Harmon stopped fostering kids not long after that, I heard."

"You're how old now?"

"Seventeen."

Pleasantries over, Ms. Clark pointed out two cardboard boxes filled with books near an empty bookcase. "All of Miss Harmon's books are yours now."

Trina got down on her knees to take a look. The boxes were filled with children's books she had read in this house and some Miss Harmon had read aloud from, a chapter at a time. *Great Expectations. Jane Eyre. Bless Me, Ultima.* Books Miss Harmon called "literature" in a reverent voice.

"I'm afraid the books aren't worth much," Ms. Clark said. "Nor are things she willed to other foster children. A bride doll, much loved. A checkers set. Calligraphy pens. A waffle iron, of all things! I mailed fifteen items to addresses all over New Mexico and beyond."

A vehicle's roar penetrated the adobe walls. "Only one other girl Miss Harmon fostered still lives in the valley," Ms. Clark said. "That must be her now."

Ms. Clark opened the door as a motorcycle sprayed gravel in a dramatic stop. A tall girl removed her helmet and strode toward the house like she owned it.

Trina recognized the mass of carroty hair. *Jill Ann Stickley. Hell on wheels.*

"Miss Stickley?" Ms. Clark asked.

"Jillian."

Trina mentally scoffed at the name change. The girl had been plain Jill Ann when they knew each other. Stepping from behind Ms. Clark, Trina said, "Hello, Jill."

A deceptively innocent smile bloomed on the girl's freckled face. "It's Teeny Treeny, the tiny señorita."

Trina bit back a retort. That she was just five feet tall usually didn't bother her. That she was Hispanic was something to be proud of. She would not let Jill push her buttons.

Ms. Clark either didn't notice or chose to ignore Jill's bad-ass attitude. "Come in, Miss Stickley. Let me get the necklace."

Trina flinched as she felt Jill tug on her braid in passing. Jill grinned and crossed bare arms surprisingly free of tattoos. The rest of her appearance was standard tough girl: tight denim vest, ripped jeans, biker boots, too much eye makeup.

"So it's Jillian now?" Trina asked.

"Why not? I like it better. You can still call me Jill. Okay, Treeny?"

"Trina."

Jill shrugged. "Whatever. Miss Harmon left me her pearls, can you believe it? I'm shocked the old lady gave me a thought after my dad came for me. What did she leave you?"

"Some books." Trina gestured to the two boxes.

"Figures. You would almost wet your pants when she took us to the library."

The estate agent returned with a necklace that she passed to Jill. "This is what Miss Harmon wanted you to have, Miss Stickley."

Trina recognized Miss Harmon's everyday choker.

"These aren't her pearls," Jill said.

Ms. Clark's voice was as dry as her face. "They're freshwater pearls. Not what you expected?"

"She had real pearls, a long string of them," Jill said. "That's what I thought you meant when you called."

"These are real, just not as valuable as pearls from the ocean. I didn't find any others in the house," Ms. Clark said. "No other jewelry at all. When Miss Harmon passed away in the hospital, she only had this necklace with her."

Jill pocketed the choker and collected herself with a familiar ease. When another little girl might have thrown a tantrum, Jill Ann Stickley would grow calm. "Oh well." She looked around her. "Ms. Clark, could I use the bathroom before I head back to town?"

"Yes, of course. You must know where it is."

"Down the hall to the left. Only one in the house."

Did Ms. Clark hear the undertone of scorn in Jill's mild remark?

"Miss Valdez, would you like to use it after her?"

"No, I'm okay."

"Look around if you like. I've still got things to put out for tomorrow's sale. Normally my daughter would help, but she's on her honeymoon."

The dining room also was packed with sale items Trina recognized: jigsaw puzzles and board games, table lamps from all over the house, embroidered throw pillows, balls of yarn, an unfinished scarf with the knitting needles attached, lots of other things.

"The old lady sure was a hoarder," Jill said from behind Trina's back.

For a girl who liked to make a big noise, Jill Stickley could sneak up like a cat. "You'd have a lot of stuff, too, if you lived to your eighties," Trina said.

"I'll always travel light." Jill gripped Trina's arm. "Let's go. I need to talk to you."

Jill swept out of the house like a queen commanding her entourage. Trina picked up one of the boxes of books and followed. She stowed it in the trunk at the Bug's front end.

"Right," Jill said. "They made Bugs bass ackwards."

Trina propped her hands on her hips in a show of impatience. "What do you want?"

"Surprise, surprise," Jill said. "Teeny Treeny's grown a tiny backbone. You won't strain it. I only need a little bit of help."

The desert heat was making the redhead crazy, not that she wasn't already. "What are you talking about, Jill?"

"Miss Harmon's pearls. Her good ones, not these." Jill waved the choker in Trina's face. "The string with the gold clasp. She'd wrap it around her neck at least twice, and it still hung to her waist. Then that whiny little kid broke it. What was she, three or four? The one whose mother got her back pretty fast?"

"Jazmin. Spelled with a 'z'."

"She was always tugging on Miss Harmon's clothes to get her attention," Jill said. "One time she yanked that necklace, and the string broke. Remember Miss Harmon clutching at her chest? Pearls rolled all over the place. It was hilarious!"

"You thought that was funny? Jazmin cried her eyes out until Miss Harmon made a game of finding those beads. We crawled all over the floor and under the furniture."

"I kept a pearl," Jill said. "My dad and I moved a lot, so I lost it. I wonder what happened to the rest."

"She put them in her pocket," Trina said.

"No, idiot. I mean after that. She never got that string fixed that I know of. How about after I left? You were here longer than me."

"About a year."

"Ever see those pearls again?"

"I don't think so. No."

Jill's eyes took on a faraway look. "She had other jewelry, too. Brooches with sparkly jewels she pinned on her blouses. Dangly earrings she'd wear for the Sunday dinners."

Formal dinners, Trina recalled. Four or five little girls, in clean clothes, seated at the table, after helping to set it with the good china and best drinking glasses. Nothing much matched; most of it came from second-hand stores. If someone broke a plate or glass, Miss Harmon would say, "Accidents happen. There's more where that came from."

"I loved how she read to us after dinner," Trina said.

"Bored stiff, I was. But I liked to look at her jewelry, and I guess she knew it. I wonder where she kept it. Not on her dresser, that's for sure. I bet all that jewelry is still in the house, and the Clark woman was too stupid to find it."

Jill stepped within an inch of Trina's face and smiled. The dad who took Jill back must never have had money for braces; Jill's front teeth still crisscrossed a bit.

"No," Trina said. "Whatever you're thinking, stop it."

"Meet me here at midnight."

"To break in? No way!"

"Not break in, exactly. I cracked open the bathroom window. Ms. Clark isn't likely to check it. She'll only lock the doors, I bet."

"I can't help you, Jill."

"Of course you can. I'll split whatever we find with you. Except for those pearls. They're mine. And if you don't help, your past as a sneaky little thief will be all over social media."

"That was a long time ago. You made me do it!"

"You were a handy lookout when we pinched things at the mall. And at that 7-Eleven, you were so cute counting your pennies out for candy while I pocketed more snacks. I bet you're flying solo now."

"I am not."

"Your high school friends will believe it. People love to dish dirt."

"I could say bad things about you, too."

"About this honest Starbucks barista? I'm twenty, but you're still a kid. You don't want to mess with me. Help me, and there'll be no problem."

"Why do you need help?"

"Because two of us can search faster. We'll meet at midnight, like I said. Bring a flashlight. You must have one in that Bug."

Trina glanced at her old car but said nothing.

"I take that for a yes. Drive up the lane in back. Don't park in front of the house. It's isolated, but we don't want to take a chance on somebody seeing us from the main road."

"Mom and Dad will know if I go out that late."

"Stay overnight with a girlfriend. You do have friends?"

Trina gave the smallest possible nod.

"Fine. Tell your friend to cover for you while you're out with a boy. You like stories. Make one up."

Jill hopped on her motorcycle. Up close, Trina noticed it wasn't very big, and its seat was ripped.

"See you at midnight." Jill stuck the helmet on her red head and roared off without bothering to wave.

Under the midday sun, Trina shivered. Jill Ann Stickley had been bad news from the moment Miss Harmon introduced her as the new girl. Jill could bruise a person's body in places nobody but her victim could see. Trina shook off the thought and went into the house for the other box of books and to say she was leaving.

In the kitchen, Ms. Clark, on a step stool, was peering into a cupboard. "Canning jars and casserole dishes. I'd best set them out."

She stepped down and wiped a hand across her forehead. "Whoo. It's stuffy in here. No air conditioning."

An electric fan, perched on top of the refrigerator, circulated tepid air. "You could open the fridge and stand in front of it," Trina suggested.

Ms. Clark laughed. "There's an idea. Clever girl, you. Like my daughter. I bet you're helpful, too."

Trina looked down at her sandals. Compliments made her bashful. "I try to be."

"Do you have any work experience?"

"Babysitting. And I help out on the neighbor's food truck at festivals. I'm saving up for college."

Ms. Clark's face brightened. "How would you like to come tomorrow at eight and help with the sale? Two strong young men are going to haul furniture, but I could use an extra pair of eyes to see that things don't walk off without being paid for. What do you say? I pay minimum wage and provide lunch."

Trina saw no reason to say no. "I'll have to ask my mom, but sure. No problem."

"Don't wear those nice white shorts. Jeans and an old T-shirt will do. Estate sales are dirty work."

* * * *

At midnight, Trina inched the Bug, headlights off, along the back lane to Miss Harmon's and cut the engine. Jill's motorcycle was parked under a pecan tree, and Jill was waiting in the darkness near the back porch. "Good," Jill said. "Thought you might chicken out."

"I should have," Trina said, hearing the misery in her voice. "We're going to get into trouble."

"Did you bring a flashlight?"

"It's in the Bug. Sorry."

"Go get it. Hurry up! Run!" Jill gave a hard push. Trina fell to her knees but managed not to cry out. She scrambled to do as she was told.

Under the high bathroom window, Jill interlaced her fingers to make a stirrup. "Put your feet here. Geesh, they're petite. Up you go."

Her heart racing, Trina felt herself being boosted. True to her word, Jill had left the window cracked open, but it wouldn't budge farther.

Below her, Jill said in a stage whisper, "Push harder, Valdez!"

Trina jammed the flashlight in a back pocket and pushed with both hands. Propelled by Jill's shove, Trina fell into Miss Harmon's deep bathtub and yelped like a wounded puppy. She struggled to her feet and looked out at Jill. "Now what?"

"Check the bathroom for those pearls. Then go unlock the porch door, dummy."

The bathroom had been emptied of everything but toilet paper. Trina scurried down the hall, through the kitchen, and to the porch that held Miss Harmon's washer and dryer. She admitted Jill, who snapped on her flashlight and pushed Trina aside without a thanks.

"Gracias to you, too," Trina muttered.

"Whatever." Jill didn't look back. She led the way to Miss Harmon's bedroom. "There's no light switches in here," she said. "Good thing we have flashlights."

Trina hesitated to step inside Miss Harmon's private space. This bedroom hadn't been off-limits exactly, but there was no reason to spend time in it. Like everyone was expected to do, Miss Harmon cleaned her own room and made her own bed. One time Trina watched from the doorway while Miss Harmon flicked a feather duster and sneezed. They both laughed at that. Another time, to avoid Jill's ire, Trina kept guard as Jill filched a five-dollar bill from Miss Harmon's purse. Then and now, Trina's stomach felt queasy.

Jill lay on the floor aiming her beam under the bed. "Nothing but dust bunnies. Don't stand there like a statue. Look in the drawers."

Trina opened the dresser and vanity drawers. "They're empty. Ms. Clark must've cleaned them out."

Jill peered into the closet. "Well, this is full of clothes. Things in bags too."

"Maybe Ms. Clark doesn't think it's worth selling."

Jill parted hangers of dresses, blouses, and slacks. She dug through shoes and purses on the floor. Trina opened a trash bag filled with night-gowns and underwear, and a smaller bag holding a gilt brush and comb set, a matching mirror, bottles of perfume, and a container of talcum powder. She sprinkled powder on her palm and smelled lilacs.

Jill stomped around the room, having a fit. "Why can't those pearls be right here?"

Trina couldn't help but giggle.

"What?" Jill said. "What's so funny?"

"Nothing." Trina moved fast to avoid a slap or pinch.

"Tell me," Jill said, menace in her voice.

"You think everything should be easy pickings. Those pearls aren't going to be where you can reach out and grab them. You should be thankful Miss Harmon left you her choker. It's not worth a lot, but it shows she thought of you. I'm happy she left me her books."

"You are so naïve," Jill said.

"I bet Miss Harmon taught you that word."

Jill wasn't listening. She was sweeping her light around the room, illuminating the pictures on the wall, four prints of flowers.

"Too bad these aren't Picassos," Jill said. "I wonder..." She went from picture to picture, moving the frames to peer behind them. Next to the vanity, she cried out, "Ohmygod, there's a niche in the wall. Look what's in it!"

The hollowed-out space for a votive candle or statue of a saint held Miss Harmon's jewelry. Jill scooped out necklaces, brooches, and a wooden dish that held earrings. She dumped it all on the vanity. "No pearls. I can't believe it! This stuff is awful. Ugly and cheap."

Trina watched from a safe distance. "I bet a lot of it was Miss Harmon's mother's."

With a swing of her flashlight, Jill knocked most of it off the vanity. Pieces skittered all over the floor. "Where are those pearls?"

Trina crawled around on the floor, picking up jewelry. "Quiet! Someone will hear us."

"No they won't. Nobody lives close enough. We have to search the rest of the house. Leave that stuff."

But Trina put the jewelry for someone else to find in the smaller of the two bags in the closet. She trailed behind Jill in a search for hidden niches in the other rooms. In the bedroom they had shared, Jill said, "Small, isn't it?" and moved on. Trina paused to recall climbing to the top bunk, glad to have a place to lay her head.

She caught up with Jill, pawing through sale items, in the dining room. "Come on, help me," Jill ordered.

Trina opened a basket stuffed with girls' socks that needed mending. A threaded needle was stuck in the toe of a white anklet.

"What a waste of time," Jill said.

But Trina got a warm feeling at the memory of Miss Harmon sewing while everyone else did homework or read quietly. After a previous, chaotic foster home, this one had been a haven until she got adopted.

"Do you still see your dad?" Trina asked. Jill's flashlight beam struck her face.

"Now and then. When he needs a handout, I give him a few dollars. He's still a drunk."

"I'm sorry," Trina said.

"No, you're not. Why should you be? Little Orphan Treeny has it made, it sounds like."

That didn't rule out feeling sympathy for another person. But Trina didn't dare say it.

Jill was examining a pair of salt-and-pepper shakers.

"They're probably silver plate," Trina said. "That's what most people have."

"Maybe they're sterling." Jill slipped them into her vest pockets.

A further twenty minutes in the front room turned up no pearls. Jill insisted on checking the hall closet, which held only cleaning supplies and a vacuum.

"Let's get out of here," Trina begged. "I don't feel so good."

In the kitchen, Jill flipped on the overhead light, peered into bare cupboards, even opened the refrigerator. "What's all this?"

The refrigerator was stocked with lunch meats and cheeses, apples, bread, and bottled water.

"Ms. Clark is providing lunch tomorrow."

"Tomorrow?"

"At the sale. She hired me to work at it. After you left," Trina said. Immediately, she wished she had kept that news to herself.

"Lucky you," Jill said. She helped herself to an apple. "But you mean today. It's Saturday already, dummy. You keep looking for those pearls when you come back. Don't think I won't know if you find them. I'll skin you alive if you keep them for yourself."

The threat would have sounded more ominous when she was nine, Trina realized.

Jill turned off the kitchen light and headed out through the back porch. Trina twisted the doorknob's button to lock up. At the ranch house across the way, a light flicked on. Jill threw herself on the ground, and Trina followed suit. What if the neighbor was calling the police? She crawled close to Jill. "What do we do? Wait or make a run for it?"

"I don't know," Jill said. "My heart's really thumping. Exciting, isn't it?"

Trina couldn't agree less. This was scary, sickening, guilt-making. Her mouth felt parched, her armpits damp.

About five minutes later, the neighbor's light went out. "Somebody probably had to take a pee," Jill said. "Let's go." She ran to the motorcycle and, with a "See you around, Teeny Girl," rumbled off.

A jolt of panic hit Trina as she fumbled to start the Bug. She drove with no headlights until she reached the highway. A mile outside of the city, she almost threw up when a police SUV headed toward her in full emergency mode. An ambulance followed, so she breathed a sigh of relief, assuming the emergency had nothing to do with her.

At her girlfriend's house, Trina submitted to a grilling about her fictional date with a fictional guy, who she'd said was a high school graduate. "You didn't do anything stupid, right?" her friend asked with a smirk.

"Virginity still intact," Trina said in an adroitly deceptive answer.

* * * *

In the morning, having been given the go-ahead by her folks to help with the sale, Trina drove straight to Miss Harmon's. At eight sharp, a good-sized crowd pushed into the house past the estate agent, who sat inside the entrance with a cash box. If Ms. Clark noticed anything amiss from the overnight search, she didn't mention it. Much of the furniture soon sold and was hauled out by her pair of young men.

Stationed in the dining room, Trina fully understood the meaning of "irony" as she watched for shoplifters. By mid-morning, there was space on the trestle tables to move up objects from the floor: two empty suitcases, a globe of the Earth, a metal bucket filled with plastic flowers, a varnished wicker sewing box.

Nearby, a woman stood clutching skeins of yarn and considering the half-completed scarf. "My nana might like to finish knitting this."

"Would she want this sewing box?" Trina asked, sliding it between them.

"Maybe."

The woman opened the box. On top was a tray that held spools of thread of various colors. She lifted it out, peered into the box, and said, "What have we here? A string of pearls? Oops, it's broken!"

Beads slid off the string back into the box.

"Can I see that?" Trina asked.

The woman shrugged. Carefully, Trina lifted out a long necklace. A quick look proved the beads weren't pearls; the coating was peeling off some of them. The necklace had a gold-colored clasp with gray metal showing through. This had to be the necklace Jill, poor kid, remembered as being valuable.

"I'll take the sewing box," the woman said. "You can keep the beads."

Trina found a basket for the broken necklace. She slipped out to the kitchen and put the necklace in a cupboard.

As the day wore on, the number of shoppers dwindled. At five o'clock, Ms. Clark waved goodbye to the hired men. To Trina, she said, "That's it for today. Tomorrow, I still have to pack up Miss Harmon's clothes and all the unsold items to take to the shelter." She asked Trina to go get her a bottle of water. "Bring one for yourself, too."

Trina returned with two bottles and the broken necklace in the basket. "This was at the bottom of Ms. Harmon's sewing box. I think she might have planned to restring it but never did."

Ms. Clark wasn't a dim woman. "Is this the necklace Miss Stickley hoped to inherit?"

"It has to be. Jill mentioned the clasp."

"You girls thought the pearls were real."

"Jill did, not me."

"Would you like to take the necklace to your friend?"

"She's not really my friend."

"I see. Well, I can contact her," Ms. Clark said. She handed Trina a check. "A full day's pay and a little extra for being such a good worker."

Good worker. Trina liked the solid sound of that.

Ms. Clark took a drink of water. She looked even more tired than when Trina had met her. "I wonder, would you like to come back tomorrow afternoon and help finish up?"

"Sure! What time should I be here?"

"One o'clock will be fine. Now, I have a surprise for you."

Near the fireplace, Ms. Clark indicated a small pine chest that Trina remembered Miss Harmon using as a footstool. The chest was tied closed with rope, and a "sold" sign was taped to the lid. Ms. Clark untied the rope. "Open it."

An old-paper smell like in the stacks at the library rose from the chest. In it were four books.

Ms. Clark didn't seem tired now; she looked excited. "I didn't know this chest contained books until someone left it open today. I secured it and marked it 'sold,' until I could give them to you."

Trina was puzzled. "Miss Harmon never read to us from these."

"They're classic adult literature. *War and Peace. Tess of the D'Urbervilles. Ship of Fools.* And here's a very special one."

The book had a blue-cloth cover. "*Women in Love,*" Trina said. "I've never heard of it."

"Look inside. It's signed by the author."

"D. H. Lawrence. What pretty handwriting. Cursive, like Miss Harmon taught us. Who is he?"

"He *was* an English writer who lived in New Mexico for a time. Today, I did some research on my phone. If this book is worth what I suspect, the sale of it could substantially add to your college fund."

Windfall. The word sent a tingle of gratitude from Trina's head to her heart to her toes.

Rita A. Popp's light and twisty crime fiction has appeared in *Fish Out of Water: A Guppy Anthology*, *Mysterical-E*, *Every Day Fiction*, and *Postcard Shorts*. Her flash fiction has earned several honorable mentions in *Alfred Hitchcock's Mystery Magazine's* "Mysterious Photograph" contests. She has completed her first mystery novel and is drafting a second. Both are set in New Mexico, where she and her husband made their home before moving recently to Fort Collins, Colorado. Find links to Rita's work at ritapopp.com.

WHO STOLE MY LUNCH?

KATE FELLOWES

When I opened the door to the refrigerator in the staff lunch room, I knew what I'd find. A big empty place where my lunch should have been. It had happened three times in the last week, and that was three times too many.

I gritted my teeth and closed my eyes, holding back the swear words I wanted to shout, since they'd have been a violation of company policy.

Behind me, I heard the shuffle of feet. Glancing over my shoulder, I saw my co-worker, Zac.

"Hi, Zac," I said, sighing and closing the fridge door with gusto.

"Oh, don't tell me. Someone stole your lunch again?"

Zac and I started at the company on the same week, nearly a year ago now. He was a great guy—smart, good-looking, willing to pull his own weight on the job and take initiative when needed. I liked him a lot. Not that way, just as a friend. A work friend.

"Again," I confirmed, shaking my head. "You know, this office isn't that big. There are, what, six of us here? So, who is it? Who is my tor-mentor? Is someone trying to send me a message that I need to lose weight or something?"

Zac eyed me up and down and then up again. "You're perfect just as you are and you know it," he scolded.

"Well, then, what?"

He shrugged. "Search me. Does this mean you're going out for lunch?"

"I guess I have to," I said.

"Want company?" he offered.

I smiled. He was such a nice guy. He'd taken me to lunch three times in the last week.

"You have to help me catch the culprit," I begged.

"We'll make a plan over lunch," he said.

It was a lovely summer day, so we got sandwiches from a food truck and took them to the park. For a whole hour, we kicked around ideas and suspects.

"My money's on Lily," I told him, dipping a hand into his bag of potato chips.

"Why?"

"Because she's always so focused on work, she probably wouldn't even notice it's not her lunch she's eating."

"Nah," Zac scoffed. "I'd guess it's Hank."

"Why?" I asked around a mouthful of veggie sub.

"Because he's trying to quit smoking. I hear that makes you want to eat anything."

"Are you criticizing my cooking?" I teased. No one would ever criticize my cooking. I'm really good at it. Just saying.

"Of course I'm not!" Zac said. "You're a great cook. The stuff you bring to share is always fantastic."

"What about Mr. Schultz, then?" I asked, picturing our plus-sized boss.

Zac shook his head. "Never."

"Why not?"

"Because he's the boss. End of story." He handed me the bag of chips. "How about Kelly? She looks guilty all the time for no reason at all," he said.

I laughed. "It's not her fault. She's just a little insecure, being new and all." She'd only joined the staff a few months ago. Zac needed to cut her some slack.

"Well, it has to be one of them," Zac said. He rubbed his hands together and jogged his eyebrows up and down. "Let's set a trap."

"It sounds like you have something in mind," I said.

"I've been thinking," he said, leaning toward me with enthusiasm.

I leaned back a little. "Let's hear it."

"It's simple, really. Let's set up a camera, so we can see the refrigerator. Then, we'll just watch." He spread his hands. "Bingo."

That was simple, all right. Simple enough to work?

"Okay. When?"

"Tomorrow?" Zac suggested.

"Let's come in early," I suggested. "So everything's in place before anyone sees us and asks questions."

"Who'd ask questions?" Zac frowned. "Lily, no. Hank, I don't think so. The boss? The new kid? We're good."

* * * *

And we were. By nine the next morning, when the rest of the staff trickled in, Zac and I were at our desks, hard at work. Kelly, the new girl, got sent off to a meeting and wouldn't be back until three, so we were one suspect down, right out of the gate. In the lunch room, Zac's tablet was artfully hidden behind a potted plant, its camera shooting video of the refrigerator.

The morning dragged by. As usual, I planned to take a late lunch, but I made a couple trips to the lunch room to refill my water glass. Once, on my way back to my desk, I passed Zac in the hall, heading to the lunch room with his own water glass. We gave each other conspiratorial winks.

It killed me, watching Lily, then Hank go back and forth for their lunches. Somewhere in there, the water cooler guy came to replace the big jug. Even though I wanted to ask him to check to see if my lunch was still there, I didn't. I'd know soon enough.

At last, it was one o'clock.

I wrenched open the door to the refrigerator and looked inside.

There sat my tidy paper bag, its top edge folded down exactly twice, the way I like it.

I closed my open mouth and reached for the bag, feeling oddly disappointed. I'd been ready to catch a thief!

But the minute I lifted the bag from the shelf, I knew that job still lay ahead. My lunch bag was empty.

"The game's afoot!" I hissed as Zac joined me.

He pulled a face. "What does that mean?"

"You don't read much, do you?" I asked. "Sherlock Holmes?"

Shaking his head, he opened the fridge door and peeked.

"Gone," he said, turning back to me.

I dangled the empty paper sack between two fingers. "It was in there, like this. Someone's onto us."

"Let's check the camera," Zac said.

I shoved aside the morning newspaper, the salt and pepper shakers, a box of ketchup packets and a scissors, clearing a space on the table, while Zac retrieved the tablet.

Sitting side by side, our cheeks nearly touching, we looked at the screen. And fast-forwarded through at least an hour of empty staff lunch room.

Here came Zac for his glass of water, his face looming large as he checked the camera. There we were, passing in the doorway. Here I was, looming large, too, then checking my lunch, which was still in place—or so it seemed.

Finally, Lily drifted in, checking her phone. She opened the door to the refrigerator, just as the water cooler guy rolled into the room. Naturally, he stopped in the perfect place to block our view of the action.

"Oh, no!" I groaned.

"Look, there's Lily leaving." Zac pointed around the guy's shoulder where we could see a bit of Lily.

Hot on her heels was Hank, moving to the fridge while water cooler guy finished up.

"Hank's in the fridge." I pointed around the guy's shoulder.

"And now they're having a chat," Zac said, as the two men exchanged pleasantries.

Then, suddenly, the view was clear as both of them departed.

Zac sat back with a sigh. "Well, that was frustrating. What are the odds?"

I gestured at the screen. "Either Hank or Lily could be sitting there out of sight right now eating my lunch," I said. "We can't see the table or the rest of the room from this viewpoint."

"True."

I drummed my fingers on the tabletop, thinking.

"Tomorrow," I said, "I'm going to bring a delicious chocolate-frosted brownie with my lunch and I'm going to put laxative in it. Then we'll know the culprit soon enough."

I watched Zac toss his head back and laugh.

"That's rich," he said. "You wouldn't."

"You're right," I said, admiring his smile. "I wouldn't. All we need is a different camera angle. From the refrigerator's point of view."

"Might work." Zac sounded skeptical.

"In fact," I got to my feet, "we already have that."

"What?" he asked.

Crossing the room, I lifted the ancient box of sugar substitute no one ever uses from the top of the fridge and carried it back to the table, setting it in front of a startled Zac.

"See here?" I poked the side of the box. "I punched out this letter O in the So Sweet label, and I put my tablet inside, so we could catch all the fridge action." I didn't look at Zac as I talked.

"Why didn't you tell me?" he said, sounding hurt.

"It's a double blind sort of thing," I said. "Need to know basis."

As I talked, I pushed buttons to view the video footage I'd recorded.

"Let's see what we see, hm?"

"But lunch break's nearly over," Zac said. "Maybe later." His chair screeched back.

I shot out my hand to cover his.

"Stay right there, buster," I said.

On screen, my face loomed large, as I fiddled with positioning before leaving the room. A minute later, I was back with Zac, my lunch and his tablet. Here I was telling him I just needed to make a pit stop in the restroom and he should start setting up without me.

Then, practically before I left the room, there was Zac—my friend, Zac—wolfing down my lunch like a starving man. With infinite care, he placed the carefully folded, now-empty bag, into the fridge and shut the door.

I backed up the video to a particularly incriminating view of him eating my poppy seed mini-muffin.

Folding my hands under my chin, I just looked at him in silence.

"I think I hear my mother calling me," he quipped and made to rise again.

"Oh, no, you don't."

"I plead the fifth?"

I shook my head.

"It's your own fault," he blamed the victim.

"What?" I turned to him, startled.

"You're such a good cook. You always have a great lunch. That muffin was fantastic."

"Thanks. New recipe," I said before I could stop myself. "However, back to the matter at hand. How could you? I thought we were friends."

"We are," Zac said, and this time his hand came to meet mine. "I like you. A lot. It's been great going to lunch with you." He dropped his voice. "I'd like to do it more often."

"And the way to make that happen is to steal my lunch?" I asked. "What are we, in junior high?"

He shrugged. "It was dumb, I know. I thought it might be funny. A harmless prank. And then you'd ask me for help, and I'd help you and be a hero," he finished lamely.

I rolled my eyes, but I felt a thrill, I'll admit. "Some hero!" I said, blustering. "You're the thief."

"Well, I always meant to confess," he said. "Maybe you could make lunch for us every day, and we could eat together," he suggested outrageously.

"You cannot be serious," I said. "What's that old saying 'give someone a fish, feed them for a day'?"

Zac smiled. "It was just a thought."

Sitting back, I crossed my arms and tried to look solemn.

"As judge and jury, I sentence you to cooking lessons at my place every Friday night for the next month."

"Make it two months," he said quickly. "Please?"

"Oh, all right."

I pushed more buttons on my tablet.

"You know, I knew it was you before we watched this," I said, smugly.

"No way. How?"

"Same way I first came to suspect you yesterday."

I turned the camera function to selfie mode and handed the tablet to Zac.

"Give us a smile," I said.

When he did, he saw what I'd seen—several tiny poppy seeds marring his toothy grin.

"Oh, busted!" he groaned.

"And you know what else?" I went on. "I still haven't had lunch. Again."

"Let's go," he said.

And we did.

Kate Fellowes is the author of five romantic mysteries, including *Thunder in the Night* for Crimson Romance. Her short stories and essays have appeared in several anthologies, as well as *Victoria, Woman's World, Brides, Romantic Homes,* and other periodicals. She is a founding member of Sisters in Crime's Wisconsin Chapter. Her working life has revolved around words—editor of the student newspaper, reporter for the local press, cataloger in her hometown library. A graduate of Alverno College in Milwaukee, she blogs about work and life at katefellowes.wordpress.com and shares her home with a variety of companion animals.

NINE LIVES OF HUSBANDS AND WIVES

CHELLE MARTIN

Emily Slater seethed as she left the divorce hearing. Her attorney, Madison Courier, a young sprite in a tailored suit tottered beside her on too-tall shoes. In an effort to keep up, or perhaps to show support, Madison hooked arms with Emily and leaned in to say, "We won't let him get away with this, Mrs. Slater... um... Miss Slater... um..."

"The nerve of that man! He has no interest in Josephine. He's just the name on the ownership papers."

"Unfortunately, that's a huge problem," Madison said. "Ownership is 9/10 of the law. Pets are viewed as property. We talked about this going in."

Emily stopped abruptly and grabbed Madison by the lapels of her Chanel suit. "You said we could negotiate. *'Give him his boat. Give him the time share.'* All I want is the cat, and now he's got his boat, the time share, and Josephine! What kind of negotiator are you?"

Madison gently pried Emily's hands from her jacket and spoke to her in a calm, albeit high-pitched voice, "I have successfully negotiated many uncivilized divorce proceedings. Your husband just happens to be an ass." With that, she turned on her heels and headed for a fellow attorney whom she quickly latched onto like a toddler running from one parent to the other.

"I'd like to see her walk in those shoes after a few drinks."

"Excuse me?" Emily asked the stranger who had decided to strike up a conversation.

"Oh," the woman waved a dismissive hand. "Nothing. I just don't know how that ditz can practice law when she's constantly focusing on how to walk in stilettos."

Emily snorted in disgust. "Maybe I should've thought of that before hiring her. But despite her appearance, she did seem competent, and a friend had used her."

"I'd lose that friend," the woman said, handing her a card. "How bad do you want Josephine?"

"Are you an attorney?" Emily asked before glancing at the business card: MAXINE'S CLEANING SERVICE 732-555-5500. "Oh, sorry. I don't need a maid. No more cat. No cat hair."

"I'm not an attorney or a maid," the woman said, "but I happened to overhear your conversation, and I can help you get your cat back. For a price."

"And why would you do that?" Emily asked, studying the woman's appearance. Her red hair stood at attention, and her yoga pants screamed at the seams.

"I'm good at my job. I like helping people. And it's cash under the table. You only pay me if I deliver."

"This sounds shad—"

"—You mean 'too good to be true', don't you?"

Emily knew nothing about this woman, not to mention her husband had single-handedly removed any remaining trust she might have in another human being. "No, thank you," she said, handing the card back. "I'll find another way."

The woman took her card and dropped it in Emily's open tote bag. "In case you change your mind."

* * * *

Emily sat on the big sectional sofa contemplating her next move when Josephine jumped on the couch. Her white fur left a trail as she curled into a ball. "If it wasn't for you, I wouldn't be in this mess. You and that cat handler, Margo." Emily opened a bag of potato chips and dug in.

"I can't believe Ryan fell for her. And I was too blind to see it." She grabbed another chip.

"If I have to, I'll get another attorney, but there's no way I'm letting him win. No cat—no cat shows, and maybe no more cat handler. That would serve him right." Emily turned the television on and found a movie.

Owner and cat startled when a phone call interrupted the solace of their Friday night. Emily checked the caller ID. "It's your bad daddy," she said, letting the answering machine pick up the call.

"I know you're there, Em. I see your car in the driveway. I just wanted to stop in for a minute. Please."

Emily bristled at Ryan's voice. *How could I ever have had feelings for that man?* she wondered. Her hand moved to the receiver, rested a beat. *No. There's nothing to discuss.*

"Emily, we have to be civil about this. We both want what's best for Josephine. She could be a grand champion if you give Margo a chance."

Oh, you've got to be kidding! It's not bad enough you left me for that skank. Now you think I'm going to let that so-called handler traipse around the country with you doing cat shows? She fumed just thinking about it. Margo had billed them for her travel and hotel stays for the east coast shows in which Josephine competed. And Ryan had been sneaking off to meet her.

"Last chance, Emily." Ryan sighed deeply. "Okay, then. I'll let my attorney know that communication seems to have ceased at your end. Enjoy your evening."

The answering machine clicked off, but Ryan's message flashed at her in an annoying shade of red that must have matched her blood pressure.

* * * *

Saturday morning, the doorbell rang, and Emily peered out to see Julius, the paper boy, standing on her porch. When she opened the door, he waved sheepishly. "Sorry, Mrs. Slater, but I didn't get your check this month. I figured it's a mistake since you're always on time."

Emily looked around her front yard, then invited Julius into the foyer. "Oh my gosh. I'm so sorry, Julius. Things around here have been a bit..."

"That's okay. My mom told me about your divor... Oh, sorry, I'm not supposed to mention that."

Emily was half-listening from the kitchen while she grabbed her checkbook from the drawer and began to scribble. "No worries," she said absently as she tore off the check.

She returned to the foyer to see a fluffy white tail escaping through the front door, which Julius must have left ajar. "No!" she cried, but it was too late. Josephine had made a break for it. Emily flew through the door with Julius on her heels, only to see Ryan tackle Josephine at the end of the driveway.

"Oh, thank goodness," Emily said, as she reached out her arms to retrieve Josephine.

"I don't think so," Ryan said, refusing to turn over the cat. "You seem a bit irresponsible, leaving the door open like that."

"What? That was an accident. Not that I owe you any explanation."

"No," Ryan said, then kissed Josephine on the nose while squishing her cheeks, "but the court might want an explanation."

"You can't be serious," she said, her hands going to her hips. "Oh, c'mon, Ryan. Julius left the door ajar. It was an accident."

"Perhaps, but you're the adult. You should've seen to it that the cat was properly confined. What if she'd run into the street and gotten hit by a car? What about the neighbor's dog? That could've been quite an ordeal if she'd gone over the fence."

"Julius is my witness. He'll testify that I did nothing wrong."

Ryan pointed to the Go-Pro camera sitting on his ball cap. "His word against my video."

"Just how long were you here? I didn't see you lurking about."

"Honey, I wasn't lurking. I came to visit Josephine this morning since you ignored my call last night." He clutched the cat to him and headed for his car.

"Ryan! Ryan, where are you going? You can't take her. The mediator hasn't made a decision yet."

"All the more reason I can take her," he said. "My name is on the papers."

Emily watched helplessly as Ryan loaded Josephine into a cat carrier on the passenger seat, got in his Ford, and drove away.

Julius pedaled off on his bike, and Emily returned to her kitchen to look for the mysterious red-headed woman's card.

* * * *

Maxine crawled along Mountainview Avenue in her '98 Chevy Malibu and followed her GPS's instructions to the address given her by Emily Slater, the cat-loving lady who was divorcing the ruggedly good-looking Ryan Slater. Good thing she'd tucked her card into the woman's tote bag. Sometimes her clients needed a nudge.

Ryan's girlfriend's house sat high up on a hill at the end of a cul-de-sac on Mountainview Road, but luckily the house number was prominently displayed on the mailbox at the end of the driveway. Ryan's Ford was parked in the circular drive along with a white convertible Mercedes, presumably the girlfriend's car.

Maxine circled back to the intersection where Mountainview intersected with Cypress Drive and pulled some real estate listings from a folder. If anyone questioned her being there, it provided a good cover story. She patiently shuffled the papers, marked notes on them as if considering the properties, and waited. Half an hour later, the white Mercedes crossed in front of her with Ryan in the passenger seat and a blond driver who fit Emily's description of the girlfriend.

Maxine turned the corner and parked in the circular driveway behind Ryan's Ford. Over the years, she discovered acting as though you belonged somewhere aroused the least suspicion.

The detached garage sat toward the back of the property, which gave Maxine the opportunity to walk up the driveway to the back porch. Sitting in what was most likely the kitchen window, was Josephine, watching her arrival. Maxine produced a bump key set and within a minute had access to the house.

"Hi there, kitty," she cooed. The cat was exceptionally beautiful with its long white fur and baby blue eyes. No wonder it won a few ribbons, she thought.

The cat jumped from the windowsill and disappeared into the great room. Maxine followed, taking in the scenery of exquisite furnishings, fine oil paintings, and several oversized credenzas filled with crystal and porcelain collectibles easily worth tens of thousands of dollars. Who'd expect less from a woman who owned an expensive convertible and had time to show cats? Ryan-the-cheater had done well for himself.

A cat carrier sat in plain sight, which would make Maxine's getaway convenient, but then she had a better thought. She chirped a call to Josephine who, as far as cats go, was pretty friendly. The feline ventured over to sniff Maxine and allowed her to pick her up. "Good kitty," she said. "We're going for a little ride." Maxine tucked the cat into the crook of her arm, retraced her steps to the kitchen, wiped the doorknob clean, and left the backdoor slightly ajar. *Let the cat-grabber have a dose of his own medicine*, she thought.

A short drive later, and Josephine was safely back at her mistress's house. Maxine pocketed a nice sum of cash for her work and declined a cup of coffee. "It's best if I don't linger in one place too long," she said. "You know where to find me if you need me."

Emily and Josephine had resumed their favorite spot on the couch when the phone rang about an hour later. Ryan. Emily grinned and answered. Would he admit that Josephine was missing?

"Hello Ryan."

"Don't play coy with me. You took the cat, didn't you?"

Emily gasped. "Is Josephine missing? Don't tell me you lost her!" She raised her voice a few octaves, but Ryan didn't buy it.

"Don't quit your day job, Emily. You'd never win an Oscar. The neighbor saw you here. I want the cat. Now!"

What a liar! She answered by hanging up the receiver.

* * * *

Maxine chatted up the guy sitting next to her at a popular Irish bar called O'Connor's. The joint featured big-screen TVs for sports fanatics, two pool tables, and daily drink specials with early bird dinners. She nearly spilled her beer when who should come walking in but Emily's soon-to-be-ex. He plopped onto the open stool next to her and ordered a beer on tap. The man looked none too happy.

"Girl trouble?" Maxine asked.

"What?" Ryan shot her a quick look, laid a twenty on the bar for a running tab, and took a hearty gulp from his glass.

"None of my business," Maxine said, sipping her own drink. "You just look a bit… flustered. Good looking guy like you… I don't mean to sound forward. I'm not hitting on you. I'm married," she said, holding up her left hand. "You just look like you could use a friendly ear."

Ryan laughed and shook his head. "If you only knew."

Maxine said, "Sometimes a stranger can offer an unbiased opinion."

Surprisingly, Ryan needed little prompting to pour out his man-done-wrong tale of woe. And if not for already knowing a bit about his affair with the cat handler, Maxine would have sworn she heard violins playing in the background while he relayed how his wife didn't understand him, how they'd grown apart, how he was forced to take refuge in another woman's arms. And now his soon-to-be-ex was even depriving him of his beloved cat. And to make matters worse, he feared his girlfriend might leave him if he lost custody of Josephine. She lived for cat shows and this cat in particular.

"I know Emily has her," he said, working on his third beer, his words beginning to slur. "I'd pay anything to get that cat back."

Maxine knew he'd be good for the cash; Ryan was getting his luxury boat and a time share as part of his settlement. She smiled and placed her hand on his, "Maybe I can help," she said.

* * * *

Ryan had been quick to agree to a plan for getting Josephine back from Emily, having no idea it was Maxine who was behind the catnapping in the first place. What a pair, Maxine thought, as she formulated a plan to once again move the cat like a chess piece.

Emily pretends to care about the cat's well-being, arguing in court that the poor feline would be distraught having to leave the only home she's ever known. *She actually looked quite content at the girlfriend's house. And she's traveled to cat shows, none the worse for wear, it appears.* Emily didn't so much as pat Josephine when Maxine brought her home from Margo's house. Odd behavior for a woman who supposedly loved her pet.

Ryan wants the cat, but his motive is to keep his girlfriend happy. This might be the only chance she gets to work with a champion, and Josephine has proved she's on her way. If Ryan loses the cat, he risks losing his lover.

Maxine realized the charade between the bickering couple would soon be coming to an end. The final divorce decree was this week. Would whoever had the cat in his or her possession at the time be able to conceal it from the other should he or she lose custody? It didn't much matter to Maxine, but this lucrative opportunity would be over, and then she'd have to move on to another mark.

Maxine's job of removing Josephine from Emily's house replicated her actions from the week before. Wait for an opportunity, retrieve the cat, and collect the reward. Ryan and the girlfriend, introduced as Margo, happily handed over the requested amount, and Ryan even threw in an unexpected cash bonus. It just got better and better with this group.

"We can't thank you enough," Ryan said, fussing over the cat in Margo's arms. "She'll officially be ours soon, but we couldn't wait."

* * * *

Maxine blended into the crowd waiting in the hallway at the court house, her hair neatly styled and now a rich shade of brown with blond highlights. The customary yoga pants replaced with a smartly tailored suit from a consignment shop. And to complete the change in appearance, she donned a pair of wireless glasses fitted with clear glass lenses. Having a background as a hair dresser came in handy for this line of work where disguises assured her success and anonymity.

Her nose was buried in a newspaper when Emily burst through the courtroom door, practically skipping in happiness with Josephine in her cat carrier. A beat later, Margo stormed past with Ryan at her heels. "Baby, wait! Don't leave me. I'll buy you another cat. A better one."

That poor cat, Maxine thought. Looks like it was going back to Emily for good. Maybe not. There was still one more opportunity to be had before Maxine left town for good.

* * * *

"This looks great," Margo said, as she looked over the documents Maxine had provided her. "Everything is in order just like you promised. I can't believe you were able to give Josephine new paperwork with a new name! Now I don't have to worry, even if Ryan and Emily come looking for her. Which they won't. Neither of them really cared about the cat, you know."

Maxine smiled as she looked at the furry white cat with the blue eyes who sat atop Margo's green velvet sofa. "I'm well aware," she said. She grabbed the duffle bag full of cash and bid Margo goodbye.

Maxine stuffed the bag into her back seat and climbed behind the wheel of her old car. She'd trade it in soon, under an assumed name, of course.

As she turned the corner at the end of the cul-de-sac, her travel partner raised her head from the little pet bed on the passenger seat and meowed. Maxine reached a hand over, and a fluffy white paw tapped her palm.

"I'll never let you go again, Josephine." She laughed. "I knew Margo wouldn't know a real document from a fake one. And she wouldn't know one white cat from another with a good shampoo and some styling secrets. Who knows? Your replacement might show just as well."

Josephine curled up in her bed and settled in for a nap. Someone loved her at last.

Chelle Martin is a Jersey girl with short stories appearing in many mystery anthologies, including the Guppy anthologies *Fish or Cut Bait* and *Fish Out of Water*. When she isn't writing, she's knitting, reading, or playing with her dog. Chelle is a member of MWA, MWA-NY (where she serves on the Mentor Committee), SinC National, SinC Guppies, and SinCCJ, where she's served as President and Vice President. She's currently working on a humorous mystery series as well as children's picture books. For more information, visit her website: www.ChelleMartin.com.

THE LOST MINE OF DON FERNANDO

ANNA CASTLE

"Here he comes." Luke Turner slid his coffee mug out of sight under the counter and shifted down to stand opposite his sole customer in the Questa Trading Post.

Flechas Velarde folded the newspaper he'd been reading and shoved it away from him. Luke tapped the bridge of his own nose, and the Apache elder hastily stripped off his wire spectacles, tucking them somewhere under the striped blanket he wore draped around his shoulders.

They called him an elder out of respect for his position of leadership, but he could've been anywhere from late thirties to mid-fifties, as far as Luke could tell. He would never dream of asking.

They quickly set the scene, both leaning over the counter pretending to study the small chunks of silver ore Velarde held in his broad palm. As the front door opened, Luke shook his head and said, "*Lo siento, amigo, pero si este es todo…*" Then he looked up at the newcomer and said, "Mornin', Mr. Wilkinson. Here for your mail?"

The tall, blond government agent nodded, striding forward to place both hands on the counter. He shot a sidelong glance at Velarde, then looked again, craning forward to get a better view of the silver. Velarde's round face turned to stone—that expressionless façade Indians showed to people they didn't trust. He curled his fingers around the ore and drew his hand back under his blanket, eyes fixed on the pine counter.

"What's the old chief got?" Wilkinson asked, not bothering to lower his voice. He couldn't imagine an Apache speaking English, even though Velarde had spent the better part of last year in Washington pleading the case for a reservation inside the Jicarilla Apache's traditional lands. But George Wilkinson was your basic greedy simpleton, while Flechas Velarde was one of the shrewdest men Luke had ever met.

"It's nothing," Luke said. "A few chunks of silver ore. Probably found 'em in some creek bed up there somewhere. Might've fallen out of a sack once upon a time and washed down the mountain."

"He probably stole them," Wilkinson said. "I should inform the sheriff."

"Don't bother," Luke said. "It ain't likely. That's pretty rich ore. You wouldn't leave it lying around long enough to get stolen. You'd smelt it down close to the mine."

"Where does he say he got it?"

Luke laughed. "Well, that's the funny part. He claims it's from one of Don Fernando's lost mines."

"Who's Don Fernando?"

"One of those old Spanish grandees used to own all the land hereabouts, outside the pueblos. Legend has it they left a lot of silver in the ground when the Indians sent them packing some two hundred years ago. Lots of old mines up there, they say, hidden in those deep arroyos. Some folks say the Apaches still remember where they are." He cast a dubious glance toward Velarde, shaking his head at the worn blanket and shabby footwear. "Me, I figure if they had a working silver mine, they'd live a little higher on the hog."

Wilkinson raised his pale eyebrows. "Unless they were hiding it from us, biding their time until they get their reservation."

Luke shook his head. "This last year would've—"

Velarde pounded his flat hand on the counter. "*Ingeniero*," he said, in a commanding voice.

"Hold your horses," Luke said. He winked at Wilkinson, then fetched his packet of letters from a pigeonhole and handed it across. "He wants me to lend him the money to hire an engineer and buy some proper equipment. He thinks if they can get this imaginary mine of his going, they won't need any more handouts from the U.S. government. Which ain't enough to keep his people from starving anyway, you ask me."

Wilkinson grunted. "They can't get it through their thick skulls that things cost money. I have to pay the going rates for seed and cattle, like everyone else. Add the cost of shipping every damn thing up to this Godforsaken backwater, it's a wonder they get anything."

A wonder, indeed. Especially when Wilkinson siphoned off half the money, splitting it with his wealthy rancher in-laws—after sending a handsome tip to Senator Teller.

"You'd know best about that." Luke jerked his thumb toward Velarde. "I'll talk him into pawning those chunks and resting content with the windfall. Maybe get himself a decent pair of boots."

He moved back down the counter, leaving Wilkinson thumbing through his letters. One was from the governor's office, which might or might not help. Another was from Special Agent MacKenzie, a friend to the Apaches and an enemy of the Wilkinson party. They'd thought about inviting him into their ring, but decided against it. The fewer, the better. Still, the letter wouldn't be friendly, so it'd ruffle Wilkinson's feathers—all to the good. A nervous mark was an easy target.

Luke shot Velarde a swift grin, knowing the government agent couldn't see it, but got only a level gaze in return. "*Ingeniero*," the Apache repeated slowly, as if speaking to a child.

"I heard you the first time, *Señor*." Luke shook his head in an exaggerated manner. "Ain't but one *ingeniero* in these parts, and he only comes up to Questa once a month."

They chatted in Spanish a bit longer to keep up the act, trying to stick to the topic, even though Wilkinson didn't speak that language. Then the door banged open, and another man walked in, almost as tall as the government agent, but with dark hair and friendly brown eyes.

"Mornin', Turner."

"Speak of the devil!" Luke grinned at him. "Mornin', Gould. You're just in time. This here fellow"—he tilted his head toward Velarde—"wants to show you some silver he found on the far side of Flag Mountain. He says it's from one of Don Fernando's lost mines."

"Does he now?" Victor Gould pretended to be impressed. "Well, let's have a look. Mornin', Wilkinson." He strolled past the government agent, who had planted himself in the middle of the store to read a letter, only his eyes spent more time on Velarde than on his paper.

"What've you got there, friend?" Gould asked, pointing at Velarde's closed fist with his chin. He got no response, so he turned to Luke. "Doesn't he speak English?"

"Don't seem to," Luke said. "But his Spanish is pretty good. I'll do the honors."

Gould shifted to a position that blocked Wilkinson's view of the silver while they carried on a stilted conversation in English and Spanish. They agreed that Velarde would take the two white men up the mountain in the morning to the place where he found the silver. They should plan on being out most of the day, because it was hard to find in the trackless wilderness.

Out of the corner of his eye, Luke could see Wilkinson practically twist himself in half to get another glimpse of the silver over Gould's shoulder.

Then Velarde tucked the pieces back under his blanket and shuffled off to study a display of horse tack. Gould and Luke sauntered back to the post office end of the counter, chuckling as if they'd just heard an amusing tall tale.

"Lost mines," Gould said, shaking his head. "How many times have I heard that story?"

Luke shrugged. "People find 'em though, every now and then. There's definitely silver up there."

"We shall see. Got any of that tobacco I like?"

Luke scouted out a tin of Virginia Flake Cut and passed it across. Then he called, "Anything else I can do for you, Mr. Wilkinson?"

"What?" The government agent acted like he'd been absorbed in his letter. "No, no. I'm off. Busy day. Have a fine morning, gentlemen." He stuffed his letters in his pocket and left, letting the door bang shut behind him.

Gould went to the door to watch him walk away, then turned back to the others. "He's gone. Do you think we got him?"

"Hook, line, and sinker," Luke said. "Don't you think so, Flechas?"

Velarde shrugged. "Let's see what happens tomorrow."

* * * *

"Slow down," Velarde said. "We don't want to lose him." He pulled up his horse and leaned out to look down into the steep canyon they'd been winding their way through.

"One way to get rid of the son of a beast," Luke said.

"Not until we get our money back," Velarde said. He scraped a handful of loose rocks from the cliff face on his right and tossed them clattering down. A small cry rose from Wilkinson on the faint track below. He'd followed them out of town that morning, trying to be sneaky and failing miserably—exactly as they'd expected. So far, he was following the plan as if he'd had his own script.

They rode for the better part of the crisp morning, passing into the cool shade of tall pines, then back out to the bright sunshine and clean tang of warm sage. Sometimes they followed narrow deer tracks, but mostly they seemed to be picking their way through untouched wilderness.

"I feel like we're riding in circles," Gould said after a while.

Velarde chuckled. "No reason for my people up there to waste a whole day." He led them on, pausing now and then to give Wilkinson time to catch up, finally stopping in a wide spot where a crude shed stuck out from the hillside. Beams had been shaped from the local pines with an axe a long time ago, judging by the weathering. Long timbers emerged from the slope as if they'd grown sideways and been carved where they grew. The hill had reclaimed a good portion of the original structure over the years. Two rickety tables stood to one side with burlap sacks filled with lumpy material at their feet.

Velarde swung down from his horse and handed the reins to an Apache boy who appeared from somewhere. The others dismounted, too. Gould stood with his hands on his hips, gazing at the shed with rapture. "I thought you were fooling, but that's a real Spanish mine!"

Velarde held up his hand, and they fell silent. Luke heard nothing but the wind sighing in the trees, until he caught the crunch of rocks and a grunt back the way they'd come. Out of the corner of an eye, he spotted a patch of black—Wilkinson's coat—moving into a jumble of boulders about twenty feet away. The Easterner was about as subtle as a buffalo.

"That thing must be two hundred years old," Gould said loudly. "I'm going inside to take a sample." He pulled a mining helmet and a small pickax out of his saddle bag, leaving his Stetson on the horn. As they moved toward the roughly-framed opening, two Apache women emerged, dressed in their layers of deerskin and embroidered cotton, with their long glossy braids. They carried flat baskets filled with rocks to one of the sorting tables under a stand of piñon pines. Something in the baskets glinted in the sun—a couple of old spoons, probably, or some mashed tin cans.

Luke removed his hat and tilted his head to show respect. "Ladies." They ignored him, playing their parts. Usually he could get a smile out of them; more amused than impressed, sorry to say. He didn't see many women these days, at least not decent ones. It was the one thing he missed. He loved the high country, and he liked the Indians he traded with a lot better than the city folk he'd left behind. But the nights could get lonely, especially in the long winters.

The men went inside the shed. "Is that your wife?" Luke asked.

Velarde nodded. "And her sister."

"A sister, eh?"

"She's already married." Velarde shook his head. "Besides, you need a white woman. One who knows your ways."

"Where'm I going to meet a white woman out here? They ain't exactly rolling up in droves, you might have noticed."

"You should take out one of those ads in a newspaper back east." Gould grinned, as he struck a match to light the candle on his helmet. "Might have to use someone else's picture, though."

Luke combed his straggly brown beard with his fingers. "I'll have you know I clean up handsome. Got my own store and a frame house. I'm a bargain."

The other men snorted their disbelief. Gould led the way through another rough opening where the top beam slanted down at an alarming angle.

"I'll wait out here," Luke said. He didn't like caves. Velarde waited with him, standing with one hand on a beam watching the glow of

Gould's candle disappear into the shadows. It soon bobbed right back out again.

"There's nothing here," Gould said. "They only dug a few yards before giving up." He took off the helmet and snuffed the candle. "Wonder what made them think there was any silver here in the first place."

"Maybe someone told them." Velarde twitched a half-smile.

Gould laughed. "Pulled the same trick twice, eh?"

They went back outside, blinking as if coming out from the depths of the earth.

"Well, you've got quite a find here, Señor Velarde," Gould said, pitching his voice toward the boulders. He held their three chunks of real ore up to the light and nodded. "It's a rich vein, all right. Could be another one farther down. I appreciate your predicament, but don't worry. I know some folks in Santa Fe who'll jump at the chance. Won't take long to line up your front man. Meantime, you'd best keep this under your hat."

Velarde led them back to town by a different route with even more twists and turns. Luke figured that was for his benefit, since Gould didn't know this country well enough to remember the trip out and Wilkinson could barely find his way from the hotel to the trading post by himself. It didn't matter. The game would be over, one way or another, in a few days.

* * * *

When they got back to town, Luke spent a few hours at the trading post, passing out mail and shaking his head whenever someone asked about the old Spanish mine the Apaches had supposedly stumbled onto. "Something going on up there," was all he'd say. "Your guess is as good as mine."

Then he closed up and went to meet Gould at Elvira's for supper. They each had a bowl of pork and bean stew, laced with those fiery green peppers New Mexicans liked. He'd gotten hooked on the stuff himself over the past year.

"How long do you reckon it'll take Wilkinson to make up his mind?" Luke asked.

"Not long. If that mine were real, he'd be too late already." Gould tore off a piece of tortilla and dunked it in his stew. "But I don't understand how this thing will play out. We can get Wilkinson to fork over the five grand easy enough, but one look inside that hole, and the game's over. There must be half a dozen ways for him to get the money back, or do them some other harm in revenge."

"I think they're hoping he'll be transferred soon. The special agent in Albuquerque is gunning for him, and the new governor doesn't like him much either. They can't prove he took the Apaches' money, or so they say, but everyone knows it's true. We're hoping they'll send him back to Washington. Or maybe he'll feel such a fool, falling for such an old trick, that he'll keep his own lip buttoned."

"A man like that doesn't have much shame," Gould said. "They'd better spend the money fast." He took a spoonful of stew, swallowed it down, then gasped at the heat, and grabbed for his beer.

"That's the plan. Chief Velarde'll turn it into cattle and horses. Heck, blankets, frying pans, sacks of corn. Everything they would've got if Wilkinson had paid out their government relief money in full, instead of putting it in his own pocket."

The Apaches had suffered a hard, cruel winter that year, struggling to survive on the pittance Wilkinson allowed them. They'd been pushed off their ancestral lands by ranchers and railroads and had no way to make a living for themselves. Luke had done what he could, even borrowing money from Gould, so he could take more of their meager possessions in pawn. He'd sold some of the women's beautiful baskets to a couple of artists in Taos, who helped him sell a few more to a museum. It wasn't much, and nothing could repay the loss of dignity.

"Five thousand dollars; no more, no less," Gould said. "If it were real, they could get twice that. But if that's all they want, that's what I'll get."

"They want justice," Luke said. "But they'll settle for the money."

They talked about Gould's travels in South America, while they finished their stew and moved on to thick slices of blackberry pie with mugs of Elvira's pungent coffee. They took their time about it, starting to think they'd misjudged their mark, when Wilkinson finally turned up, throwing both halves of the saloon doors open and striding in like he owned the place. He went straight to the bar and ordered a shot, tossed it back, and ordered a beer. He took a sip, turning around to lean his elbows on the bar. Then he made a show of noticing Gould and Turner sitting in their usual spot, halfway back along the outside wall.

He tilted his chin at them, tossed a couple of coins on the bar, and sauntered over, taking a seat without being invited. "What do you know about that silver mine? The one your pals the Apaches found. Rumors are flying all over town."

"Five grand," Gould said.

"What's that?"

"Five grand. That's how much they're asking."

"They can't ask anything," Wilkinson said. "They can't file a claim. Apaches have no legal standing."

"'Course they know that," Luke said. "That's why they're looking for a white man to go partners with 'em. They're offering a sixty-forty split. Pretty fair, I think, since they'll do the hard labor."

Wilkinson shook his head, a contemptuous smirk on his lips. "Sixty percent of nothing is still nothing. Whoever files the claim owns the mine, not them. He could just shut them out."

"If he could find it," Luke said, watching the smirk disappear. "It ain't exactly on the Old Spanish Trail."

"That's why they want the money up front," Gould said. "They're not expecting to get their fair share of the silver in the long run. Once the mules go back and forth enough times to beat a track into the ground, they'll fade away." He traded a knowing glance with Luke and added, "If I had the money, I'd be on it like mud on a pig. There's a load of silver under that hill."

"What d'you reckon?" Luke asked. "Ten thousand? Twenty?"

Gould blew out a breath. "Could be a lot more. Get some skilled miners up there with proper tools… Might keep that mine going for years. If it was me, I'd snap it up and start selling shares on the international markets. They're ravenous for American silver."

Wilkinson's blue eyes glittered. "How do they want the money?"

* * * *

A week later, Luke and Velarde were standing at their usual places on opposite ends of the counter at the trading post. Luke entered sales in his account book, while Velarde read yesterday's *Santa Fe Daily*.

"Heard anything from MacKenzie?" Luke asked. The special agent in Santa Fe had agreed to help manage the financial end.

"All done. Wilkinson wired the money from the Bank of California. Now it's in the government account where it was supposed to go in the first place. Only this time, they put MacKenzie's name on it. I already have forty head of cattle coming in from Texas."

The stage from Santa Fe rumbled past. "Mail's in," Luke said.

They went out to the porch to see who arrived. Most notable was a young woman in a gray dress with a long black coat trimmed in velvet. The hat sported a heap of black bows on top. Light brown curls hung free, jostled loose on the long drive. She had a bright expression on her face, like she was looking forward to something big. She watched while they got down a battered suitcase and said something to the coachman, but she didn't follow the bag into the hotel. She marched right past it like a woman with a mission and went inside the assay office.

"Where do you suppose she's going?" Luke asked.

Velarde shrugged. "She's pretty. You should go meet her."

"And say what?" Luke fingered his tangled beard and grunted. Could do with a trip to the barber that evening, maybe. Then the driver came up with the mail bag, so he went inside to start sorting letters into pigeonholes.

Not fifteen minutes later, Gould came tearing into the store. "The jig is up, boys!"

"What's a jig?" Velarde asked, folding the newspaper and hiding his specs.

"Kind of a dance," Luke said. "But it doesn't mean that. What's the problem?"

"Did you see that woman came in just now on the Santa Fe stage?"

They nodded. "Pretty," Velarde said.

"Is she married?" Luke asked, shooting a look at the Apache elder.

"How the hell would I know?" Gould glared at him like he'd gone right off his rocker. "She's a Pinkerton agent, you damn fool, come all the way from Saint Louis. Worse, she specializes in mining fraud. She's here on account of that fake Spanish mine."

"It's a real Spanish mine," Velarde said. "It just doesn't have any silver in it."

"Well, that's what makes it a fraud, now, doesn't it?" Gould looked angry and a little bit scared. "It's my reputation on the line here, need I remind you? I'm the one told Wilkinson that mine was good."

"That's not the way I heard it," Luke said, grinning. "I heard you say only a fool would believe tall tales about lost mines."

"I never said that." Gould blinked at him. "You were sitting right there."

"Me and nobody else. Get it?" Luke winked broadly.

"Who's going to believe you over George Wilkinson?" Gould scoffed. "We know he's a thieving scoundrel, but he's still the official Indian agent in these parts."

Luke shrugged. "Nothing we can do about it now, *amigo*, except stick to our guns. We all tell the same story. We'll get through it."

"That woman's no fool, I tell you. She copied out the details from the claim and went straight to the telegraph office. I don't know how she got onto this so fast, but she knows something fishy's going on here. She means to take a look at that mine herself, tomorrow. We could be in real trouble."

Velarde frowned and nodded sympathetically. "Let's see what happens tomorrow."

* * * *

Luke got himself a haircut, a beard-trimming, and a hot bath to boot, just in case. But he didn't see the Pinkerton gal all evening, even though he lingered over his blackberry pie at a table right in front of the windows. She must've had her supper at the hotel. Nothing like as good as Elvira's, but maybe she was too proper to take a meal in a whorehouse.

The next morning, he opened up the trading post at the usual time. Chief Velarde came in a few minutes later for a cup of coffee and yesterday's paper. They barely had time for one cup before Luke spotted the Pinkerton gal trotting past on a horse from the livery stable, wearing one of those split skirts that showed off a lady's backside. She had a good seat for a city girl. More to the point, she was riding toward Flag Mountain.

Only a couple of hours later, she rode past the trading post again. "She's back," Luke told his partner in crime.

"Huh." Velarde strolled over to the front door. "I want to see what happens."

"What could happen?" Luke asked, following him out to the porch. "She couldn't have gone all the way up to the mine. She hasn't been gone long enough."

"It's not far, as the crow flies. My brother took her."

"Your brother!"

Velarde shrugged. "She wanted to see it."

Before Luke could demand a better explanation, Gould quick-stepped down the boardwalk from the assay office. "She's seen it. God help us, she's been inside!"

"Flechas says his brother took her up there."

"What?" Gould's jaw dropped open. "Keeping that damn thing lost was our best strategy. I thought we all agreed on that."

Velarde's gaze shifted to one side and then down to the floor.

Then the Pinkerton gal came up the street, taking long strides in that two-legged skirt, arms swinging, a look of determination on her face. No bows on her hat today. This woman was all business. She went straight into the sheriff's office and out again in two minutes, leading the sheriff and his deputy. They all stomped across to the hotel and went inside.

"What the hell?" Luke traded a worried look with Gould, who shook his head. Velarde said nothing.

A few minutes later—just about long enough to go upstairs and roust a man out of his room—the Pinkerton gal came back outside. Right behind her came the sheriff and his deputy, each gripping one arm of Agent Wilkinson, whose hands were cuffed behind his back. The party marched down the center of the street toward the sheriff's office.

As they passed the trading post, Wilkinson shot a dark look at the three friends standing on the porch. "Arrest that damn Apache while you're at it, Sheriff. He's the one sold me that mine in the first place."

The Pinkerton gal answered. "Now, Mr. Wilkinson, you know Apaches aren't allowed to file mining claims. You told me last night you found that mine while hunting and verified the ore yourself. Were you just bragging? And you've been selling bogus shares on the London Exchange. I've got the telegraph records to prove it. The British take a dim view of stock fraud, I'm afraid. We're going to make an example of you as a show of friendship."

She smiled sweetly into his scowling face, then gave him a little wave goodbye, as the sheriff tipped his hat and moved his captive on along. She stood in the street, watching, until they disappeared inside. Then she cocked her head at the group in front of the trading post. This time, her smile was the real thing.

"You must be Señor Flechas Velarde," she said, stepping up into the shade. "You look a lot like your brother."

Velarde nodded. He'd been watching Wilkinson's slow march to the jail like he was memorizing every last detail, storing it up to tell his grandchildren.

"Uncle Teddy sends his regards," she said. "And I wanted to thank you myself. My cases aren't usually this easy. This'll be quite a feather in my cap."

"Wait a minute," Gould said. "Are you saying this rascal here sent for you?"

"Didn't I mention that?" Her blue eyes sparkled as she turned to Luke. "Louise Beck, Pinkerton Agency. You must be Luke Turner." She held out a hand.

Luke wiped his on his trousers first. He hadn't shaken many women's hands, but it turned out they did it the same way men did. He couldn't think what to say to her beyond, "Welcome to Questa," even though she looked like she wouldn't mind if he said more. He wondered what Velarde had told her about him.

She gave him a few seconds, then turned to Gould. "I could use some help with the paperwork. Any comparable mines in the area? Working ones, I mean." They went back to the assay office, leaving Luke and Velarde alone again.

"You knew about her from the start," Luke said.

Velarde nodded. "I met her uncle in Washington. He's a missionary with the Shawnees. Speaks their language. He told me about his niece one day while we were waiting for something. We spent a lot of time waiting. Her father was a mining engineer. I told her uncle about the old

Spanish mine. He said she was good at her job. And the way he talked, she sounded pretty."

"Sounded pretty," Luke muttered. "How long ago did you two cook this thing up?"

Velarde shrugged. "Not long."

"Why didn't you let me and Gould know she was coming? He about laid an egg yesterday. He was so scared of being caught out."

"You are both good men, my friend, but you are terrible liars. And you're not very good at keeping secrets either."

"I can keep a secret."

Velarde chuckled, shaking his head. "She likes the mountains. She doesn't have a husband." Then he pointed his chin toward the assay office. "I owed you a favor. Now we're even."

"I helped keep your people from starving last winter!"

"And I found you a wife."

Luke gave him a long look, poking his tongue into his cheek. Then he shrugged and took his hat out from under the counter—his best one, with the silver band. "Fair enough." He left the Apache elder in charge of the store and moseyed on down to the assay office.

Anna Castle writes two historical series: Francis Bacon mysteries and the Professor & Mrs. Moriarty mysteries. She's earned a series of degrees—BA Classics, MS Computer Science, and PhD Linguistics—and has had a corresponding series of careers—waitressing, software engineering, assistant professor, and archivist. Writing fiction combines her lifelong love of stories and learning. Find out more at www.annacastle.com.

SCRABBLE-ROUSERS

K.M. ROCKWOOD

"Read 'em and weep." Eb slammed his cards down on the table. "Hee, hee, hee," he cackled, as he swept the pile of pennies from the center of the table.

Miss Shannon marched over. Her left eye twitched. She frowned, as she gathered up the cards. "You know there's no gambling at the Rich-cove Senior Center," she said. "In fact, it's illegal. And here we are, in the same building with the county emergency services! Including the police."

The people in the other groups smirked. At least, they weren't the ones targeted by Miss Shannon today.

As she went to put the cards away in the cupboard, Eb stuffed the pennies into his pockets. The other players at the table glared at him.

"If'n you didn't gloat so loud, Eb, she never would have noticed," Harold said.

Eb shrugged. "Miss Julie, she never did mind us playing poker."

"Be that as it may, Miss Shannon's in charge now, and she does mind." Gwen shook her head. "Now what are we gonna do 'til lunchtime?"

That question was answered by Miss Shannon, who came back to the table with a box of Scrabble, which she plunked down in front of them. "You can exercise your minds with this." She turned and headed toward the kitchen.

"Playing poker exercises your mind," Eb grumbled, but he took his seven letter tiles.

"Wish Miss Julie hadn't retired." Martha reached for her tiles. "She wasn't but 70 years old. Lots of life left in her."

Gwen played "axle" on the double-word score.

Eb began cackling again. He added three letters to the *a*. "*Anus!*"

"That's only four points," Martha pointed out. "It's a waste of an *s*. And you used your *u*. Suppose you get the *q*?"

"I'll worry about that when I get the *q*."

Miss Shannon was busy setting up the lunch tables, but when Eb's turn came again, he shouted, "*Vagina*! With the *v* on a triple-letter space." She looked over.

"Hush up," Harold whispered. "She's not gonna like that."

Sure enough, Miss Shannon hurried over. "What in the world..." She stared down at the Scrabble board.

"It's time for lunch," she said through gritted teeth.

"We're almost done with this game," Martha said, although that wasn't true.

"Now." Miss Shannon picked up the game board and poured the letter tiles into the box. "We're going to begin playing chess."

"What's this 'we?' *You* don't play anything," Eb muttered under his breath. If Miss Shannon heard, she chose to ignore him.

Harold stared at the window, as if plotting an escape. His daughter brought him to the senior center every day. He didn't have much say in the matter. "We don't know how to play chess."

"I have arranged for members of a chess club to come teach you. They've volunteered to come all the way from Columbia to give lessons."

"Only two people can play at a time," Gwen protested. "We like group games."

"We'll get several chess sets, so more people can play. Then winners can play winners, and losers can play losers. Now, come have lunch."

With a sigh, Martha grabbed Gwen's wheelchair and turned it toward the lunch tables. Eb groped around behind himself, until he felt his walker. Harold picked up his cane, and they followed.

Miss Shannon pushed the multi-shelved food cart over to the tables and began plunking compartmentalized plastic trays in front of everyone.

They sat and stared at the food. It was utterly colorless.

"What's that?" Martha asked, as she poked at a white slab of something on her tray.

"I dunno. But I think this is cauliflower." Eb lifted a forkful of white lumps and sniffed at it.

Harold looked mournfully at his tray. His daughter would figure he'd eaten a good lunch and not offer him anything else until supper.

Gwen put some white paste in her mouth. "Mashed potatoes," she said. "I think."

"Well, at least, we know this is white bread." Martha picked up a slice and poked at it. "A bit stale. Is there any jelly? Or at least butter?"

"Maybe, if we put some salt on some of this..." Gwen looked around the table. "Where's the salt and pepper shakers?"

"And the ketchup," Eb added. He tended to put ketchup on everything.

"Oh, Miss Shannon!" Martha called. "We don't have salt and pepper!"

"Or ketchup," Eb grumbled.

The twitch over Miss Shannon's left eye seemed worse. She straightened up from putting the last tray in front of a feeble lady, who just looked at it, as if she had no idea what to do with it. "I've put the salt and pepper shakers away in the cupboard," she said. "Salt isn't good for you."

"But I'd like just a little. The food's kind of bland without it."

"It's nutritious food, prepared in a healthy manner. You need to give it a chance. Your taste buds will adjust."

Martha flaked a piece off the white slab and lifted it to her mouth. "Fish."

Eb slammed his fork down. "I don't like fish. Except tuna salad. That doesn't taste like fish. Anyhow, this needs ketchup."

"I'm sure everything is properly seasoned," Miss Shannon assured them. "We are quite fortunate that I was able to arrange for a different catering company to handle our meals. It's a local company that does a thriving business delivering dinner to people's houses on weeknights after work. We're lucky they could take us on."

Gwen pushed some lumps of cauliflower into the mound of mashed potatoes. "Sure doesn't look lucky to me."

A man stuck his head through the door that led into the kitchen and beckoned to Miss Shannon. "Excuse me. May I see you for just a minute?"

Miss Shannon hurried toward him. "Eat up now!" she called back over her shoulder. "Tapioca pudding for dessert."

"I don't like tapioca pudding," Eb growled. He reached for his walker. "I'm gonna find the ketchup."

"Bring the salt and pepper shakers, if you see them," Martha asked.

Eb lumbered over to the cupboard where the salt and pepper were kept. He tugged on the handle. "Locked."

"Ketchup might be in the refrigerator," Gwen said. "In the kitchen."

"Probably." Eb pushed open the door and peered in. "Nobody's here," he said, and entered.

He hurried back a few minutes later, a red squirt bottle in his hand. His eyes were wide, and his breath came in short gasps.

"Any luck with the salt and pepper?" Martha asked. "Or the ketchup?"

"Not really. They got a lock on the refrigerator, too. I did find this one little container. I think it's ketchup." He unscrewed the top and sniffed it. "But I did find out they're trying to poison us!"

"That's ridiculous." Gwen stabbed at her slab of fish.

"Don't eat that!" Eb reached over and knocked the fish off her fork. "That's the poison!"

"What do you mean?" Martha put her fork down.

"It's there on the box it came in. In the kitchen. One side of the box says, 'fish.' The other side says 'poison.' Right on the box."

Gwen looked up. "What else does the box say?"

"I could only read one side. It said 'product of Canada.' And something about individual fish servings. The other side—the one that says 'poison,' is mostly in some other language. Not English."

"Well, if it's from Canada, the other language is undoubtedly French," Martha said. "French for fish is 'poisson.' With two s's. Did it have two s's?"

"I dunno. But we have to do something before she kills us all." Eb rested the ketchup on the handle of his walker.

Gwen folded her napkin. "Don't be silly. She's not trying to kill us. For one thing, she'd be out of a job."

Harold put his fork down. He'd tried to swallow some of the cauliflower, but it stuck in his throat, and he coughed. "What do you propose doing?"

"Get rid of her!" Eb grinned.

"Get rid of her!" Martha rolled her eyes. "How could we do that, and if we did, how would it help?"

"I dunno. But there has to be some way to get her out of here. Kidnap her or kill her or *something*."

"Don't be absurd," Martha said. But she looked interested.

"If we could get her to the depot, we could put her in an empty boxcar on the siding. There's always a few cars there."

"And what would prevent her from climbing out of the boxcar and reporting us for kidnapping?"

Eb's eyes gleamed. "We could tie her up and put her in a mail sack."

Martha sat up straighter. "I don't believe they carry mail by train anymore."

"And why would she let us do that to her?" Gwen chimed in.

"Well, she'd have to be knocked out or drugged or something. At least in the beginning."

"How do you propose to accomplish that?"

Eb eyed them. "Just leave it to me."

Miss Shannon swept through the door from the kitchen. She saw Eb standing there with his back to her. "Why, Ebenezer. Do you need help to get to the restroom?"

Eb stuffed the ketchup container under his shirt before she could see it. "No, ma'am." He tried to maneuver his walker around the table.

One of the legs of the walker got caught on Gwen's wheelchair.

Eb turned sideways and tried to yank the walker free. It didn't come.

He yanked again, harder. Then he tottered, swaying back and forth. He fell over, landing face down.

His walker flew up in the air and hit the table with a clanging sound. It bounced once against the wheelchair and landed on his head.

Eb lay there, winded. A red stain seeped from under his shirt and spread on the floor around his chest.

Miss Shannon looked on in horror for a second, her eye twitch going a mile a minute. "We need paramedics!" She turned and raced to the kitchen, where a phone hung on the wall. "I'll call 9-1-1."

"You could just go down the hall to the fire station," Gwen suggested. But Miss Shannon didn't hear her.

The smell of ketchup filled the air.

Since both the dispatcher and the first responders were in the building, help arrived immediately.

A hefty paramedic felt the side of Eb's neck. A petite woman in uniform carted a backboard in.

"Heart attack?" she asked.

"Accident! He fell, and he's bleeding." Miss Shannon sat down abruptly. "I feel faint."

The paramedics transferred Eb to the backboard and hurried him out to the ambulance.

Another paramedic turned his attention to Miss Shannon.

The siren wailed, as the ambulance pulled out on the road.

Miss Shannon pushed the paramedic away. "I'm fine." Then, she looked at the red spot on the floor and turned her head, gagging. "So much blood!"

"So much ketchup," Harold muttered.

The building custodian showed up with a bucket and mop.

* * * *

At ten thirty the next morning, when the senior center opened, Eb used two canes to struggle over to his usual seat. His walker, with a new dent in one of the legs, was in a corner by the coat hooks.

He looked longingly at the locked cupboard with the decks of cards, but Miss Shannon brought the Scrabble game out. He sighed and unfolded the board.

"They take you to the emergency room?" Harold asked.

"Uh huh."

"You okay?" Martha selected her seven tiles.

"Yeah. After I had a shower to get the ketchup off."

"But your head was okay?"

"My head?"

"Yeah." Gwen frowned at the letters in front of her. "Your walker hit your head pretty good."

Eb rubbed his head. "So that's where this lump came from."

On his first turn, Eb came added a *pis* to an *s* already on the board. "Hee, hee, hee."

Martha shook her head disparagingly. "Waste of an *s*."

"Hope they have a better lunch today," Harold said and added *en* to the *p*.

When his turn came, Eb added an *is* to the *pen*. "Penis! Triple word score!" he chortled. Loudly.

Miss Shannon strode over, looked at the board, and frowned. She rubbed her twitching eye. "The chess club members I invited over will be here for lunch," she said. "They will start the lessons afterward. Let's get this picked up."

"It's a bit early to eat," Gwen said.

"The food's here." Miss Shannon reached for the board, but the door opened, and four diminutive people entered. She hurried over to greet them.

"Are those the chess players?" Harold squinted at them. "They're tiny. Are chess players supposed to be small?"

"What do you mean?" Martha drew herself up straight in her chair. "Nothing wrong with being small. I myself am four foot eight and one-half inches."

"Of course, there's nothing wrong with being small," Harold muttered. "I just wondered if it was an advantage. You know, like it's an advantage to be tall if you want to play basketball."

"I never heard that." Gwen looked over at the new-comers. "But you're right. None of them look like they're over five foot tall."

Miss Shannon announced that lunch would be served in a few minutes and asked that everyone please take their place.

After much shuffling of walkers, clanking of canes, and squealing of wheelchair brakes, the seniors were assembled around the lunch tables. Miss Shannon introduced the chess instructors and gave a speech on "wholesome, challenging" games. She glared at Eb, but the effect was somewhat diminished by the tic over her eye.

Martha and Gwen turned their hearing aids off. Eb took his out. Harold's daughter said he didn't need a hearing aid. Besides, they were expensive, and he'd probably never wear it anyhow.

Miss Shannon's words were a low drone, but she raised her voice at the end. "After we eat, our guests will have more to tell us!"

Some items at lunch today were a bit more recognizable than yesterday's, but the whole meal was no more appealing.

Martha shoved her fork into a pile of rice and pushed it around the plate.

Harold, who was genuinely hungry, lifted a white round to his nose and sniffed. "Meat?" He tasted it. "Maybe pork. Or turkey loaf?" He took a bite. "Probably pork," he decided.

Gwen dipped a spoon into a pale yellow semi-liquid and announced, "Applesauce. I think."

"More like congealed piss," Eb said under his breath. Then he picked up a limp white spear and dangled it from his fingers. "What the hell is this?" he asked loudly.

From across the room, Miss Shannon frowned. "White asparagus, Ebenezer. It's a specialty item."

"I don't care how special it is. I don't even like green asparagus," Eb mumbled. "I can't see as white asparagus would be any better."

Harold took a bite of his white round that was probably pork. "At least it's better than yesterday." He shoved the whole piece in his mouth and started in on the rice.

The others pushed the food around on their plates.

"We have ladyfingers for dessert!" Miss Shannon announced and sailed into the kitchen.

"What are ladyfingers?" Eb asked.

"Well, they're sponge-cake-biscuit-type things." Martha picked up an asparagus spear and peered at it. "Usually, you use them to make something, like trifle or tiramisu. I've never heard of them being served by themselves—they're kind of dry and tasteless."

Eb stood up. He hobbled over to where his walker sat against the wall, exchanging it for the two canes. "This has got to stop."

Gwen stared at him. "And just what are you going to do about it?"

"I'm not sure," he said. "But something." He steadied himself on his walker and headed for the kitchen door.

Martha sighed. "He's just going to get himself in trouble. And maybe thrown out of the senior center."

Gwen shook her head. "Or worse. Thrown in jail. Do you think he was serious yesterday about kidnapping Miss Shannon?"

"Who knows what Eb will do?" Harold said. "I wish I had his courage."

A long time passed before Eb came back out of the kitchen. His cheeks were red, and he was wiping his nose on his sleeve. "It's chilly outside."

"What were you doing outside?" Martha asked.

Eb grinned. "Taking care of our problem."

"And what problem is that?"

"Miss Shannon. She's going away for a while."

"What do you mean?"

Eb sat down again. "The chess people, they came in a van. And I guess you do have to be small to join their group. The van says 'Wee Knights.' She's in the back of their van."

Gwen leaned back in her wheelchair. "Did you have anything to do with her ending up in the back of their van?"

"Only a little," Eb assured her. "She was leaning into the back there, trying to get something out, when she slipped and hit her head. She kind of fell half in and half out. I just lifted up her legs, so she was all in."

"But won't she just get up and climb back out?"

"She hit her head pretty hard. I think she passed out. Anyhow, I slammed the door shut and latched it. She can't get out. They'll take her back to Columbia with them."

"Suppose she's hurt and needs to go to the hospital?" Martha asked.

Eb shrugged. "Not my problem."

"But she called for an ambulance for you yesterday when you fell."

"Yes. And I wish she hadn't. It was embarrassing, explaining about all the ketchup."

With Miss Shannon locked inside the van instead of in the kitchen, the ladyfingers never showed up. And no one collected the still-full food trays.

The chess club members conferred among themselves, then started giving a presentation on the game of chess. All pretty boring—the origins of the game, how some people became champions, etc. A few people carried on a low conversation. Most of the audience snoozed.

At last they stopped. "Well," one of the little chess players said brightly. "I guess we'll see you next week. And maybe we can set up some chess games then."

They started out the front door.

Eb stirred himself. "Hey. Isn't your van out back?"

"Oh, no. We came in a car. It's parked out in front."

"But there's this van in the back..."

"I think that belongs to the caterers. It's a refrigerator van. The writing on it says something about delivering meals right to your home on busy week nights. Pretty clever idea. They even named their business 'Week Nights.'"

The chess players left.

Eb sat still.

"Well," Martha said. "She won't get all the way to Columbia in that van. The caterer is right across town."

"A refrigerator van?" Gwen shivered. "She could freeze to death in there!"

"Oh, I bet they'll check it before they put it away for the night. Don't you think?" Harold said.

"I hope so."

Eb didn't say anything.

Harold located his cane and got to his feet. "Time for me to go out front to meet my daughter. She gets mad if she has to get out of the car and look for me. If I see any of the firefighters or cops, I'll say something to them about Miss Shannon. Not that I think they'll believe me."

* * * *

The next morning, a substitute site manager showed up at the senior center in Miss Shannon's place. He didn't seem to have a very good idea of what he should do, and didn't even introduce himself. He had a clipboard in his hand.

"Did you say something to anybody yesterday about Miss Shannon?" Gwen asked Harold.

"Yep."

"What did you tell them?"

"Just that I thought she'd fallen in the van and might need some help."

Martha turned to the man with the clipboard. "What happened to Miss Shannon?"

"She's indisposed," he said.

Eb glanced up. "Not dead?"

The man shook his head. "Of course not. What made you think she might be dead?"

When Eb just looked down at the table and didn't respond, the man shrugged and checked his clipboard again.

"I see we have an exercise session first."

"Miss Shannon stopped doing that," Gwen said. "Nobody but her would do the exercises."

"Then we have game time."

"Yes!" Harold pointed to the cabinet in which the cards were locked away. "The cards are in there."

Frowning, the man examined the paper on the clipboard. "On here it says you play Scrabble. Or chess."

Harold looked alarmed. "Not chess! Nobody knows how to play chess!"

"It goes on to say that some volunteers are teaching chess."

"Yes. But they aren't coming today."

The man got out the Scrabble games and distributed them. "You sure nobody wants to try chess?"

Eb shook his head. "Nope."

"It's a great, challenging game," the man said.

"Nope."

They settled down to the game. Gwen had just put down *rhea*, a kind of bird, and Eb added *dia* to it to make *diarhea*. Nobody seemed to notice that it was misspelled.

The door to the kitchen burst open, and Miss Julie, the old site manager, popped out.

The man looked relieved. He handed the clipboard over to her. "Thank you for substituting on such short notice."

"My pleasure." Miss Julie looked around the room and smiled. "I miss these old codgers. Do you know how long it will take Miss Shannon to recover enough to come back to work?"

"Well..." The man shook his head. "I understand she was pretty traumatized. We'll re-evaluate when she gets out of the hospital. And maybe transfer her to another site."

"Hospital?" Miss Julie's eyebrows raised. "I didn't realize she was hurt so badly she had to be hospitalized."

"It wasn't really the fall, I don't think. She did hit her head. But she was pretty upset, so they kept her for observation. In the mental ward."

Eb leaned over and whispered, "I *knew* she was a mental case."

"Is it all right if I leave now?" the man asked. "I've got lots of work to take care of at the office."

"Of course." Miss Julie smiled. "It's almost lunch time, anyhow."

She went into the kitchen and came back with the food cart. When she got to the lunch tables, she pulled out a tray and stared at the contents. "What's this?"

The lunch trays were once again colorless.

She lifted the tray to her nose. "It doesn't even *smell* like food."

"No." Harold grabbed his cane and went over next to her to look at the tray. Martha followed.

Harold picked up a white meat round and nibbled at it. "Turkey loaf, I think. Not great, but it could be a lot worse."

"Like the poison fish?" Eb asked.

Gwen shook her head. "It wasn't poison. But it was pretty bad."

Miss Julie poked at a sticky mound. "What's this? I don't think it's mashed potatoes."

Martha held a forkful up to her nose and sniffed. "Mashed parsnips?"

"Parsnips?" Harold stuck a spoon into the mound and lifted it to his mouth for a nibble. "I like parsnips. These are pretty good."

Eb snorted. "You must be really hungry."

"I am." Harold stuffed the parsnips in his mouth.

"And," Miss Julie moved some white spheres around on the tray. "What could these be? Marbles in white sauce?"

Eb's eyes grew wide. "I knew it. Now they're trying to choke us to death. On marbles."

"Not marbles." Martha took a sniff. "Creamed pearl onions."

"Can you eat those?" Eb asked.

Harold finished the parsnips and was licking the spoon. "What's for dessert?"

Miss Julie pulled another tray out of the food cart and uncovered it. It was filled with small glass bowls filled with whitish paste. "Vanilla pudding? Egg custard?"

Harold dipped his spoon in one and brought it up to his mouth. "Something tasteless. But probably edible." He shoved the spoon into his mouth.

"Enough of this nonsense." Miss Julie put the cover back on the tray. "Let's order pizza."

K.M. Rockwood draws on a varied background for stories, among them working as a laborer in a steel fabrication plant, operating glass melters and related equipment in a fiberglass manufacturing facility, and supervising an inmate work crew in a large medium security state prison. These positions, as well as work as a special education teacher in an alternative high school and a GED teacher in county detention facilities, provide most of the background for short stories and novels, including the Jesse Damon Crime Novel series. Find out more at www.kmrockwood.com.

THE RETIREMENT PLAN

MARY FERN ROSS

Robert Lawson lunged for a flute of champagne as a server balancing a silver tray on one hand glided past. His nerves were frayed from attempting small talk, and Tarrington House held nothing but bad memories. Dozens of guests swarmed around the Great Hall, a mix of landed gentry, celebrities, and tabloid vermin caught in a morass of heavy red damask walls and matching carpet. The restoration of the ancestral home of the Parkers had taken five years, outlasting the seventh Earl of Harrow by mere weeks, which allowed his son Harold to take credit for the work.

"Easy, brother. Don't get sloshed before the main event," Christopher Lawson said as he raised his hand to summon another server.

Robert placed his empty glass on the tray when his brother snagged two more drinks.

"I'm a wreck. You look like you're enjoying yourself."

"I've been paid to look happy to be here."

"They paid you—"

"I instructed my agent to charge triple the usual appearance fee because I loathe Harold Parker." Christopher threw his sonorous voice into a high nasal affect. "What a coup for the Parkers to lure a celebrity of Lawson's stature, even though one could say he's in descent, to a party in the middle of nowhere."

Robert laughed. "I was trying to puzzle out why you accepted the invite. So, for revenge?"

"And spending a few days with you. The fee bought you this fine new suit." Christopher tugged at the lapel of the tuxedo he had custom tailored for Robert. "I have more planned than the appearance fee, though, more than you or the Parkers could fathom. Everything will change tonight." Christopher held a glass aloft to an elderly couple who were staring at him. "Smile for the people, Robert." The woman's face grew red beneath a puff of white curls.

"I don't know how you can bear always being watched and talked about, especially here, with all the memories."

"No matter where I go, I am watched and talked about. Why not get paid to do it alongside my dear little brother?"

The elderly couple approached, and the woman held out a gossip magazine. She touched Christopher's arm. "I'm Lady Joanna. Oh, Mr. Lawson, I so enjoy your films. Might I trouble you for an autograph and a picture?"

Christopher held the magazine at arm's length and read aloud. "Will the Brosnan look-alike Christopher Lawson be the next Bond?" While he signed the page, he said, "Don't believe a thing you read, Lady Joanna. I must apologize to Pierce that I should be favorably compared to him."

The woman clasped her hands together. "Oh, but Mr. Lawson—"

He leaned in close as Lady Joanna's husband attempted to use her phone to photograph them. Robert stepped in, took the picture, and handed the phone back to the still confused husband. When the couple walked away, Robert said, "Imagine the money the Parkers spent to make the estate this dreadful."

"I don't have to imagine. Their construction manager's daughter wants to be an actress. He has been emailing me regularly asking for advice, and he's quite forthcoming with his employer's secrets."

"Is his daughter a good actress?"

"Don't know, but I find the restoration details fascinating."

"Why would you—"

"Bollocks, here comes Parker." Robert gasped to see the thin, balding pale shell of a man, who had been his childhood tormentor, walking down a curved staircase with an equally curved brunette on his arm.

"He's aged terribly. Same pained look on his face."

Christopher grabbed two more glasses of champagne as they floated past. "I'm not nearly drunk enough to deal with him."

He handed one glass to Robert and raised the other aloft.

"To the *nouveau riche*."

A high-pitched voice called, "Bad form to toast yourself, Lawson. I know you are not referring to me."

"Rest assured I would never toast you, Harold."

A man who looked like a shorter, younger version of Christopher slipped beside Harold and offered his hand. "Good to see you, Lawson. How have you been?"

"Excellent, Taylor. Let me introduce my brother, Robert, a newly minted Detective Inspector."

Taylor slapped Robert on the back. "Congratulations, your brother did nothing but talk about you when we were on location last year. Pleased to meet you."

Robert guessed from the set of Christopher's jaw that Taylor was the "grasping upstart" he had complained about stealing his scenes.

Harold laced his arms across his chest. "I am now the Earl of Harlow, Lawson. Surely even you know that the proper way to address me—"

"Goodness, my manners. Congratulations on the death of your father, Harold."

Harold kept eye contact with Christopher while speaking. "Taylor, did you know that Chris and Bobby's parents were servants here at Tarrington House?"

Taylor's face went red, but he forced a smile. "How jolly. You've known each other since childhood? My family moved so often—"

Harold held up a hand to cut him off. "Occasionally, I was ordered to play with the servants' children. That is, until their parents were fired. Sticky fingers." Harold looped an arm around the brunette, who hadn't taken her eyes off Christopher except to scribble in a notebook. "Lawson, do you know Felicity Solon, from the *News of the World*?"

Robert hoped his face didn't give away the anger he felt. Over twenty years since Harold's family had falsely accused their parents and he was trying to humiliate them all over again.

Christopher reached for Felicity's hand. She stopped scribbling, blinked, wide eyed, at him, and stammered.

"I'm a big fan of yours, Mr. Lawson."

Christopher kissed the back of her hand.

"Not more of an admirer than I am of your beauty, my dear Ms. Solon. And do please call me Christopher."

She ripped the page from her notebook and handed it to Christopher. "I won't need my notes if we could chat over a drink later?"

Harold inserted himself into the space between Felicity and Christopher. "This is my party and my guest—"

"Then run along and enjoy your party. Harold."

Harold's face went as red as the walls, and he pulled Felicity into the crowd.

Christopher balled up the reporter's page of notes and slipped it into his jacket.

Robert shook his head. "I've been getting up before dawn for the last five years trying to climb the ladder; you get your way with a wink and a smile."

"Coming from a face you've seen 20 feet tall in the cinema, it takes on new meaning." Taylor leaned in towards Christopher. "Hope the prig is paying you premium to be here. Better go earn my keep. Pleasure to meet you, Robert. Oh, um, Christopher, I don't suppose you've heard if Marty has completed casting yet, have you?"

Christopher raised an eyebrow but didn't speak until Taylor hurried away.

"He knows damn well the part is his," Christopher said. "I saw Marty last week, and he couldn't look me in the eye. Three of the last four parts I went for, Taylor won them. And that idiot Harold, bringing up the theft accusations from thirty years ago."

Robert snorted. "As if Father would steal—"

Christopher glanced at his watch, but Robert caught his changed expression.

"Christopher, what don't I know?"

"Not here."

Robert pointed to a set of French doors in the library. "Outside then."

"The doors are alarmed." He cocked his head to the right, and Robert followed him to a quiet corner. "I am sorry, Robert, but father really is a thief, rather, a klepto."

Robert grabbed a chair to steady himself, and a wave of nausea shook him. "I looked up to him, thought he worked so hard."

"He always did. He couldn't help himself and lost a lot of jobs. That's why I went into the Army instead of going to University. I had to help support them. I am sorry I kept it from you."

Robert looked across the room where Harold was gesturing toward a portrait of an ancestor. "I am sorry you had to carry that burden alone."

"Tonight, Harold Parker will pay for all the years of bullying, and I am happy you are here to see it. I'm playing my greatest role tonight, that of a grateful plebeian invited to mingle with the nobility." Christopher gestured towards the portraits of Parker forebears along the north wall. "I've found a way to tip the scales, you might say." Robert cocked an eyebrow. "I will warn you that you won't like it, but everything is in place. It needs to be done."

Robert saw a coldness in Christopher's eyes that sent a chill up the back of his neck. Before he could speak, the quartet stopped playing, and Harold motioned for the room's attention.

"Lords, Ladies, members of the media, honored guests, welcome to the new Tarrington House, painstakingly restored to its past and future glory." Harold paused for a smattering of applause. "Won't you all step through into the library for the *pièce de résistance* of our vast collection?"

When the guests had assembled in the library, Harold motioned for the reporter, Felicity, to stand on the other side of a shoulder-high plinth made of ash with inlaid strips of brass. Robert tensed, wondering if Harold was about to unveil an urn of the previous earl. Felicity lifted a purple satin cloth to reveal a stunning necklace and earrings dripping with sapphires and diamonds. "This set has been worn by many genera-tions of Parkers." The guests applauded, and Harold beamed. "Everyone, please enjoy the breathtaking Parker wedding parure and help yourselves to more champagne."

Robert lifted his glass. "New drinking game, every time they say, 'Parker'."

"Here, here." Christopher drained his glass.

"This is appalling. Where is the security? He invites the guests to paw the jewelry. Anyone could walk up and—"

"Surely not anyone. It would have to be someone exceedingly clever with a deep-seated loathing of this tasteless family."

Robert blanched. "That's an odd thing to say."

"I am an odd man."

"I suppose that so many of the people here, except me, are rich, so they've nothing to worry about."

"In your professional experience, the rich are morally superior?"

"I didn't say that. Wait—how did they pay for all of this? Rumor was they were selling the silver a few years ago. Now they've spent a fortune on thirteen bedrooms, formal garden, all restored. For what?"

"The construction manager said Harold mortgaged everything and hopes to write off the cost when they open the house to tourists in the new year."

"Neighbors will hate that. Tacky. Not surprising."

"Excuse me. I think Felicity is about to become very useful."

Christopher smiled broadly and waved across the room. Felicity hur-ried to his side.

"My dear, you are the most beautiful woman here."

"Mr. Lawson, I'm not—"

"Now, now, I asked you to call me Christopher." A rush of pink rose up her slender neck. Robert pulled at his jacket collar as the space be-tween the reporter and his brother closed.

"I have a feeling that journalism is not your first love, and I have the perfect role for you in my next film, should you be interested."

Her hand flew up to her face. "Of course, I'd love to."

"I thought as much." Christopher turned towards Robert. "If you'll excuse us, Felicity and I will go for a breath of fresh air in the garden." After a few steps, Christopher stopped. "My dear, I forgot my smokes in the car. Why don't you head out, and I'll be right behind you."

When she sashayed to the French doors, Robert grabbed Christo-pher's arm.

"You said the door was alarmed."

"Did I? And I don't smoke. Where is my mind tonight?"

Felicity pushed open the door, and a burglar alarm pierced the air. The few remaining guests in the library ran from the room towards the alarm. Christopher gave a quick glance towards the commotion as he slipped on a latex glove. Then, he pulled a rope of sapphire and diamonds from his pocket and deftly replaced them with the necklace on the plinth. Robert grabbed his arms, but Christopher pulled away and pocketed the jewelry.

"Christopher! What have you done?" he hissed.

"Steady, brother. I've pulled off the biggest acting job of my career." Christopher nodded towards the plinth. "Cost me three hundred pounds for the replacement. Good trade. Wouldn't you say?"

Christopher turned on his heel and headed out of the house. Robert watched his brother open the rear door of his car and slip the necklace into a padded box then wedge it into a divot carved from the underside of the headrest.

Robert grabbed his brother's arms. "Christopher, you can't—"

"Can and did, little brother." He pulled his arms out of Robert's grasp. "Never crush Armani."

"I fail to see the humor—"

"Don't you see what perfect revenge this is? They sack father for something he didn't do—"

"You said he did steal—"

"There's more to it—"

"You'll go to prison. Please put it back before they notice."

"These people used our parents for thirty years, only to rob them of their pension. It is time for the Parkers to make things right."

"Wait, the fake—you brought it, the hiding place—you planned this? That's why you accepted the invite—"

"I've been planning every detail for months."

Robert sputtered as he paced around the front of the car. He weighed his sworn duty to uphold the law against the thought of putting his brother behind bars. He saw his mother waiting in the visitor's lounge to see her eldest son, sent up by her youngest. Christopher slid past Robert and walked towards the house. Robert caught up, grabbed his hand, his fingernails digging into Christopher's flesh. "We can't go back in. What if they realize it's a fake?"

He watched a smile slowly grow on Christopher's lips. "If? I'm counting on it."

* * * *

Christopher's heart raced. He positioned himself near the fake wedding set and pretended to take a phone call, while Robert stood nearby, still in shock. Christopher hoped to lure his rival to eavesdrop. Christopher called out the name "Marty" several times, feigning delight with his non-existent call. He caught Taylor's eye and laughed heartily. Taylor stepped closer with Harold at his heels.

"News on the role?" His already impressive baritone lowered another half octave.

"What a nosy old hen you are, Taylor. You will be receiving a call from your agent shortly. Let's enjoy the evening, eh?" He shifted slightly, so Taylor's only path to leave was to awkwardly back up or slip past the plinth.

He held out a hand. "May the best man win."

As they shook hands, Christopher took a step towards Harold causing him to lose his footing and send the plinth to the ground. The necklace and earrings thudded to the marble floor as a roomful of England's upper crust gasped in unison.

"Too much champagne, I dare say," Christopher said, helping Harold to his feet. Felicity dropped her glass of champagne and screamed when Harold dropped back to his knees.

"It can't be, my diamonds, shattered—"

Christopher patted him on the shoulder. "There now. It's only a display model, right? Isn't the real necklace in a safe—"

Harold shook his head. "The copy wasn't ready. Call the police."

Christopher stepped forward and clapped his hands together. "Indeed, call and report a fraud."

Harold hissed. "A fraud? What the devil—"

"Isn't it obvious?" Christopher looked around the room of gape-mouthed faces. Robert held his breath.

"My dear man, you brought in a priceless heirloom and were given back a fake." He picked up the earrings and replaced them on the stand. "The earrings must be genuine. Look. Not a nick. Real diamonds."

Harold picked up the biggest piece of glass and threw it to the floor. "The repairs were done from a jeweler of the utmost reputation, appraised by three experts. There's no way—"

"Then, there is a thief among us. Yes, please do call the police. Search us all." Under his breath, he muttered, "Lovely headline. Felicity, you have your lead story for tomorrow. Tarrington House guests accused of theft."

Harold glanced around the room, his face drained of color. Reporters invited to broadcast the renewed glory of his great triumph were now poised to write of dukes and earls accused of theft. He nodded towards the servants who had gathered behind him. "Clean this up, please. Mind you, don't cut yourself."

"Everyone, shall we move back into the great room?" Harold called out and swept his hand towards the door.

In moments, the crowd had thinned, and Christopher bent over to pick up a piece of glass. "I'd say the Earl of Harrow is a broken man." He dropped the glass into a waste bin.

"Let's go, now, Christopher."

"Patience, brother—"

"I dare say you've pushed your luck enough for one night."

"One lifetime, I would have thought. As you wish."

Harold was standing in the foyer, going through the motion of thanking guests as they left. Christopher slapped a hand on Harold's shoulder. "Thank you for a most entertaining evening. Robert has an early morning. Chasing after the bad guys is a never-ending task." Christopher bit back a smile on seeing the sadness in Harold's eyes. "Really remarkable what you've done with the place."

Felicity batted her long lashes and mouthed, "Call me."

Christopher tossed his car keys to Robert as they walked down the driveway. "Mind driving? I'm a bit revved up."

Robert raced around the car and shoved Christopher against a door. "Good God, Christopher, I really should turn you in. You've flouted everything I believe in tonight."

Christopher grasped Robert's hands and moved them away from his jacket. He smoothed out the front of his tuxedo. Then, he folded his lanky body into the passenger seat. Robert stomped around the car and slunk behind the wheel.

"Everything you believe in? What about family? Our bond as brothers?"

"I'm sworn to uphold the bloody laws of our country, and you committed a felony, right in front of me. You knew I was too weak to turn you in, and I am so angry at myself that you were right. Tomorrow, I'm resigning."

"Oh, don't be so dramatic. I'm the actor."

"You're a thief, a common criminal."

"There's nothing common about what I did tonight. It took months of planning—"

"You're proud of yourself?"

"Yes."

"What? You're proud of committing a felony?"

"Our parents will never want for anything in their retirement."

"You've supported them for years. They have everything they need."

"Except their dignity. I'm going to tell them that Harold had a change of heart, knows Dad didn't steal those tools, and is providing their pension. In a way, it is true."

"But Dad knows he stole the tools—"

"I only had time for half the story. Dad always insisted he didn't steal from the Parkers, and usually, he confesses to Mum immediately. A few years after they were fired, I saw Harold in a restaurant. His date made a fuss over me, insisted I join them, and in no time she was playing a very one-sided game of footsie with me. Harold was furious with me, and just like tonight, he told the story of Dad being a thief, but he could never prove it, so he made sure he got caught."

"He set Dad up."

"He all but admitted it."

Robert started the car. "Suddenly my world isn't so black and white. How are you going to turn the loot into cash? Every jeweler will be alerted—"

"I know a fence, advisor on a movie. He'll take the stones out of their setting and then sell them individually when he can. For now, I'll use my own money to give them the back pay of their pension. Oh no, rookie mistake, telling a copper about my clever plan."

A hint of a smile tugged at Robert's lips. "You've thought of almost everything, but what about Felicity? She said to call her, but you never got her number."

"You disappoint me." Christopher pushed a hand into his left jacket pocket and pulled out a clutch of business cards and a napkin. He thumbed through the papers, then handed one to Robert. Felicity Solon's business card with a red heart drawn around her mobile number. Robert started the car down the driveway.

Christopher knew his brother would never admit it, but he must be a tiny bit proud of him. He felt so alone in the world of Hollywood gold diggers, agents, and fans. It warmed him to know his brother would always be there for him. He fought to keep his eyes open when the adrenaline ebbed. Then his phone rang. Through heavy lidded eyes, he saw his agent's number. He slipped the phone into his jacket pocket and closed his eyes. To learn he had lost yet another role to Taylor was a sting he could not face sober. Learning he had won the role could not make him feel better than knowing he got away clean with the necklace and that his brother had his back. He closed his eyes as Robert turned south towards London.

Mary Fern Ross is a systems analyst in the better town of the Twin Cities. She started her writing career in third grade by taking over a group project to write a play, which sadly, closed on opening night. When Mary isn't writing or reading she can be found birding with her son, rowing at the gym, or spending a weekend on the North Shore of Lake Superior. She blogs infrequently at mary-fernross.com.

ROOM AND BOARD

VINNIE HANSEN

"Dude, I know a way you can pay."

Jayden cracked open a crusty, pink-rimmed eye, his gaze traveling up brown fabric to a blurry figure hovering above the back of the couch. "Huh?" His stomach tumbled. From the meth or from the dawning Matt had another scheme for him, Jayden wasn't sure.

Matt walked around the couch to face him, swigging a Red Bull breakfast and tossing messy, sun-bleached hair from his eyes. "Yeah, bro, Tasha is sick of this shit." Matt swirled a finger to indicate the cheap ball-point pen on the coffee table—traces of crystal at the end—and the tiny empty plastic bag beside it. "You can't keep couch surfing without contributing. Least not here."

Jayden blinked and propped himself onto elbows. Without Matt's assistance, he'd be living in his truck, shooed from place to place by the cops, competing for available toilets with the hordes of homeless in Santa Cruz.

Matt paced back and forth, like he meant to deepen the groove in the worn carpet.

"So I have a plan." He drained his drink, crushed the can under his Converse sneakers, and threw the flattened metal onto Jayden's stomach.

Drops of liquid shocked his skin. He'd been sweaty last night and stripped down to his boxers. He brushed the cold metal to the floor and sat up, wrapping his arms around his torso. Epically groggy, he squinted at Matt, trying to follow his words.

"They need a docent at the Surf Museum."

Jayden rubbed the goosebumps on his arms and scanned the room for a possible cigarette. "What's a docent?"

Matt lit a cigarette, then fished another from the package and lobbed it to Jayden. "Someone who shows people around, answers questions."

Matt had not yet untacked the sheet covering the window, so Jayden peered through the dimness at him. "Why does anyone need to be shown around? That place is like the size of this room."

"I know, huh?" Matt flicked his burnt-out match to the floor and resumed pacing. "It's perfect. You just sit there and answer questions about surfing." He pitched the book of matches to Jayden.

"How much does it pay?"

Matt stopped walking. "The thing is, it doesn't."

* * * *

Jayden's flip flops slapped the concrete floor of the lighthouse, home of the museum. He followed black hair swaying above a tight butt. Peach-colored yoga pants gripped curves so closely that the girl might as well have been naked. *Dude, if you don't stop, you're going to give new meaning to Woodies on the Wharf.*

Biting his chapped lip, Jayden forced his attention to the displays. On a bulletin board beside him, yellowing newspaper articles showed photos of record waves.

What Matt wanted, as payment for a place to crash, was an early Johnny Rice longboard. According to Matt, it was hanging on the far wall. Surfers lusted after the artistic boards shaped by the dead, local surfing legend. "It'll be epic riding that thing," Matt had said.

Jayden wasn't surprised at Matt's plan. As long as Jayden had known him—since middle school—Matt had survived by posing as a Greek god with Jayden, a useful dark shadow, following his glory.

Problem was, in the little museum, boards leaned and hung everywhere—dozens of them.

The hottie in front of Jayden explained the duties, adding, "The docent gig is really chill."

In front of an exhibit of black-and-white photos of Hawaiian prince surfers in Santa Cruz, the girl turned to face him, all smooth skin and blue eyes. "If you surf Steamer Lane," she burbled, "you can come straight out of the water and be at work."

He hitched up his long shorts, sagging off his hips. "Awesome." *Especially if my schedule overlaps yours.* His gaze roved up the brick walls. "Some of these displays are way high," he said, scratching an ear.

She eyed him. "Yeah, it must have been crazy hanging the big boards." She pointed at a board propped in sand behind a cordoned-off area. "That plank weighs 95 pounds."

The board reached to the rafters.

"Check this out." She motioned to a surfboard missing a chunk from its bottom. "Shark attack."

"That's dope," he said.

"Totally, huh? Better than a leg, though."

* * * *

Lighting a cigarette, Jayden sank into Matt's couch. Or, to be more accurate, Tasha's couch. "I had to fill out an application," Jayden whined, "*and* interview with the Santa Cruz Surfing Society." He threw the burnt match onto the littered coffee table. "I hope you appreciate what I'm going through here."

In front of him, Matt, shirtless, resumed wearing out the carpet. Broad-shouldered and bronzed, Matt attracted babes like a sale at Forever 21. "Another option," Matt offered, "is you could get a real job."

Jayden snorted. This from a guy who'd never worked a day in his life.

After Jayden's parents kicked him out the first time, he'd bagged groceries, but that schedule seriously interfered with surfing. He'd quit to take a night gig at a theater. Leave it to Matt to get him fired for letting him and Tasha sneak in. But what could he do? Just a room in Santa Cruz ran $800. "If I'm gonna go through all this," Jayden said, "you better be sure Tasha will let me stay."

Matt stopped and smirked. "She *loves* me."

Jayden frowned. "If you have that much influence, why do I have to go through all this bullshit?"

Matt leaned over the coffee table and drilled a finger into Jayden's chest. "You're in no position to negotiate." He fished a cigarette from the package in the pocket of Jayden's flannel shirt. "So, how's our plan going?"

"Your plan, you mean."

"Yeah."

"Okay, I guess," Jayden said. "I asked for the least busy day, like maybe I wasn't sure of myself, you know."

"You'll want to park in the spaces beside the lighthouse."

Anxiety welled up in Jayden. "If I can get one." This was all easy for Matt. He was taking none of the risk.

"Well, if you can't, wait until someone leaves and go out during your shift to move your truck. It seems pretty loosey-goosey over there."

Jayden scratched at his arm, sprinkling himself with cigarette ash. "Damn." He swiped at the burn, smearing gray along the top of his hand. Matt's whole scheme depended on the laid-back vibe of the museum, and the idea that with surfboards all over, no one would miss one. At least, not right away.

"Relax, dude," Matt said. "Even if someone sees you, in that vicinity, lots of people are walking around with boards."

"Not Johnny Rice longboards."

"Who's going to pay attention to that?"

Jayden stubbed out his cigarette in a jar lid and scrubbed at his forehead. Tasha's couch squished under his weight but at least he could stretch his feet over the arm rest and get comfy. There was no way to get comfortable in the cab of his truck. "Seriously, do you have anything better than cigarettes?" he asked.

* * * *

Jayden sagged on a wobbly stool behind the counter, feeling as noodled as if he'd surfed all day. He appreciated the divider between him and the museum visitors. People flowed in and out of the single room, kids on rollerblades, old farts with canes, and foreigners.

These people with their questions: "Is this the original Jack O'Neill wetsuit?" "Which surfboard is worth the most?" "What do you do with Sex Wax?"

In between answering questions and selling keychains and beanies, he'd been busy checking out how he might climb up to reach a surfboard. At least a dozen of them hung from the rafters in rope cradles. He might be able to use the sandwich-board sign that said SANTA CRUZ SURF-ING MUSEUM T-SHIRTS FOR $20 as a step-stool to clamber on top of the postcard display rack.

At ten minutes before four, Jayden pushed upright and used his hands like a megaphone: "The museum closes in ten minutes."

The last few visitors straggled toward the door. A young man with a heavy accent stopped to ask him, "When will there be more surfers?"

"When the surf's up?"

The man blinked at him. "When will that be?"

"Call a surf shop," Jayden said. "They can tell you."

Finally, the place emptied, and he locked the door. He circled the room, reading the labels. *Epic good luck.* A custom Johnny Rice surf-board leaned against a case housing old surfing DVDs.

He hefted the glossy redwood board out of the sand display. He couldn't tip it without banging into stuff, so holding it in a vertical posi-tion, he duck-walked it across the room. Damn the thing was heavy. Peering out the exit, he tipped the board to carry it under his arm. The rush of adrenaline was almost as good as meth.

The esplanade veered away in a horseshoe around the lighthouse, so walkers and bikers weren't paying any attention to him. *Just like Matt said.* The ocean vistas, their cell phones, their dogs riveted their atten-tion. Heart racing, Jayden lifted the board into the back of his old Toyota truck.

He trotted back to lock up the building, looked around again to see if anyone was watching, and then drove off. *Piece of cake.*

Matt stared into the bed of Jayden's faded red Toyota. "Dude, this is made of redwood."

Jayden ran his hand over the glossy finish. "Pretty sick, huh?"

"This is the wrong board."

The juice drained out of Jayden. "It's a Johnny Rice longboard. That's what you said."

"There's a balsawood one. With a trick design of different woods on the fin." Matt clapped Jayden's shoulders and spun him to face him. "It's hanging up. Was this one hanging up?"

Jayden gulped. "What am I supposed to do?"

"Take it back. Get the right board."

"That might be better to do at night."

Matt nodded. "Do you still have the key to the museum?"

"You think I drove to the Surfing Society with that board in my truck?" Jayden said. Matt could be so dense.

"Well, before you turn it in, make a copy." Matt dipped his hand into the pocket of his shorts and fished out a baggy. "We'll celebrate later."

* * * *

Pen knife in his pocket, Jayden putted across Santa Cruz, taking surface roads. He was pumped, like Scott Lang in *Ant Man* traveling into the quantum realm. When the Toyota hit a pothole, the heavy surfboard bounced and whammed precariously against the tailgate.

Even at midnight, the esplanade was not deserted. Moonlight silhouetted a few walkers. In the parking lot, a homeless man rattled by, his supermarket cart piled high. He headed toward the field across the street. Jayden swallowed, sweat gathering in his armpits. Without some luck, he could end up like that guy. At least he had his truck, though.

He climbed from the cab. The quiet of night amplified the crashing of the waves below the cliffs. In front of him, the lighthouse threw its beam out to the water. How amazing that with the duplicate key, he could just waltz right into this place. His heart hammered with excitement.

Inside the dark interior, Jayden lugged the board back through the clutter, hefted it over the velvet ropes, and propped it in the sand. Using his phone's flashlight, he hoped to spot the Johnny Rice board suspended conveniently above the counter or over the flat, glass-covered display case across the room, but the light-colored board of Matt's wet dream hung above the housing for an old DVD player and monitor.

Jayden lit a cigarette and wiggled the stool from behind the counter, placing it beside the tall housing case. Holding the cigarette between his teeth, Jayden scrambled on top of the stool. It rocked beneath him.

Jayden yelped, latching on to the display. His cigarette tumbled down, like a surfer wiping out.

Jayden gripped the top of the case. The stool leg cracked. His foot slipped into the air, the sudden weight yanking one hand loose. Jayden let himself drop back to the floor. *Damn!*

He scouted around on the floor for the cigarette but couldn't spot it. He couldn't waste time looking for it. Kicking the stool aside, he dragged the sandwich board over, scraping it across the concrete.

He sniffed. *Smoke!* He no sooner smelled it than a displayed newspaper article curled into flame. Jayden slapped at it with his palm.

Holy shit! That hurt.

Sucking a burned finger, Jayden considered. The fire would consume the old newspaper and die. The best idea was to get the board and get out quick.

He lifted himself on top of the sandwich-board sign, as the flames licked another article. Glancing at the longboard, Jayden pulled up and belly flopped on top of the case.

Pushing up to all fours, Jayden coughed as smoke drifted upward. With shaking hands, he sliced at the nearest rope around the longboard. *Damn this knife is puny.*

And dull.

But, if he could cut the first loop, he could probably tug and tip the board out of its cradle.

The flames below him devoured the newspaper clippings, then died back as he'd expected.

Jayden sawed at the last fibers of rope. Black smoke coiled up, worse than before, choking him. He squinted down, eyes burning. The newspapers had been consumed, but the wood-framed cork board behind them was smoldering. He hacked at the rope.

The final thread gave way.

Pulling the board toward him, Jayden pushed the end downward, but the board was too long. The part remaining in the ropes held it in place.

Leaning precariously from the top of the case, Jayden chopped at the next loop of rope.

The smoke thickened. Closing his eyes, he slashed blindly. When the rope snapped, his body pitched forward. He grabbed at the board for balance. Unsupported, it crashed to the floor. Jayden's body plunged after it. Flinging out a hand, he grabbed a rafter and dangled like a monkey.

His heart raced, but damn, this was fun, like making the drop on a big wave.

He released his hold, bending his knees for impact. His feet landed on the surfboard. The glossy wood skidded on the concrete. Jayden sailed backward. He threw out a hand to break his fall, but his ass slammed against the concrete. Pain shot through his wrist and hipbone. *A total wipeout.*

Above him, the tail of a Santa Cruz Surf Club t-shirt ignited. The ancient shirt burned well, the blaze shooting toward the ropes. A fire alarm shrieked.

Time to bail!

Dragging the board to the door, Jayden glanced, wide-eyed, over his shoulder, as the fire crackled along the rope. A surfboard plummeted, hitting a standing surfboard, which toppled another surfboard to the floor.

Holy shit!

He jammed out the door and tucked the surfboard under his arm, his wrist protesting. Behind him, the alarm was squealing his crime to the world, and through the windows framing the entrance, light flickered.

He pitched the board into the truck bed, scurried to the cab, and would have burned rubber—if there'd been any left on his tires.

As he swerved onto West Cliff Drive, the surfboard slid along the top of the tailgate. He hadn't put it in far enough, but he wasn't going to stop now. Late-night strollers, the people in the houses along West Cliff, everyone could hear that alarm.

Jayden careened onto a side street, the board bumping and hopping. He checked the rearview. The board had slipped around, so it was practically sideways, sticking far out on the passenger side.

A fire truck wailed. Jayden started at the nearness of it.

He flew around the next corner, the board bouncing, teetering from the bed of the truck. The fire engine shrilled toward him. Jayden swerved to the side of the street and hit a pothole. The end of the board lifted, and the Johnny Rice launched into an aerial ride, its final performance, taking the drop, before riding across the pavement into the far lane.

Jayden stomped on his brakes and scrambled from the cab in time to watch the fire truck roll over the fin, crushing wood and hope.

At the side of the road, Jayden stood, arms dangling and mouth agape, staring at the bits of board sprinkled across the road. *Matt's gonna be so pissed.*

Jayden darted into the street and started picking up the bigger pieces—the evidence. If everything in the museum burned, they might never know about the theft. And if the door burned, maybe they wouldn't know he'd left it unlocked behind him.

After collecting and tossing bits of surfboard into the bed of the truck, Jayden climbed in and drove slowly away, his hands shaking on the steering wheel. *Maybe the fire experts will figure it was an accident, caused by a smoldering cigarette. Dropped by a tourist.* He hoped they never figured out it was him.

He didn't want to be known as the guy who burned down The Surfing Museum. Even the surfers he hung with would hate him.

If he didn't end up in a bunk at the county jail, he faced a future of sleeping scrunched up in his truck. For reasons Jayden couldn't explain, he found himself back at the museum, parking on West Cliff Drive. *Returning to the scene of the crime.*

Why did criminals do this?

A few spectators had gathered in the eerie yellow parking lot light. None of them looked in Jayden's direction. Through his windshield, he watched a silhouetted firefighter tug on the hose. The others were inside.

The lighthouse might be gutted, but at least it was going to stand, beaming its signal to save lives. If only it could save him. Jayden pounded the steering wheel. What did he have to show for all this? An epic zero. No board. No room.

Vinnie Hansen fled the howling winds of South Dakota and headed for the California coast the day after high school graduation. As a child, she read while huddled on top the dryer. She's now the author of numerous short stories, the Carol Sabala mystery series, and *Lostart Street*, a cross-genre novel of mystery, murder, and moonbeams. Still sane(ish) after 27 years of teaching high school English, Vinnie has retired. She plays keyboards with ukulele bands in Santa Cruz, California, where she lives with her husband and the requisite cat.

PAYOUT PAYBACK

SUSAN BICKFORD

For a few days in early summer, Caroline Cooke thought she was a wealthy woman. Perhaps not Silicon Valley rich, but at least comfortably well-off, at the ripe young age of thirty-two.

Striking gold in Silicon Valley was tougher than high-tech mythology might lead many to believe. The layoff paperwork in her hands proved that.

She tilted her head back to savor the typical Silicon Valley summer day—not too hot, not too cold, not humid, not a cloud in the sky—and headed indoors to the year-round climate-controlled office of XIM, now her former employer.

A tall woman with long black hair was pounding her head against the window under the XIM logo in slow thuds. As she drew closer, Caroline recognized Mita Srinivasan, head of the testing group. Caroline was the lead engineer of the development team. They had been to hell and back on many projects.

"You'll give yourself a concussion," Caroline said.

Mita paused but didn't turn. Her hands and forehead rested on the glass. Her breath fogged the window. "I won't kill Daniel if I'm unconscious. What kind of CEO lays off over half the company, just before we're acquired?"

"The kind of CEO who wants all the money for himself. And his cronies."

"We've been…" Mita's face crumpled into a scowl.

"Screwed. That's the American term."

* * * *

Caroline stomped up the stairs from the lower lobby and made her way to Pat's office. Pat was XIM's Human Resources director. She had been meeting with other laid-off workers all morning and looked a bit frayed around the edges. Not that Caroline had any sympathy.

"Word is you aren't part of the layoff, Pat. Why do they need a Human Remains department if there are no remains left to manage?"

"Don't start with me, Cookie. You're better off than most," Pat said, as she smoothed her hair and adjusted her twin-set sweater.

"My name's Caroline, Patty. And there are about thirty people who are better off than me who are still employees of XIM."

"Well, here's a silver lining you might like. We want you to stay on as a contractor for approximately four months until the final payout goes through. There's a lot of work that needs to be coordinated with our new home, TDI."

Caroline suppressed a gag and picked up the papers. TDI had a terrible reputation as a place to work—a fact she would have been willing to overlook for ten or twenty million dollars.

"As you can see, we will pay you very good money. Much more than you earn now, and it's hourly, so you'll be fully compensated for all those long days," Pat said, tapping her fingers on the edge of her desk.

Caroline grunted. She didn't dare open her mouth for fear steam—or something worse—would come out.

"And at the end, you'll get a bonus. Twenty thousand dollars." Pat leaned forward and winked, as if she and Caroline shared some secret bond. "Don't forget that you may want a good recommendation for your next job."

"Do I have a choice?"

"Not if you want to maintain your reputation in Silicon Valley." Pat winked again. "Or maybe you could move back to Iowa."

"Central New York," Caroline said. She picked up a pen.

* * * *

Caroline cornered Daniel in his office on her third day as a contractor. His admin, Zoe, was at lunch. Pat was in a meeting. Caroline didn't expect to achieve anything, except a bit of self-respect. If she slunk away with her tail between her legs, she would never be right in her soul.

She stepped inside his glass-walled sanctuary and slammed the door.

If Daniel was startled or nervous, he didn't show it. He leaned back in his big leather chair and put his feet up on the desk. Caroline ground her teeth at the insult.

A slow grin oozed across Daniel's face. "Cookie. Now, now, don't be mad. You remind me of my wife. She's mighty pissed I divorced her last year. Fifty percent of next to nothing wasn't much of a settlement."

"I never liked Amanda, but I'm beginning to sympathize."

"I warned you. I told you to play nice. Multiple times." Daniel paused to lick his lips. "You got on your high horse, and now you're a loser. Just like Amanda."

Caroline turned and left. So much for soul soothing. It was time for revenge.

* * * *

The next day, Caroline arrived around 10 a.m. to find she had a new companion sitting in the big open bullpen—Mita.

"Welcome to the transition team," Caroline said.

"I had to think about it a couple of days." Mita slammed down her laptop and slumped into a chair. "I decided, if I wanted to kill Daniel, I'd need better access."

"You'll have to stand in line. Besides, he's always in meetings now with his new peeps. I do wonder if I would be any better off if I had slept with him."

"Don't count on that. Barbara slept with him, and she was laid off."

Caroline stood and wandered around to make sure they were alone. "Any great ideas on how to extract our pound of flesh?"

"Run him over in the parking lot?"

Caroline stroked her chin. "The problem is, he can only die once. I'd prefer something more agonizing and protracted."

"How are you going to do that? Too complicated. We should take remote control of his Tesla and flatten him."

"Daniel treasures money and status. We need to find a way to deprive him of one of those. Preferably both."

* * * *

Caroline pushed Mita out onto a small balcony overlooking the parking lot, climbing through one of the only windows that was not hermetically sealed. Mita took the opportunity to enjoy a smoke, far away from the eyes of tobacco usage enforcement.

"We shouldn't talk inside," Caroline said. "There are too many ways for people to eavesdrop—cell phones left lying around, laptops recording video, hidden cameras."

"You don't have to lecture me. I tried to figure out if I was on the layoff list doing all those things."

Caroline stepped back to study her friend. "I'm impressed."

Mita blew smoke over Caroline's head. "Video surveillance stuff is highly overrated. Very inefficient. The only thing I learned was that Daniel and Pat are having an affair."

"Everyone knew that. No video recording required."

"Exactly my point."

Caroline turned to face the parking lot and drew imaginary diagrams in the air. "I think our best bet is to execute a man-in-the-middle attack." She wiggled the fingers of her right hand. "At some point, TDI has to send acquisition payout money to the incoming XIM people." She pointed to the wiggling fingers of her left hand. "Where we need to be is right here." She clapped her hands together in the middle. "We'll nab the payout money in flight."

Mita snapped her cigarette butt over the side of the balcony. It struck Daniel's Tesla on the hood before bouncing into the parking lot. "No problem. Figure out the date and time of the payout. Create a fake account to receive the money. Slip that into the list somehow. Make sure Daniel doesn't know, and live happily ever after. Did I miss anything?"

"Don't get caught," Caroline said. She stepped back through the window.

* * * *

The strategy was clear: intercept Daniel's payout. The tactics were not as apparent.

Caroline spent several fruitless hours each day hunched over her laptop, considering their options. Quick glances at Mita seemed to indicate no bright ideas were forthcoming from that direction, either.

Around them, the half-filled bullpen buzzed with former XIM contract employees like herself, as well as a handful of soon-to-be TDI workers. Caroline did her best to encourage professionalism and collegiality with team meetings and paid for a happy hour at the local Mexican hangout.

It was a lost cause. Within a week, only the contract workers came into the office. Within two weeks, Mita and Caroline were the only workers of any kind in the bullpen while everyone else worked from home.

The company Caroline had worked so hard to help establish was dead, and she was stuck propping up the corpse. She would have preferred to work from home as well, but the summer weather turned brutally hot, and she did not have air conditioning in her tiny apartment. She stayed in the arctic chill of the office until late at night, warmed by the fury in her blood.

* * * *

Caroline's father was fond of saying, "You make your own luck."

By hanging out in the office, pretending to be content, keeping her head down, and paying attention, Caroline managed to be in the right place at the right time one afternoon in early August.

She was alone in the bullpen. Mita was in a project review. Pat, Daniel, and Zoe all had offices on the opposite side of the building.

Eventually, nature called, and she went to the Ladies Room, located off an internal corridor in the middle of the building. As she left, she caught a glimpse of Pat standing at the shared combination printer-copier with a hefty stack of papers.

Caroline stepped back into the bathroom alcove. The last thing she wanted was another round of fake cordiality with their HR stooge. She smiled a mirthless grin as she watched Pat struggle with the notoriously balky machine.

The problem was obvious—the original sheets of paper had been previously folded to fit in letter-sized envelopes, and they weren't feeding into the copier smoothly. Caroline could have stepped in to help, but there was no way she was going to reach out to the hapless Pat.

After several false starts and a lot of cursing on Pat's part, the copying job proceeded, stopped, and started again. A jazzy tune jingled, barely audible over the grinding of the machine. Pat moved away from the copier to answer her cell phone.

"Hold on, hold on. I'm at the copier. It's too noisy in here." Pat walked away from the machine, phone to her ear, and headed for the second-floor lobby.

Caroline snaked in behind Pat's retreating form. She flipped through the copies as they popped out into the collator. Personal documents. Employee names. Social Security numbers. Birth dates. Amount of payout.

She grabbed the pile of finished copies, fed it back into the hopper, and pressed *Copy*. She prayed the copies would pass through faster than the originals.

Edging to the wall, she could see Pat's phone call was wrapping up. She snatched the new copies, swapped in the first copies onto the collator and made a dash back to the Ladies Room.

Safely locked in the large handicapped stall, Caroline sat and studied her acquisition. This was better than she had hoped. Every page contained critical information about each XIM employee eligible for a payout. She sorted the pile so that XIM executives were at the top. At the very top, she put Daniel's page.

* * * *

Mita strolled in after her meeting. "Ugh. As if our XIM meetings weren't bad enough before. This transition work is torture." She stopped to study Caroline, who was slumped in her chair, her gaze fixed on the printer-copier. "Hey. What's with you?"

Caroline looked up and gestured toward the balcony. "Let's step outside for a smoke."

After Caroline had explained her close call with Pat, Mita lit a cigarette. "That is very cool but too risky. How can we possibly monitor that machine twenty-four/seven?"

Caroline leaned over the railing and hawked a wad of phlegm toward Daniel's Tesla, parked below. It fell short.

"We don't have to."

"Please explain."

"Here's a funny coincidence. As an undergrad, I wrote printer software as my summer job. I'll have you know I speak Printer."

"Okay. I'm impressed. So what?"

Caroline leaned back against the balcony rails. "These multi-function things are computers, just like our laptops. They sit on the network. They have operating systems. They have disk drives. They have USB ports."

Judging by Mita's squint and wrinkled forehead, Caroline could see the wheels in Mita's brain were turning. She continued. "Every single job that you send to the printer from your computer or feed into the machine to copy is stored. Think of all the company secrets still on that piece of junk."

Mita turned to look through the window at the printer-copier. "Wouldn't that be a rather large security hole?"

"Agreed. There are a number of measures IT can take to make sure the data is encrypted, not retained, and so forth. But for many companies, investing in security is at the bottom of the list. I'm betting that unit has never been secured. Data is probably stored unencrypted, and copying jobs aren't cleared. I can log in and pull off all that information. There will be a lot of junk, but there will also be nuggets of gold—personal information, schedules, dollar amounts, signatures—stuff we could use to figure out how to siphon off Daniel's money. I'd bet my bonus on it."

"You'll need that bonus for bail if you get caught." Mita stubbed out her cigarette. "So do it."

"Patience. I have no intention of getting caught. It's probably impossible not to leave a few footprints, but if we're careful, we won't be trackable."

"Now that you mention it, they did gut IT."

"It's not IT I'm worried about." Caroline grabbed Mita's arm. "If we make off with millions, we'll have every agency around looking for where it went and how. Each employee who was laid off will be top on their list. We need to make certain nothing can be traced back to us."

* * * *

After work, Caroline and Mita paid a visit to an obscure computer supply store and picked up the cheapest and smallest laptop they could find. At the public library, they set up the computer, including an anonymizing browser and related encryption tools.

"We need to figure out what kind of bank or brokerage account TDI needs to process Daniel's payout money. There's no way they will accept some sort of offshore or numbered account." Mita tapped her pen. "We will need a standard account to receive the money. We'll transfer the money out right away to something like a numbered account and then split it up between us."

"We have Daniel's information from Pat's documents. We can set up a dummy account, no problem."

"I'll figure out how to set up the anonymous accounts. It might require a bit of upfront money. A couple thousand? Can you do that?"

"I'll come up with it somehow," Caroline said. She closed the laptop. "The bigger issue is to figure out how to slip the bogus account information into what needs to go to TDI. And when."

"I thought that was what hacking the printer was for." Mita stood and stretched with a yawn.

"That should tell us what we need and when we need it, but not how to do the swap. One step at a time."

"For now, that step is home to bed."

* * * *

In the morning, Caroline plugged the little laptop directly into a Local Area Network port in the small conference room near the lobby. She hoped this would be more anonymous than a wireless connection.

Once on the network, she connected to the printer-copier, now nicknamed "Junior," using its IP address in her browser. Within minutes, the Junior was retaining all copy, fax, and print jobs, plus sending backups to the USB drive she plugged into the back of the device. She disconnected the laptop and turned it off.

She had a new routine. Every night she removed the current USB drive, handed it to Mita, and replaced it with a new one. Mita scoured the day's data with the enthusiasm of a gold miner and reported back the next day.

* * * *

"We need to come in earlier for Junior's disks. I caught Pat prowling around, looking into drawers and lockers. She gets in really early," Caroline said to Mita in the bathroom as they ran water in the sinks to mask their whispered conversation. "We don't want to be the most obvious suspects."

"Yes, I get that," Mita said.

"I'm not sure we need much more information from the printer." Caroline washed her hands for the third time. "We know the date TDI will direct Daniel's payout to an account, and we want that to be ours. Time has come to insert our information into a list. That's the last tough task to figure out. At least, the next part is easier. Pat will send an email to everyone when those go out. We need Daniel's email login information to intercept and delete that message."

Mita gawked. "And how is that easier? He always locks his laptop."

"Simple. This is social engineering. Not the real stuff. If we need to intercept Daniel's email, we need the weakest link."

* * * *

Sitting in her own cubicle around the corner from Daniel's office, Zoe was Daniel's admin and also assisted Pat. Zoe was cute, a bit of a dim bulb, and she was on The List of employees moving to the new company, thus due to receive a nice payout.

Being on Zoe's good side had benefits. In return for help with technical issues, Zoe was a good source for office gossip. Zoe also had full access to Daniel's email and calendar.

The weakest link.

Caroline resisted the temptation to search out Zoe. Patience was hard to come by these days, but she knew Zoe would be around soon to ask for help on some oddball problem.

She was rewarded several days later when Zoe appeared in the bullpen, red in the face. "I need to send Pat some information on the payout accounts, but I can't figure out what she really wants. And she needs it now."

"I'll be right there," Caroline said. She unlocked a drawer and extracted a copy of Daniel's false account information. She selected *Record* on her phone's camera app and set out for Zoe's cube. Standing behind Zoe, she could see the admin's laptop screen was locked. *Good girl, Zoe.*

"Turn away," Zoe said. "I need to enter my password."

"No problem." Caroline turned her back but held her phone up facing over her shoulder to capture every one of Zoe's keystrokes.

Over the next hour, Caroline worked steadily with Zoe, helpfully substituting the sheet of paper with Daniel's new information into the stack of forms Zoe needed to process.

When Zoe left for lunch, Mita kept watch as Caroline logged into Zoe's machine. The email application Daniel and Zoe both used stored account passwords under a protected area in the Tools menu. Within seconds, Caroline had what she needed to access Daniel's account from any computer on the network.

As a test, she sent an email from Zoe to Daniel using her little laptop. She read it as Daniel, deleted it, and removed it from his Trash folder.

All the pieces were in place to step into the middle and snatch Daniel's payout. Now it was about timing—and patience.

* * * *

The month leading up to Payout Day was so tedious, Caroline could barely sit still. Work that required her attention was tapering off, and she was forced to appear busy most of the day. The information flowing from Junior was less and less interesting, but they dutifully checked every day, in case there was a change in dates or updated documents required.

With only three days to go, she overslept and didn't arrive until 10:30 a.m.

She knew something was wrong as soon as she entered the bullpen but needed to turn around in a slow circle twice before she figured it out.

Junior was gone, as was her personal USB drive, dangling out the back.

Once Caroline's breathing returned to normal, she wandered over to Zoe's cube.

"Hey. Where's our printer? I need to print my resume for a job interview."

Zoe looked up. "Some guys took it away first thing. The office is moving at the end of the month. It was as old as the hills and so unreliable."

"How are we supposed to print?"

"Daniel lets me use his private printer. If you really need something, I'll print it for you."

"What if it's private?"

Zoe raised her eyebrows. "Then you shouldn't be using a work printer in the first place."

Caroline strode back to the bullpen. She unlocked her personal file cabinet and pulled out a small disk drive and a set of tools in a palm-sized case as she mentally kicked herself. She should have taken care of cleaning up Junior weeks ago.

She rushed to the upper lobby and ran into Mita coming up the stairs.

"Hi Caroline—" Mita said. "Yikes. Don't grab my arm like that. It hurts."

Caroline pulled Mita back down the stairs. "Shut up," she said in a hiss. "We need to rescue Junior from the eWaste pile."

Mita's eyes were wide and round. "Rear loading dock. Let's go."

* * * *

Caroline and Mita ran through a maze of windowless corridors until they found a door with a wired glass window set about nose high.

Mita stood on tiptoes for a better view. "I see it," she said. "There's one of those big bins on the right. Junior is sitting right next to it."

"Any people?"

"Maintenance guy. Tony?"

"Manny."

"Let me go first." Mita opened the door and slipped through.

Based on hand gestures, Caroline could see Mita was enticing Manny outside for a smoke. Once they had disappeared out the roll-up door, Caroline entered and ran in a crouch to Junior.

First, she yanked the USB backup drive out of the port. Next, she removed three screws at the back of the printer and lifted away the panel hiding the guts of the machine.

She didn't dare look up. Time was too precious. She listened to Mita's banter with Manny and tried to estimate how long a cigarette would last. She disconnected Junior's disk drive, set it down, and plugged in her encrypted and blank replacement.

With the panel back in place, she was halfway through turning the second screw when she heard Mita's voice grow louder. *Leave now.* She picked up the third screw and stuffed it into her pocket before she scurried along the far wall toward the door.

The door clicked shut behind her, and she slumped against the wall, sweat dripping from her face. She jumped when the door opened. Mita stepped through and offered a thumbs up.

"I think I need early lunch," Caroline said. She leaned on Mita's arm on their way back to the unattended lobby.

* * * *

Daniel was swiping his badge to enter the building as Caroline and Mita reached the door to leave.

"Well, well, ladies. Not much time until we will part ways for good. Where're you heading?" he asked.

"To celebrate on your behalf," Caroline said.

He had already turned his back and was heading upstairs and out of earshot. Caroline offered him a middle-finger salute.

After early lunch, Caroline placed Junior's hard drive on the pavement behind the left back wheel of Mita's car.

"Back up about two feet. Now forward. Now back. Good job." She tossed the crumpled drive into a trashcan and jumped into the passenger seat.

* * * *

"Payout Day tomorrow," Mita said, leaning far out over the railing of the balcony to send smoke rings into the sky.

"I've got a new job," Caroline said. "I start in two weeks. It's a good job. I won't be a director, but they're encouraging. Great pay. Stock options. Real HR."

"I've got a job, too. I'll miss you."

"Me, too. But I don't know if I can stand this much fun ever again."

"We don't have to do this. There's time."

"Not impossible. I could change the routing information for Daniel's payout."

"No one would notice?"

"No one would ever double-check."

Neither woman spoke for several minutes.

"Is that what you want to do?" Mita asked at last.

Caroline spat a wad of phlegm at Daniel's Tesla. This time, it hit the window with a splat.

"Nope. Game on."

* * * *

Caroline picked Mita up at midnight, and they rode to the public library. Although the library was closed, the wireless network was accessible by parking close to the building.

They took turns snoozing and monitoring the laptop. Mita gave a yelp when the notice of the payout transfer came in at 4 a.m.

Caroline snatched the laptop, deleted the message from Daniel's Inbox and then from his Trash folder. She handed the laptop back to Mita, who started moving the money.

"I can't close out the brokerage account right away," Mita said after a few breathless minutes. "How much money should I leave?"

"Ten thousand five hundred and thirty-four dollars," Caroline answered.

"Why that amount?"

"Read it like the numbers were letters. Flip the four."

"1-0-5-3-4. *LOSEP*?" Mita chortled. "No. *LOSER*."

* * * *

When Caroline reached the office at 10:00 a.m., several police cars were parked in the round plaza in front of the main entrance, blue lights flashing. She slid her car into the spot beside Mita's and forced herself to breathe steadily before she climbed out and started for the front door.

When they arrest you, ask for a lawyer.

The double doors of the main entrance sprang open as she reached them. She jumped back to avoid being hit by a team of two paramedics, pushing a gurney toward an ambulance, parked in back of the cop cars. The man on the gurney was holding a bloody wad of bandages and icepacks to his head.

They were followed by another team of a man and woman in police uniform, dragging someone in handcuffs between them. *Daniel!*

Caroline rushed upstairs to study the parking lot with Mita on the balcony.

"Who the hell was on the gurney?" she asked.

"Fred Wheeler, CEO of TDI." Mita's eyes were twinkling. "Apparently, Daniel had a fit when he couldn't find his payout this morning. He lost it. He accused poor Freddy of cheating him out of his money and—get this—sleeping with Pat. One thing led to another."

"Of course, someone did take his money," Caroline said, trying not to giggle.

"Yes, but this should throw a twist into the whole investigation."

"Don't you want a cigarette to celebrate?"

Mita emptied her cigarette pack over the side. "Nope. I am suddenly inspired to quit."

* * * *

Due to all the excitement, Mita and Caroline had to wait until Pat returned from making a police statement before they could officially part ways with XIM and TDI.

At 1:00 p.m., Mita coughed and closed her laptop. Caroline followed suit. She slipped all of her desk items into a shopping bag and tucked her work laptop and power cord under her arm.

The two women cooled their heels outside Pat's office.

"I almost feel sorry for her," Mita said, wiping away a fake tear.

"Save it for someone who deserves it."

"Like you?"

"I only need your prayers that we don't get caught."

Pat's door opened. She appeared composed despite a prominent black eye and split upper lip.

She turned and beckoned to Mita. They stepped inside and closed the door.

Caroline slouched down in the chair until her neck rested on top of the padded back, and studied the ceiling. After today, she and Mita wouldn't dare see each other often.

Caroline wasn't certain she would ever be able to tap into those ten million beautiful dollars sitting in the numbered account Mita had created for her. Maybe in a few years, she could suck it over in little sips.

The money didn't matter. Much. She had her sights set on other opportunities. The fiery anger burning in her gut for months had been quenched by revenge.

Ten minutes later, Mita came out and headed downstairs. Per their arrangement, they would each leave right away without speaking and meet for margaritas later and to destroy the little laptop sitting in the trunk of Caroline's car.

"Cookie?" Pat was waving to Caroline from her desk.

Pat pulled out a folder and spread the contents out like a deck of cards. "Please put your laptop and badge on the credenza. Here is your final contractor paycheck and the bonus check. Not as much as you'd like, I know, but still a nice bit of money."

"So it is." Caroline cleared her throat. "I'm sorry to hear about Daniel." She stretched her hand out to sign but found Pat's hands covering the documents.

Pat glared with her one good eye. "No need to feel sorry for Daniel. I understand he was upset, but I'm sure it is a simple mix-up. Going after Fred and me was completely unjustified. We are the ones who were assaulted." Pat's voice was tight with emotion.

"Of course. I didn't state that properly. I'm glad you are reaping your just rewards."

"Thank you." Pat sniffed. "The good news is he won't be working in Silicon Valley ever again. He's looking at jail time. No more big payouts for Danny Boy. There will be a big media circus around this."

You have no idea.

"Pat, if you call me by my name and not 'Cookie,' I'll sign my name to those documents and be on my way."

Pat swallowed and released the papers. "Caroline Cooke, please sign."

Caroline picked up the pen and scrawled her signature.

Pat's shoulders slumped. "Thank you. It's been quite a day. Lots of drama." She stood and escorted Caroline to the door. "I'm sorry this didn't work out the way you hoped. Better luck with your next company."

Caroline shook Pat's hand and looked her in the eye. "Don't worry. I'm good."

Susan Alice Bickford was born in Boston, Massachusetts, and grew up in Central New York. Her passion for technology pulled her to Silicon Valley, where she became an executive at a leading technology company. She now works as an independent consultant and author. She splits her time between Silicon Valley and Vermont. Her first book, *A Short Time to Die*, was released in January 2017. Look for *Dread of Winter* in 2019. Find out more about Susan at www.susanalicebickford.com.

MY NIGHT WITH THE DUKE OF EDINBURGH

SUSAN DALY

I shifted my body for the third time. Even in a black leotard and tights, behind the magnificent Haida totem pole in the center of the marble stairwell, I still wasn't convinced I was invisible to the guard. Across the darkened grand entrance hall of the Royal Ontario Museum, Ted was hidden by the other totem pole.

We waited, timing the guard's second round.

* * * *

How had it come to this? Three weeks ago, we'd all been sitting around the living room of Donovan's comfortable off-campus apartment, enjoying his excellent rye and discussing life and politics and, as ever, the Leafs' chances for the upcoming season.

We really should have known better. As modern history majors in our final year at the University of Toronto, we knew about cause and effect and how international incidents could arise out of the most innocuous actions.

Not that kidnapping Princess Elizabeth's husband could be considered innocuous.

In the early autumn of 1951, there wasn't a soul in Canada unaware of the upcoming Royal Tour. Princess Elizabeth, the lovely young daughter of King George VI and Queen Elizabeth, would be arriving in Canada for a month-long visit. She and her husband—her fairy-tale prince—would travel from one end of the country to the other, as far west as Vancouver Island and then out to the eastern tip, to our newest province, Newfoundland, before sailing home aboard the Empress of Scotland.

"I expect you're all starry-eyed at the prospect, Cathy," Donovan teased. "No doubt you'll stand by the side of the road among the cheering hordes, as though waiting for the Santa Claus Parade. Waiting hours in the glaring sun or miserable rain, just for a fleeting glimpse of the future queen and her golden sun god of a husband."

"Oh, I promised to go with my sisters," I said with a martyr's air. "They're all excited about it." I took refuge in my glass of Northern Spirit Rye. Granted, I was two months short of twenty-one, but our little group had no use for such arbitrary, state-imposed nonsense. A person could either hold their liquor, or they couldn't.

"Come on, Donovan," Ted said. "Hardly comparable to the Santa Claus Parade."

"True," Donovan conceded. "After all, Santa Claus is real."

I tuned myself out of the discussion that followed, nursing my drink. Twelve years ago my family—three generations of us—had gone to Riverdale Park to enjoy the historic sight of the King and Queen themselves, the first time a reigning monarch had come to Canada. I'd returned home, enchanted with having seen them. In person! *In my own city*. My sisters and I had talked of little else for weeks before and after. Grandma swore the Queen had looked directly at us and smiled.

Now, I was damned if I was going to miss this chance to see their daughter when she dazzled her way through Toronto.

I was equally damned if I was going to admit any of this to my fellow students at Victoria College. This year, I had somehow fallen in with the most desirable sub-subset of intellectuals, and I wanted to keep it that way. A clique, furthermore, that revolved around the star that was Donovan Grant.

While Ted and Peggy and Gordie and I were the products of Toronto collegiates and small-town Ontario high schools, Donovan, newly transferred from McGill University, seemed somehow more highly evolved. He was everything we weren't. Bohemian to our bourgeois. Cosmopolitan to our suburban.

"So if I'm to understand what you're saying—" Gordie's verbosity poked its way into my consciousness "—the adoration of the masses heaped upon these peripatetic figureheads is more than harmless amusement; that it can actually be detrimental to Canada's growth as a nation?"

Wow. What had I missed?

Donovan's slight nod indicated Gordie had summed it up nicely. "Indeed. The financial cost of supporting the monarchy aside, the cost to our autonomy as a sovereign nation is even greater."

"And you're suggesting the overthrow of the monarchy is our only hope?" I wasn't sure if Ted was for or against the idea. "Like Cromwell's republic?"

"Which didn't actually endure," Peggy pointed out. "You need to look closer to home for a lasting example." She glanced in a more-or-less southerly direction.

"A re-enactment of the American Revolution on Canadian soil?" Gordie said. "Hardly going to improve our graduating marks. In fact, it could conceivably get us executed for treason."

Before Peggy could offer the statistics of how many Canadians had been executed for treason, I needed some clarification.

"Wait a minute," I said. "Are we talking about *applied* historical science here? Applied by us as a graduating class project?"

Donovan leaned forward to refresh my drink. "Not quite, Cathy. A symbolic act against the monarchy would be quite sufficient, I think, for the purposes of presenting the anti-Royalist sentiment among the students at U of T."

While not exactly wholehearted about participating, I had no wish to forfeit my place among the members of this charmed circle, with their promising vision of a modern Canada at the midpoint of the twentieth century.

"A banner saying *Lizzie Go Home*?" I offered.

I swear I heard Peggy's eyes roll at my suggestion.

"Perhaps something a *little* more original, Cathy. Something that will make the Monarchists sit up and take notice."

"But avoiding anything felonious," Gordie added.

The Northern Spirit flowed freely, along with ideas.

* * * *

Ten minutes since the guard's last appearance. No sound of his return yet.

* * * *

Nothing had been decided that night in Donovan's apartment, and by the time we headed back to our respective residences, I was ready to believe it would come to nothing. But the following week when we got together again, the others were still gung ho, and Peggy accused me of being half-hearted, having contributed nothing. (The others had come up with lots of suggestions, ranging from impractical to idiotic, so I was hardly delinquent.) To keep my end up, I mentioned an article I'd seen in *The Telegram*.

"I read there are going to be wax figures of the royal couple, on loan from Madame Tussaud's, on display at the Royal Ontario Museum for the duration of the Royal Tour." For what it was worth.

"Yes!" Peggy cried. She rummaged through yesterday's papers. "Here it is. They've been shipped from London, and are being installed today. Perfect!"

We crowded around to read the article, complete with a picture of the waxworks, each dressed in formal splendor. Princess Elizabeth in swaths of tulle and jewels and the Duke very impressive in evening wear, like they were off to some swanky party.

"Large as life and twice as natural," Donovan murmured. "Certainly there are possibilities."

"Really?" I hadn't been serious, but if Donovan thought we were on the right track...

The ideas buzzed around us. Commit an indignity, perhaps? Put them in a compromising position, place cigarettes between their fingers, switch their heads.

But Donovan merely said, "Perhaps a tad sophomoric?"

"Donovan's right." Peggy's voice held a laying-down-the-law tone. "Those are nothing but high school pranks, the kind of games first-year meds play with their skeletons. We want to do something impressive that will display our disdain for the monarchy."

Like what?

"I think we should kidnap the Princess."

* * * *

As it turned out, Her Royal Highness's princess finery was deemed too cumbersome for us to manage, whereas the Duke, in his svelte evening wear, was more conducive to being wrapped in a blanket and spirited away.

Sure. Piece of cake.

Gordie worked out how we'd get into the museum. He'd read it in a true-crime book. You don't break in after hours. You go during the day and hide until closing time. When the coast is clear, you get into position. Then, you wait.

Right. Another piece of cake.

Ted and Peggy and I did some cautious casing of the ROM. *Very* cautious, since we didn't want the staff to notice the same people kept returning to the scene of the future crime.

Okay, not *crime*. A political statement. Standing up for the idea of a progressive, independent nation, not a satellite of an antiquated monarchy.

And after all, it was just a wax dummy. Our plan was to spirit him into place at a public event, bearing a sign saying "*No Figureheads Ruling Canada*."

But then, out of the blue, it all hovered on the verge of cancellation. Not our plot. The entire Royal Visit. King George's health was worse than his loyal subjects had been allowed to believe. The massive logistics of plotting the Royal Tour down to the finest minutia went into a holding pattern, and Canada—the entire Commonwealth—held its breath.

Much as I didn't want the King to be *very* ill, or worse, to die, I knew that either of these events would mean the Princess would stay home by her father's bedside—or take up her duties as Queen. The waxworks would be shipped back to England, and I could, with honor, avoid taking part in this whole plot.

But the King underwent lung surgery, and he appeared to benefit by it. The world exhaled, and the Royal Tour was on again. Every state dinner and prairie whistle-stop, every flower presentation by a Brownie, and Native dance demonstration—they were all pushed back exactly one week.

Along with our plot to kidnap the Duke. Except with a slight change of cast. Yesterday, Donovan had announced his mother would be visiting Toronto, so he'd be tied up entertaining her. And during the week's delay, Peggy had taken a fall in a field hockey game and broken her ankle.

Which is why, on the very day the royal couple arrived in Toronto, I found myself hiding behind a totem pole at the Royal Ontario Museum, twenty paces from where the facsimile Princess and Duke stood on a cordoned-off dais, left of center in the entrance hall.

If I peeked out from my hiding place, I could see them, calm and regal, as though ready to greet visitors. Hordes of school children on a day trip, a visiting paleontology professor, an American honeymooning couple fresh from the wonders of Niagara Falls.

The guard made his next appearance exactly when expected. Good. His full round took precisely twenty minutes. When he went off down the stairs for the third time, Ted and I went into action.

We stepped onto the dais, and I found myself at eye level with the well-dressed chest of this gorgeous man. I looked up, way up, to his waxen face.

Okay, it sounds crazy, but lifelike recreations of actual people can be creepily off-putting. I froze.

"What's wrong?" Ted whispered.

"He's looking at me."

Ted made a sound of disgust. "Get a grip, Cathy. He's just a dummy."

Uh-huh. Then why had Ted said "he"?

I got a grip. With a little awkwardness—he was heavy as a human— we eased him down to horizontal, wrapped him in the blanket we'd brought, and between us, we carried him off the dais.

I glanced over to see what Elizabeth was making of all this. The look she gave me was frigid with disapproval. Well, who could blame her?

"It's okay," I assured her in a whisper. "We'll take good care of him."

"Are you nuts?" Ted's voice was almost a squeak. "Let's get out of here."

To my amazement, it all went according to plan. We'd scoped out an escape route to the back passageway where an unobtrusive door led to the loading area out back. Hours earlier, just before closing time, Gordie had propped the door ajar with an old hockey stick.

Now, bang on schedule, Gordie waited outside with his third-hand Hillman Minx.

The Minx is not a big car. Certainly, we now realized, not big enough to accommodate a tall man in the trunk. Originally, we'd planned to use Peggy's father's station wagon. But it was with her and her broken ankle back in Bobcaygeon.

"We'll have to put him in the back seat," I said. We'd already discovered that the Duke had articulated limbs. Bless Madame Tussaud's for that.

We unwrapped him (we could hardly drive around with a mummy in the back seat) and arranged him in a more-or-less natural pose. I got in beside him.

"You two make a lovely couple," Ted observed.

We drove off through the night, with my arm tucked through the Duke's to keep him steady every time we turned a corner.

* * * *

The next stumbling block was where to stash him, since the back of the station wagon was now out. So was Donovan's apartment; his mother might have asked questions.

We decided on Gordie and Ted's room in their residence. Gordie went in to see if the coast was clear. It wasn't. A party was going on on their floor, and guys were everywhere.

"Cathy's residence," Ted declared. "Girls don't have wild parties."

"Not a chance!" I protested, aghast at the potential consequences. "It's after nine, so no guys are allowed in the residence. And if you think I'm dragging him up to the third floor by myself—"

"No, it's perfect!" Gordie said. "Your room is right at the end of the corridor, by the staircase up from the side entrance. We can get him into your room and slip out again, and no one's the wiser."

"How do you know where my room is?"

"Uh…" Ted and Gordie exchanged glances.

I got it. Peggy. My roommate.

"Okay," I said with a sigh. "And we do *too* have wild parties." But not tonight, I hoped. Because by this time I just wanted to get it all done and get into my bed.

It was easier than I'd expected. We parked the car near the side entrance, where it was hidden by a row of cedars. The boys positioned themselves on either side of the Duke, his arms around their respective necks, and they really did look like a couple of frat boys escorting a drunken friend home from a party.

I waited just inside the door to let them in, then ran up the stairs. When the coast was clear, the three guys slipped into my room.

"Where do you want him?" Gordie asked, as if they were delivering a chesterfield.

I looked around. "In the chair, I guess." Probably lying down on Peggy's bed would have been better, but something about that idea unsettled me.

Within a few minutes, His Royal Highness, Philip Mountbatten, Duke of Edinburgh, was settled into the one armchair in the room, sitting there in stately disdain.

"Okay, goodnight," I told the boys. "We'll talk tomorrow."

"Wait!" Ted cried. "We still have to—"

"Call me in the morning. You guys are leaving now, before anyone finds you."

They protested, but I escorted them down the stairs and practically kicked them out the door.

Back in my room, I regretted not having put my new roommate to bed after all. He could have lain hidden under the bedspread. Now, I had to get undressed under his imperious gaze.

I got into bed, reminding myself my visitor was an insentient dummy, and that the real Duke of Edinburgh was sound asleep in the royal railway carriage, his arms around his princess. My last waking thought was, *Do they sleep together…?*

* * * *

The pounding on my door came all too early. I cracked my eyes open and nearly had a heart attack at the sight of a large, imposing man sitting across the room staring at me.

Right. The Duke.

"Who is it?" I called out in a voice far too loud for 6:30, while dragging my body out of bed.

"It's me. Alison," came the would-be whisper. "Open up. I can't stand out here yelling."

I opened the door a crack. "What?" I demanded, blocking any possible view inside my room.

"There's a message for you." The bank of phones stood near Alison's room down the hall, and while she complained of being everyone's social secretary, I think she liked being in the know. "Some guy named Ted wants you to call him right away."

She pushed on the door to hand me a slip of paper, but I stood firm. This seemed to make her suspicious.

"Have you got a man in there?" She tried to look around me.

"Of course not!"

"Because I know Peggy's away, and I thought I heard voices last night…."

Oh damn. As I hesitated, she managed to peer past me.

"You *do*—"

"Shut up!" I opened the door enough to drag her in and then shut it behind her.

Alison's mouth fell open at the sight of Princess Elizabeth's husband, sitting there in my guest chair, a look of —amusement?—on his handsome face.

Her expression held a mixture of shock and admiration.

I couldn't resist. "Alison, you must promise *never* to breathe a word of this to anyone. If anyone found out—if *Elizabeth* found out. Or the King…"

She shook her head emphatically and turned back to my visitor. I swear—she practically curtseyed.

"Oh no, of course not. Sir, Your Highness—I mean, Your, Your Grace—"

I had to put her out of her misery.

"It's all right, Alison. He's just a waxwork." I stepped over and put my hand on my new boyfriend's knee. When he didn't react, Alison's mortification turned to fury.

It took me a good ten minutes to calm her down and explain it all, though granted, it sounded pretty foolish in the telling. Meanwhile, she kept stealing glances over at the Duke, perhaps not completely convinced of his inauthenticity.

I finally got her to leave, having sworn her to secrecy (for real this time) with an implied threat to reveal her naïveté about my having a tryst with the Duke of Edinburgh. Then, I got dressed and went down the hall to call Ted.

He wanted us all to meet in the Junior Common Room as soon as possible. At that hour on a Saturday, we'd have it to ourselves.

When I got back to my room, Alison was waiting at the door, looking even more distraught than before.

"Oh my gosh, Cathy. You are in big, *big* trouble."

* * * *

I got to the JCR just before 8:00, to find Ted and Gordie, along with Peggy, who'd just arrived on the night train from Peterborough. Still no Donovan.

"Okay, let's move on to today's agenda," Gordie said as I closed the door.

"Never mind that. We have a problem. Put on the CBC news."

Peggy and Ted looked uneasy as Gordie switched on the radio. It took a long minute to warm up. After the lead stories involving the Royal Visit, the war in Korea, the Leafs' season opener tonight against Chicago, the announcer reached our event.

"*And finally, in Toronto, His Royal Highness, the Duke of Edinburgh has gone missing. No, not the real one, but the wax figure at the Royal Ontario Museum. The effigy, along with that of Princess Elizabeth, is on loan from Madame Tussaud's in London as part of the celebration of the Royal Tour of Canada. It was last seen Friday night when the museum closed and was discovered missing this morning.*"

"They didn't notice until morning?" Gordie said with glee. "Some guards!"

"Just listen," I snapped.

"*A spokesman for the museum says the thieves must be highly professional and well organized*—I noticed Ted smirk at this—*to have pulled off such a daring theft.*

"*Madame Tussaud's creates images of members of the royal family only with special permission and doesn't actually own the figures, all of which are possessions of the Crown. As such, in order to secure the loan of these waxworks, both the Canadian government and the Royal Ontario Museum had to post bonds to guarantee the safety of the figures. The Duke's figure has a value of 4,000 pounds, or over 12,000 dollars.*"

"Oh shit…" Gordie murmured. "For a wax dummy?"

"It's just a prank," Ted protested to the room in general.

"I thought we agreed that's what it *wasn't.*" Peggy said. "The whole idea was to make a political statement. Remember? '*No figureheads*'?"

Matters got worse with the 9:00 news. It included an interview with Toronto's Chief Constable about security for the Royal visit.

"*We're fully prepared for this sort of thing. Police at all levels across Canada have been issued with the identities of known anarchists, crackpots and Reds in every city on the itinerary.*"

"*So you think this theft might be part of a Communist plot?*"

"*Let's say we're not ruling it out. But rest assured, due to the serious-ness of the theft, the RCMP may have to be called in.*"

The newscast ended and I switched off the radio. We all stood silent for a few seconds, then Gordie murmured, "The Mounties?"

"We need to return him…" Ted sounded far from confident.

"That's out of the question," Gordie said. "We wouldn't get within a hundred feet of the museum now."

"We'll leave him somewhere else," Peggy decreed. "A public place, but private enough we won't be seen."

Phone booth? Not enough room. Bus station? Too busy.

At length, we hit upon Allan Gardens. A public park with lots of foli-age. Not too far from here, but far enough to be unconnected with U of T.

* * * *

That Saturday night in Toronto, the streets were relatively quiet fol-lowing the tumultuous celebrations of the big day. Hundreds of thou-sands of royal watchers had gone home exhausted and happy, excitedly reliving their long-awaited once-in-a-lifetime moment.

Isn't he dreamy? She's so lovely! She looked right at me and smiled.

The diehards who hadn't yet got enough were down on Front Street waiting outside the Royal York Hotel, where a gala banquet was being held, while others were camped out by the York Street railway siding, where the royal carriage was parked for the duration of the visit.

Meanwhile, tonight was the season opener for the Toronto Maple Leafs. They were playing Chicago, and Maple Leaf Gardens would be jam packed, as always. Those without tickets would be home glued to their radios listening to the play-by-play from Foster Hewitt.

We would have the streets more or less to ourselves at 10:00 p.m.

At 9:00, we began removing the Duke from my room. I recruited Alison's help to keep lookout at the far end of the hall. She didn't realize I was making her a conspirator to ensure keeping her mouth shut later on.

Peggy, still on the injured list, had a sedentary but crucial role to play. She was waiting in a coffee shop at the corner of Gerrard and Sher-bourne, kitty-corner from Allan Gardens.

We got my unwelcome guest back into Gordie's Hillman, and in a repeat of last night's arrangement, I got in beside him. This time, I tied a silk scarf over my hair, and put a tweed cap on Philip, to make him look a little less regal, more sporty.

It was a matter of some twelve blocks. We kept to the side streets until our final turn onto Gerrard, a few blocks from our destination.

And there was a police car. With a policeman. He signaled us to pull over.

"Oh, shit," the guys murmured in unison.

Gordie rolled down the window, and I could hear his innocent, co-operative tones.

"Evening, constable. Anything wrong?"

"No, sir. Just want to caution you one of your headlights is out."

"Oh. Oh, yes! Thank you. That's very helpful." I swear Gordie was ready to add, "my good man."

I suppose our collective nervousness was filling the air, because the policeman didn't move away, but leaned in closer and raised his flashlight. Before the beam could reach the back seat, I pulled my new sweetheart towards me in an embrace and planted a long, passionate kiss on his unresponsive lips.

"Uh, miss, are you all right?"

Did he think the Duke was attacking me?

Gordie jumped in. "Oh, she's fine. She and Phil just got engaged, so they're a bit lovey-dovey right now."

"We're just heading home from their big announcement party," Ted added. "He wants to introduce Cathy to his mother."

Shut up, Ted. I came up for air, and, keeping my fiancé turned away from the policeman, I smiled and tried to look starry-eyed. "I'm fine. Thank you for asking."

My would-be protector nodded. "Congratulations, Miss. Sir. And you, sir, be sure and get that light repaired on Monday."

"I will."

The constable stepped away. Gordie put the car in gear, and we drove off.

* * * *

We stood back and looked at our handiwork. After parking the car around the corner, we'd carried him through the darkened park to the statue of Robbie Burns, a few yards from the Sherbourne Street sidewalk. The statue is surrounded on three sides by trees. On the steps of the substantial plinth sat his new friend, the Duke of Edinburgh, leaning back against the column.

For good measure, Gordie put an empty bottle of Northern Spirit Rye on the step beside him.

Having assured ourselves he was stable, we went back to the car. The boys got in, ready for our getaway, while I ran across the street to the coffee shop.

I gave Peggy a nod, and she got up and maneuvered herself into the phone booth, crutches and all. I stood in the doorway. Peggy called the police number and for some reason put on a plummy but not-terribly-convincing English accent.

"Yes, hello… I wish to report a drunken reprobate hanging about Allan Gardens. I was walking my dog along Sherbourne and saw this *man* sitting by the statue of Robert Burns. Just lolling there, desecrating the memory of the greatest poet that— no, certainly not! Well… he was dressed like a gentleman. In fact, I rather thought he looked like the Duke of Edinburgh, but I daresay— Oh, let's just say I'm a concerned citizen. Goodnight."

* * * *

We all needed a drink after that, so we went round to Donovan's apartment to see if he was back from showing his mother a good time in the big city. It was late enough that she should be asleep, and we could tell Donovan how it had all panned out.

Just as we drove up to the apartment block, so did a taxi. The driver held the door open for a lady and gentleman, dressed no less elegantly than the royal waxworks. I took a second look. *Donovan*—in a tuxedo? The lady had to be his mother, in a formal dress, fur stole and—were those diamonds?

As the taxi drove off, we piled out of the Hillman and greeted the stylish couple. Donovan didn't look thrilled to see us, but made the introductions. Mrs. "Walter" Grant was delighted to meet us, her eyes filled with stars, glad to have someone to share her excitement with.

They had just come from the gala dinner at the Royal York Hotel. With the Princess and the Duke and nine hundred high-end invitees.

At last, I broke the stunned silence.

"How lovely for you, Mrs. Grant. Donovan never told us, uh…."

"Yes, Donnie was thrilled to step in as my escort tonight. His father, Justice Grant, hasn't been well lately."

"Uh, the Supreme Court Justice?" Gordie hazarded.

Mrs. Grant nodded and went on about Donnie's elegant bow and correct manners. "And Princess Elizabeth even chatted with him for a few moments."

Donovan mumbled something about getting his mother out of the night air. She bid us goodnight, and we watched them disappear into the building.

"I hope he was polite," I said.

* * * *

We tuned in the news the next morning. The Princess and the Duke were leaving for Niagara Falls at noon, following one last public outing at Riverdale Park; the Leafs had blown the game against the Black Hawks 3-1; and the missing waxwork of the Duke of Edinburgh had been restored unharmed to its rightful place at the ROM. No mention was made of any drunken carousing in Allan Gardens or the anonymous phone call to the police. Whether the theft was still deemed the work of anarchists and Reds was not mentioned.

At last, I went off to keep my date with my sisters and 100,000 other royalty lovers, all held at bay by stalwart Boy Scouts and valiant Girl Guides, as the motorcade circled Riverdale Park. Listening to the resounding cheers of the rapturous crowds, it was clear to me that not one of these people, myself included, would give a damn if we'd actually made some kind of anti-monarchist statement using our friend the Duke.

And as for Donovan—Donnie—had we really allowed ourselves to be so bedazzled by all that pseudo-anarchist rhetoric, hiding his high-class background and his ease with royalty, that we'd risked possible expulsion and loss of our various scholarships?

As I said, we should have known better.

When the car swung past us, bearing the stars of the commonwealth in all their glory, my youngest sister grabbed my arm.

"Did you see that? She looked right at me! She smiled at me!"

"Wonderful!" I said. But I knew better.

The Princess had looked right at *me*.

She was *not* smiling.

Susan Daly has found her niche in the world of short crime fiction, where she rids the world of deserving victims. Her stories pop up in a surprising number of anthologies: *The Whole She-Bang 2 & 3*, The Guppies' *Fish Out of Water* and the Malice Domestic anthologies for 2017 and 2018. Her story "A Death at the Parsonage" won the 2017 Arthur Ellis Award for best short story from the Crime Writers of Canada. She lives in Toronto, a short commute from her grandkids, and can be found at www.susandaly.com.

THE A-LIST

C.C. GUTHRIE

Susan Marcus reached for the oversized glass of merlot like a parched three-year-old grabbed for a juice box after an exhausting play-date. "I'm taking that self-proclaimed power couple down. They will be shunned, ignored, and disinvited from every A-list event in the five-county area." She narrowed her eyes. "By the time I'm finished with them, the Texas Feral Hog Rescue Society won't want Krystyle and Reid Bransted as members."

The other three women in Susan's living room shared an uneasy look. Their friend was the calm one. The one they counted on when their lives spun out of control. Her advice was usually rational and measured. As a sought-after PR executive, Susan was always in control, often the only adult in the room.

"Stop, eat," Lynn McDowell said. "Take a sip of wine, then tell us."

Susan grabbed a handful of olives from the antipasto platter in front of her and leaned back on the couch. "You've heard of the Bransteds, right?"

Carmen Epperson nodded, but Lynn and Blair Christopher looked uncertain.

"Tell them, Carmen." Susan tossed an olive into her mouth.

"Krystyle and Reid are Austin's newest power couple, or at least, they say they are. They moved here about a year ago from, um, one of those states…" Her wrist flipped vaguely toward an east-facing window in Susan's condo overlooking Lady Bird Lake.

"Okay, so they aren't from here," Blair said. "Austin has changed. I work with people from somewhere else. Some I like, some, not so much."

"The Bransteds are expert party crashers and photo-bombers," Carmen said. "Apparently, they think brute force will get them on the Austin A-list." Carmen was a partner in a large international law firm and always knew the best gossip. "Reid is an heir to the Bransted Corporation. You've heard of it, right?"

Carmen brushed breadstick crumbs off her knit suit and waited for Blair and Lynn to nod and then continued.

"It's a massive conglomerate with a finger in everything, but it flies under the radar. That's a problem for Reid and Krystyle, because they love publicity. From what I've heard, he's been exiled from the business. Reid and Krystyle say they moved here to evaluate company expansion opportunities in the Austin, San Antonio, and the Hill Country areas. Bransted Corporation insiders say the couple was sent to Texas to keep Reid from screwing things up in the head office."

Lynn raised her wine glass and gestured at Susan. "Okay, but what does that have to do with you?"

"The Bransteds issued a press release today announcing they chose Fairweather & Associates to represent Krystyle's new business venture," Susan said.

"So? You've been competing with Fairweather for years," Blair said. "This can't be the first time your company lost a potential client to them."

"I wasn't competing for Krystyle Bransted's account. I've met that unprincipled couple exactly once."

Blair and Lynn shared another confused look, while Carmen grabbed her tablet and began to type. She read for a moment and looked up, a stunned expression on her face.

"Tell us," Lynn commanded, as she stretched out her long legs and crossed one clean but well-worn hiking boot over the other.

Carmen read a disjointed and grammatically incorrect press release. It extolled the Bransteds for their brilliant choice of Fairweather & Associates to handle Krystyle's strategic communication needs. Then, the document degenerated into a rant that trashed Susan's company.

"I can't believe Fairweather put this out. It's libelous," Carmen said. "I've never read anything so reckless."

"Marty Fairweather said his company had nothing to do with the announcement, and I believe him," Susan said. "At the end of the release, it says the Bransteds issued it. When I talked to Marty this afternoon, he was spitting mad, no doubt looking for the out-clause on Krystyle's contract."

"Even better," Carmen said. "It will be easier to take on Reid and Krystyle without Fairweather's support." She held up her wine glass. "I've definitely been overserved tonight. I'll review the press release again tomorrow, when I have a clearer head." She stood up. "I've got an early morning deposition, so I need to scoot." She leaned over and gave Susan a no-nonsense look. "I'll draft papers for a lawsuit against the Bransteds in the next day or so."

After a flurry of good-byes and assurances that Carmen had a cab waiting, the remaining three women sat quietly, looking at an Austin skyline that did not exist when they first met as freshmen at the University. After graduation, they scattered to graduate school and first jobs. Eventually, they all drifted back to Austin and began their Thursday night Wine and Whine decompression sessions.

Finally, Lynn broke the silence. "If you've only met the Bransteds once, why did they go after you?"

Susan opened another bottle of wine. "Reid Bransted made a fool of himself last week, and he blames me. I wish I'd never accepted the invitation to their dinner party."

"Oh, tell us more," Lynn said, as Susan topped up everyone's glass.

"Wait. Before you get to the part about making Reid look foolish, tell us about their house. If they are so status-obsessed, it must be a showplace," Blair said.

"It is amazing," Susan said. "It's in West Lake above the Colorado River. Straight modern lines, soaring windows." Susan sighed. "I'd sell my kids for that house, if I thought I could get enough money for them."

"And inside?" Blair asked. She was an avid HGTV fan, always on the lookout for ways to enhance the character of her 1930s Arts and Crafts bungalow.

Susan started laughing and paused to wipe away tears streaming down her cheeks. "The interior décor no more matches the house than Duncan Phyfe furniture belongs in a double wide. One guest," Susan named a well-known actress who lived in Austin between movie roles, "called it 'Western-chintz.'"

Blair grabbed a handful of almonds. "Who else was there?"

Susan rolled her eyes. "The guest list was as jarring as the décor. Krystyle must have used the Chinese-restaurant-menu method to select their invitees. You know, a choice from column A, column B, and so on. There were the usuals, local business types, probably why I was invited, politicians and academics. There was an entertainer from each category—an Oscar, Emmy, and Country Music Award winner." Susan thought for a moment. "An American Book Award recipient, oh, and those four University of Texas professors always short-listed for Nobels. All A-listers in their fields, but little crossover between the groups."

"Okay, enough scene setting," Lynn said. "Get to the good part."

"By the time cocktails were out of the way," Susan recalled, "everyone knew Krystyle hates to cook, uses a landscaper, finds crafts messy, and has a personal shopper."

Blair twirled her finger to move Susan along.

"Before the caterer finished slicing the smoked brisket," Susan said, "Reid Bransted was well into a full-on rant about how only MBAs should be in charge of anything. And surprise," Susan paused dramatically, "he was the only MBA in the room."

Lynn and Blair leaned forward in anticipation.

"The silence in the Bransted dining room was deafening," Susan said. "And then, Reid jammed his foot further down his throat and said only B-School graduates could think, analyze, and make decisions without getting sidetracked by emotion."

"Uh, oh. How did that go over with the four scientists?" Blair asked. She was an electrical engineer with a PhD in computer science and knew Austin's scientific and technical community well.

"About how you'd expect," Susan said. "The quiet one, the physicist? He lit the fuse."

Blair nodded. "No surprise there. People tend to underestimate him. What did he do?"

Susan paused to pour more wine. "In a very soft, unassuming voice, he asked Reid if anyone with a scientific or engineering background, or even an attorney without an MBA, could be an effective corporate leader."

"And," Lynn prompted.

A big smile spread across Susan's face. "Reid said non-MBAs can't handle complex business decisions, and if a corporation wants to succeed, its leadership team must have MBAs from top-tier schools."

"So I asked Reid if he meant like Zuckerberg at Facebook?"

Blair laughed. "And Reid agreed?"

"He did," Susan said. "Then, a UT Dean announced Zuckerberg dropped out of Harvard his sophomore year. At that point, a senior state senator suggested Bill Gates at Microsoft was a better example. So, a South by Southwest Festival marketing executive jumped in to tell us that Gates left Harvard after two years." Susan sat back against the couch, a satisfied look on her face. "At that point, the dinner party started to resemble the lightning-round in a very unruly game show."

Lynn cocked an eyebrow.

"People began to shout out names of successful non-MBAs," Susan said. "Poor Reid. His guests didn't just disagree with him. They competed to prove him wrong. Never had I seen such unified disdain for one person. Republicans and Democrats high-fived at the mention of a successful non-MBA. Senior professors from the Schools of Natural Science and Engineering chugged shots at each new name."

"How did Reid take the feedback?" Blair asked. Her voice put quotes around the word 'feedback.'

"Based on his flushed face, not well," Susan said. "Krystyle looked confused, but she tried to rally." Susan rolled her eyes. "She changed the subject and told us about her new business venture."

Blair and Lynn exchanged looks.

"Krystyle is launching herself as a Texas-lifestyle expert." Susan grinned as she watched her friends' eyes widen. "That's why Fairweather was hired, to handle her branding." She shook her head. "I can't believe Marty Fairweather got taken in by those two con artists."

Ever the analytical one, Blair focused on the inconsistency of Susan's announcement. "Krystyle is from somewhere else, so what qualifies her to be an expert in anything Texan?"

"These days you don't have to do anything to be famous," Lynn said.

"Yep," Susan agreed. "You only need to use someone else's knowledge and brand it as your own." She stood up. "And that's how we're going to take down the Bransteds."

The Wine and Whine night ended soon after Susan gave Lynn and Blair a broad outline of her plan.

* * * *

The next night in Lynn's kitchen, Susan sighed with contentment as she popped a tortilla chip in her mouth. "Beer, chips, and Ro-tel queso. An unbeatable combination." She wiped a drop of cheese-food off her lip. "Ok, let's get to work. We're going to expose Krystyle for what she is. A fake." She twirled a hand with a flourish that would have made a vaudeville magician envious. "A poser."

"Look, distributing that press release slamming you was low. Lower than low," Blair said. "Why don't you sue Reid and Krystyle? Carmen said you have a case."

"Because, no offense to Carmen, when attorneys get involved, they are the only ones that win." Susan pointed a finger at Blair and then Lynn. "I'll deny it, if you tell her I said that." She grabbed another chip and dipped it into the queso. "I assume Reid and Krystyle will have Bransted money behind them in a lawsuit, which means their funds are unlimited. Mine are not." Susan narrowed her eyes. "Those two publicly questioned my professional abilities, so we're going to use those skills against them."

Lynn bit her lip, as she poured more chips in the bowl. "What does Carmen say about your scheme?"

Susan reached for another chip and dipped.

Blair glared at her friend. "You haven't told Carmen, have you?"

"Not exactly," Susan said. "I spoke to her today and told her I need more time to think about a lawsuit. Then, I asked her about our plan."

Blair flinched at Susan's use of the word 'our.'

"So you told her what you are going to do?" Lynn asked with an emphasis on the word 'you.'

Susan reached for her beer. "I asked her about websites and what's legal and what's not. I might have suggested I need the information for a talk I'm giving to the University Public Relations Society next month." She took a sip of beer. "Carmen said that, as long as a website doesn't sell anything, accept money, or make promises that violate Federal Trade or FDA regulations, it's not illegal." She put down the beer bottle and started writing. "First, the website. Blair creates that, while Lynn and I work on content and create a buzz around Austin. When our website goes live, we drive traffic to it." By the time Susan stopped talking, Lynn and Blair were on board and contributing ideas for the plan.

"The comment sections of high-end glossy magazine websites are our priority," Lynn said. She ticked off the magazines aimed at Capitol-area residents who aspired to a higher rung on the social ladder.

"Exclusivity is the key," Susan agreed. "Our target markets are Lake Travis, West Lake, Circle C, Dripping Springs, downtown high-rise, and Round Rock residents." Susan finished her beer. "Phase two will be a self-congratulatory, successful post-launch announcement. If we don't have Krystyle at that point, we've failed and need to re-evaluate our assumptions."

Lynn shot Blair a look and said with more confidence than she felt, "We won't fail."

"When do we make the pitch?" Blair asked.

"Phase two. Krystyle will panic if she thinks she missed out."

"You really think other people will get involved?" Lynn asked.

"I'm betting on it," Susan said. "Krystyle isn't the only social climb-er around here."

Blair bit her cheek. "Should we run this by Carmen to make sure we're not crossing a line?"

Susan shook her head. "If she doesn't know the details, she'll have plausible deniability. Now we create the bait that snags Krystyle."

* * * *

"Wow, I never knew you had a talent for pretension," Blair said as she read over Lynn's shoulder. "Who knew a mild-mannered botany PhD could write such ridiculous descriptions? Your talents are wasted working with plants. It's very fitting that you use the word 'forage.'" She reached for the keyboard and scrolled down. "A 'collection of decon-structed starters?'"

"I've often thought twenty dollar starters are too constructed," Susan said with a straight face. She joined Blair and read over Lynn's shoulder. "Great weasel words, especially 'essence,' 'foam,' and 'toothsome.'"

"'Toothsome?'" Blair bent down and took a closer look at the screen. "I don't like the sound of that. Maybe you should rethink that one."

"It has a modern vibe that should appeal to Krystyle," Lynn said.

Blair nodded at the logic. "Probably." She stood up and stretched. "I've got the website elements in place, pictures, banners, and tabs. We've settled on the name, right? And who has the phone? I want to double-check the number." She looked at Lynn. "What about the message for the reservation line?"

Lynn pushed back from the table. "A friend in the theater department recorded it. He does a killer English accent," she said.

Blair wrinkled her brow. "Where's the phone?"

Lynn reached into her tote and rummaged around. "Ah, not sure. I think I had a different bag the day I bought the burner. It's probably at home."

Susan tilted her head.

Lynn threw up her hands in a push-back gesture. "I'll find it. But it's not like we plan to answer the phone."

"But we will need to change the message to up the demand factor," Blair said. "How will your friend feel about recording a new message every few days?"

"I had him record different versions. Three weeks, four, five, three months, and so on. In a wild fit of optimism, I even had him do a version that says we have no availability until next year. With all those options, we can edit the message on a laptop and change it whenever we want."

Susan sat down and grabbed her notepad. "About the timeline. I think we should go live Sunday, so we can announce that our successful soft opening was the previous night." When Lynn and Blair nodded, Susan scratched through the item and moved on. "While Lynn finishes up the website content, I'll write the comments to post on the magazine websites," Susan said. "Blair, about that. Are you sure no one can trace anything back to you?"

"I'm a white-hat hacker," Blair said without the slightest hint of irony. "Leave it to me."

"Is it legal?" Lynn asked.

"Do you really want to know?" Blair asked.

* * * *

"I'm glad you invited Carmen tonight," Blair said, as she walked back into her kitchen for the last plate of crudités. "I hope she isn't hurt that we haven't included her lately."

"She doesn't know we've been meeting without her, and she won't, if you don't tell her," Susan said. "Besides, she'll be happier not knowing."

Blair opened her mouth.

Susan glared at Blair. "Not one word. If Operation A-list goes off the rails, we might need an attorney, so she can't be a part of this."

But to the surprise of the three women, Carmen brought up the subject. "Have you heard of a new restaurant called Capitol Taste? One of the partners was talking about it today, but when I asked for more information, he shut up."

Lynn shrugged. "Budget season has me tethered to spreadsheets."

"Big defense project," Blair mumbled.

Susan grabbed her tablet and started typing. "Ah, they have a website." She leaned forward and read from the comments section. "I love Capitol Taste. The exclusive feel of the restaurant enhances the experience." She looked up at Carmen. "That sounds promising."

She scrolled to the next review. "My husband and I were privileged to dine at Capitol Taste's inaugural night. The restaurant's undisclosed location and our personal invitation to dine made the evening so elegant. With the impeccable food and service, I know Capitol Taste will become the new Austin-insider favorite."

Carmen rolled her eyes. "As we used to say back in the day, gag me with a spoon."

She reached for a baby carrot on the platter in front of her and stopped, her hand poised mid-reach. "Wait. The restaurant doesn't advertise its location? Does that even make sense?"

"Clearly Capitol Taste isn't interested in riffraff that might stroll in off the street," Susan said.

Lynn sighed. "The restaurant probably uses exclusivity to justify exorbitant prices."

"Here's another review." Susan wrinkled her forehead. "Oh, good grief. This one is even worse."

"Read it," Blair urged.

"I felt so privileged to receive an invitation to the Capitol Taste launch event." Susan looked up. "Note the use of the word 'privileged' again. The restaurant is clearly aiming for the A-list crowd."

"What's on the menu?" Blair asked.

Susan looked back at the screen. "This is so ridiculous I can't read it out loud." She passed the tablet to Carmen and stood up. "You do it. I'm going to powder my nose."

Carmen put on her glasses and began to read. "Starters include a duo of hand-selected, rustic artisanal cheeses." She looked up. "Twenty dollars for two types of cheese? Seriously?" She shook her head and looked back down at the screen. "The food is 'toothsome'?"

"Probably not the best description for food," Lynn said.

Carmen put the tablet on the coffee table. "That settles it. I'm never going to Capitol Taste, nor do I want to associate with anyone tempted to go there." She took off her glasses and rubbed her eyes. "And for that reason, I guarantee people will be fighting for a reservation."

"No doubt," Blair said.

"If there are only three reviews, Capitol Taste can't be much of a hit," Lynn said.

"There are eighteen reviews," Susan said as she entered the room.

Lynn raised her glass to hide a grin and took a sip.

"I wonder how many are legit," Carmen said.

"Wha?" Lynn sputtered and then choked. Wine dribbled off her chin as she coughed. Blair leaned over and slapped her on the back.

Susan reclaimed her place on the couch and kept her head down as she retrieved her tablet from the coffee table. "What do you mean 'legit'?"

"Oh, come on, you three can't be that naïve," Carmen said. "I bet a restaurant's staff, its owner, and even family members post fake reviews to generate positive publicity." She turned to Susan. "You're in the biz. There must be metrics about the percentage of real reviews versus fake ones."

Susan held up her palms. "My analytic people would know, but I've never asked."

Carmen topped off her glass. "I stand by my statement. Some of those reviews for Capitol Taste are fake."

Lynn, Susan, and Blair exchanged a look. "Could be," Blair said.

* * * *

Lynn squinted at her tablet screen. "Krystyle took the bait. She just posted a glowing review of Capitol Taste's launch event and signed her name." Lynn shot a fist into the air. "Mission accomplished."

Across the room, Susan and Blair high-fived.

"Lynn, your email to Krystyle did it," Susan said. "I'm sure that's what reeled her in. I knew she couldn't resist a personal invitation to tell everyone about her special dining experience at Austin's newest, most exclusive restaurant."

Blair sat down at the breakfast bar and pulled the Capitol Taste website up on her laptop. "We're getting bombarded with hits." She grinned at Susan. "You were right. I completely underestimated the importance of being an insider." Her fingers flew across the keyboard. "Time to make this all go away, and let the Internet trolls do their thing."

* * * *

"Our new CFO starts next month," Blair said as she selected a piece of ahi from a plate of sushi selections.

Susan, Carmen, and Lynn stared at Blair. They had never known her to comment on the executives at her company.

"He's from California and likes the idea of living in West Lake, near the river," Blair said. When the other three women failed to respond, Blair jumped to the headline. "He bought Reid and Krystyle Bransted's house."

"Ah," Susan said.

Lynn shook her head slowly. "That couple came as close to being run out of Austin on a rail as anyone can in this century. Texans do not like to be set up, especially by someone from somewhere else."

"I heard Harvard Business School plans to use the whole episode in a case study on how not to brand a business," Carmen said.

"There is a lesson there," Susan agreed. "It doesn't do much for your credibility as a lifestyle expert when you post a glowing review for an event that never happened at a restaurant that doesn't exist."

Blair looked over at Susan. "Like you always say, branding and promotion are best left to professionals."

C.C. Guthrie lives near Fort Worth, Texas. Her short stories have appeared in *Fish Out of Water* and *Busted! Arresting Stories From The Beat*.

THE GREAT NEGOTIATOR

RAEGAN TELLER

Jerry tried to tune out Hilda's high-pitched voice. His mother-in-law was annoying under the best of circumstances, but this afternoon, her screeching grated on his nerves. His wife Trudy was usually the one who entertained Hilda during her twice-a-year visits, but Trudy had been called to an unexpected business trip, leaving Jerry alone with her mother. He tried to ignore Hilda, but that voice of hers pierced right through his thoughts.

"Well, did you get the job or not?" Hilda asked.

"We're still negotiating."

"How difficult can it be? You need a job. They've got a job. Take it and count your lucky stars."

"It's not that simple."

"Let me guess. You think you're worth more than they're offering."

Jerry shrugged. "Like I said, I'm negotiating with them."

"I don't call that negotiating," Hilda said. "You'd better be glad they didn't offer you what you're really worth." She stood up to walk to the kitchen. "Do you have any chocolate ice cream?"

Jerry stayed focused on the TV screen.

"Well, do you?" she asked.

Jerry turned to face Hilda. "No, we don't. Why don't you go in the kitchen and find yourself something else to snack on?"

"I want chocolate ice cream."

Jerry reached into his pocket and pulled out his car keys, tossing them to Hilda. "Here. There's a store down on the corner."

Hilda muttered something Jerry couldn't hear, as she walked out of the room. She returned shortly with her purse on her arm. "I'll be back soon." Then she added, "Not that you'd care."

Jerry waved goodbye, pretending he didn't hear that last comment. As soon as the door slammed shut, he leaned back in the chair and enjoyed the peace and quiet of her absence.

An hour later, the ringing phone interrupted his sleep. "Hello," he answered, still groggy from his nap.

"Listen carefully, and do exactly what I tell you," a male caller said. His young voice sounded a bit shaky.

"What kind of dumb joke is this?" Jerry was about to hang up when he heard a familiar screech in the background.

"Listen to him, you jerk."

"Hilda, is that you?" Jerry asked.

"We got your mother," the caller said. "If you want to see her again, it will cost you $25,000."

Jerry laughed. After being out of work for two months, he didn't have $100 of his own, much less $25,000. Thank goodness Trudy had a good job and managed their budget with the same rigor she had learned from her mother. After Trudy's father died, Hilda learned to stretch their meager inheritance and to invest wisely. She paid for Trudy's college and later footed the down payment on Jerry and Trudy's house.

Hilda had plenty of money, and she made sure Jerry knew it. She reminded him constantly that her hard work and careful planning had paid off—and that Jerry still owed her for the down payment. The large diamond ring on her hand that she liked to wave around would pay off the mortgage on Jerry and Trudy's house, plus all their other bills. "Look, if she's put you up to this as a joke, it's not funny. Now quit bothering me." Jerry hung up.

Muttering to himself, Jerry walked to the kitchen to get a beer from the refrigerator. The phone rang again. He was tempted to ignore it. "Hello," he answered.

The same young male voice whined. "What's the matter with you, man? You want to see your mother killed?"

"She's not my mother."

In a bolder voice, the caller said, "If you call the police, we'll kill her."

Another male voice in the background added, "Yeah, we really will."

Hilda screamed, "You're both idiots. You too, Jerry."

"Put her on the phone," Jerry said.

The caller put his hand over the receiver, and Jerry heard a muffled conversation, but he couldn't make out what they were saying.

Then, a familiar voice blared into his ear. "Jerry, you jerk, they grabbed me in the parking lot at the store. This is no joke. I demand that you give them the money now." She paused before adding, "I'll repay you."

Hilda's offer convinced Jerry it was no joke. Hilda was as tight with her money as the E string on a Laplander's mandolin.

"That's enough," the caller said. "Now write down this address." He proceeded to provide Jerry detailed instructions on where to leave the money. "You got all that?"

Jerry's temples were throbbing. "Yeah, I got it. But there's just one problem. I'm not paying." He hung up. Her kidnappers, if they actually were that, sounded like a couple of young kids hoping to score fast cash. He debated on whether to call the police but convinced himself Hilda would be released, once they realized he wasn't going along with their little scheme.

For the next thirty minutes, he busied himself straightening up the kitchen, enjoying the quiet. Until the phone rang again. He ignored it, but the ringing was persistent.

"What?" he asked as he picked up the receiver.

"You think we're kidding, don't you?" the male caller asked. "Shut up!" Then he said to Jerry, "Sorry, I wasn't talking to you. The old woman's driving me crazy."

Jerry laughed. "Tell me about it."

"She always yap this much?"

"All the time, man, all the time."

"Look here, maybe our earlier demand was a little high. Give us $10,000, and we'll drop her off at the corner."

"Sorry, man, I'm broke, and my wife isn't here. I'm not allowed to make major purchases on my own." Jerry hung up again.

He checked the football schedule and was upset to see that the game he had been waiting for all week had already started. He threw a pack of popcorn in the microwave, opened another cold beer, and turned up the volume. A few minutes later, the home team was on the five-yard line, ready to score, when the phone rang again.

When Jerry answered, the caller said, "Okay, you win. We'll take $5,000, and drop her off, if you promise not to call the police."

Jerry pulled a bill from his pocket. "I got a fiver, that's it. But here's the problem. My team is playing for the division championship, and I'm kinda enjoying not having her here. Know what I mean?"

"You're killing me, man. Come on. Cut us some slack."

"Yes!" Jerry yelled into the phone. "My team just scored."

Hilda was muttering in the background. "You no good bum. I told Trudy not to marry you."

"Shut up," the caller yelled at her. "She's driving us crazy."

"I gotta go. I'm missing the game." Jerry hung up.

The opposing team fumbled the ball on the return, just as the phone rang again.

"How many times do I have to tell you? I don't have the money," Jerry answered.

"Jerry? What's going on?"

"Oh, Trudy, I didn't know it was you. Where are you? Everything okay?" Jerry asked.

"The meeting got cancelled. I'm in New York getting ready to board a flight home. What did you mean about not having the money?"

"Nothing, honey. Just one of my buddies wanted to bum some cash. I told him I was broke." Beads of sweat were popping up on his forehead. "Should I pick you up at the airport?"

"No, I had to take a connecting flight, so I won't be home until nearly morning. You stay there with Mother. I'll grab a cab."

"Sure thing," Jerry said, wiping his forehead. "Safe travels, hon." He hung up and sat in a chair, wringing his hands. "Crap," he said aloud.

When the phone rang again, he jumped. Not taking a chance this time, he said, "Hello, who is this?"

"What you mean, who is this?" the young male asked.

Jerry weighed his dwindling options. "Tell you what. You pay *me* $5,000, and I'll take her off your hands and keep my mouth shut. Just leave her where I can find her." He looked at the clock again, calculating how much time he had before Trudy arrived. "Give me another couple hours, though. You know, until the game's over."

There was silence on the other end.

"You still there?" Jerry asked.

"I'm thinking."

"Otherwise, I'll call the FBI, the state police, and the CIA to come after you," Jerry said, picking a piece of popcorn from his teeth.

"I can't think. Let me call you back."

Ten minutes later, the phone rang. Jerry answered. "You got the money? Otherwise, you can keep her." Jerry tried to erase Trudy's impending arrival from his mind.

"We don't have that kind of money. Just let us drop her off." A brief pause. "Please."

"Son of a...." Jerry shook his fist in the air. "We got sacked."

"Aw, that's tough, man. Sorry about that."

"Tell you what," Jerry said, "throw in a six pack of Budweiser. Not the light stuff, the real kind. One more thing. Make sure she gets her chocolate ice cream before you drop her off."

Hilda's voice chimed in, "The car is still at the store, you idiot. I can drive myself home."

The male caller added, "She's right. We didn't bother her car. It's still there. Needs a tune-up, though. It was skipping when she pulled in. Might be the spark plugs."

"Okay, I'll take care of it," Jerry said.

"No problem, man. We'll drop her back off at the store, you know, in a couple hours. Give you a chance to finish that game."

After the call ended, Jerry settled into his chair and watched his team lose by one point. He laid his head back and had almost dozed off, when he heard a knock on the door. Opening it, he saw Hilda standing there with a six-pack of Budweiser in one hand and grocery bag in the other.

She pushed past him and walked inside. "Was that little stunt of yours supposed to impress me?"

"Well, it worked, didn't it?" he said, reaching for the beer. "I told you I was a great negotiator."

Raegan Teller is an award-winning mystery author in Columbia, South Carolina. Her debut novel, *Murder in Madden*, received Honorable Mention in the 2017 Writer's Digest Self-Published Book Awards. *The Last Sale* is the second novel in the Enid Blackwell series. Both books were inspired by real-life cold cases in her hometown.

Before writing fiction, Raegan was a business writer and copy editor, a communications consultant, executive coach, and insurance manager—among other things. While working her way through school, she even sold burial vaults at a cemetery. How apropos is that for a mystery writer! Learn more at RaeganTeller.com.

FOR WANT OF A GRADE

T.Y. EULIANO

Blake Rhodes breathed in the crisp March air. The air was different on the outside, even if the outside was still Baltimore. Ten years. He had a lot of catching up to do, beginning with his daughter. Erica wouldn't bring her to the prison. He could understand that, most of the time. At least she'd allowed his mama to be a part of Jessica's life, and Mama brought pictures. He'd kept them all. His daughter's life from birth to seven years old. She was nearly ten now, but the photos stopped coming when Mama died. Those photos, and a few official documents, were all he took from the prison, his only possessions of worth.

From the bus, he watched the fenced-in compound shrink from view. He thought freedom would be more exciting, instead the amends he needed to make weighed on him. The counselor had him list them in order. First was his mama. She'd worked so hard, in order for him to finish high school. He'd failed—school and her.

Two bus transfers later, he held his GED certificate out. "I did it, Mama. I finished." A tear rolled down his cheek. Her grave-marker read only, 'Belinda Rhodes, 1934 – 2004.' Three years she'd been gone. When he made some money, he'd buy her a tombstone, with an angel on it.

He wiped his eyes as he returned to the bus stop. The next amend would be tougher. He considered just showing up at Erica's, knocking on the door and demanding to meet his daughter. But the counselor told him to take it slow. He sat on the bench at the bus stop and called.

"She doesn't want to see you," Erica said. "And neither do I."

"I understand. I don't deserve your forgiveness. Either one of you." He'd practiced these lines. "Tell me what I can do to make amends."

"Unless you can help her ace the Maryland Christian Academy Test, there's nothing she needs from you."

"A test?"

"Yes, Blake, a test, to get into the best grade school in Baltimore. But she can't go unless she qualifies for a scholarship, so she has to ace the entrance exam."

"I'm sorry," he said, because what else could he say? He couldn't send his daughter to private school, and his genes weren't going to help her ace any test. "Tell her I love her?"

"Good bye, Blake."

The counselor warned him it might take a while, that not everyone responded to amends right away. He would earn his daughter's forgiveness. She needed help, and he was her daddy.

He climbed on the bus and sat near the back. How to help his daughter? No way he could come up with the tuition, and stealing it was out of the question. He'd never stolen money. Stealing tests, though, that he was good at, until he got caught.

One problem—besides making amends, he'd also promised not to break the law. Which took priority? He should have asked. Maybe it was better he hadn't. After he made amends to his little girl, he would stay right with the law.

Time to call on Simon.

The neighborhood bus stop had changed little, except for the 7-Eleven across the street. It was gone. No more Slurpees. The walk to Simon's took Blake past his boyhood home—his mama's beautiful garden reduced to a tangle of weeds, the white picket fence no longer white, with gaping holes like missing teeth. He tripped over the uneven sidewalk, worse now than when he and Simon skateboarded over it twenty years before.

Two doors down, the garden was intact. Not beautiful, but intact. Blake knocked and was suddenly a child again, asking if Simon could come out to play.

The door creaked open. Mrs. Slocum's face had changed—sort of melted. But her eyes were the same, sparkling gold flecks in milk chocolate. "Blakey, it's so lovely to see you."

"Hi, Mrs. Slocum." While most things seemed smaller, she was twice the woman he remembered. She pulled him into her ample bosom for a hug. Everything was squishy, but he didn't resist.

"I'm so sorry about your mama."

"Thank you."

She held him at arm's length, looking him over. "Simon's downstairs." She led him to the familiar basement, where he'd spent many a contented afternoon listening to music and playing Nintendo. The theme song from Super Mario Brothers completed the flashback.

"Turn that down, Simon." Mrs. Slocum hadn't changed so much, after all.

The music faded.

"Someone's here to see you."

Simon's bald head turned, and his expression morphed from irritation to delight. "You made it!" He stood and pulled Blake into a man hug—more slapping than hugging. Simon was less squishy, but they'd have to revise his title. 'The lean, mean, computing machine' no longer fit.

"I'll leave you two to catch up," Mrs. Slocum said.

They sat in low curving chairs, about the only new addition to the basement playroom, besides the enormous screen.

"Video games haven't changed much," Blake said.

"Not if you're using a Nintendo system from 1995."

"Ah. So, how are you?"

He raised an eyebrow. "What do you think? I'm living in my mom's basement, playing decade-old video games."

"Awesome, then?"

"Totally." The men high-fived like high schoolers before the fist bump. A blue light flashed in the corner of the screen as a beep sounded over the game's music.

"How about some fresh-baked cookies?" Simon's mom waddled in and set a plate on the ground between them. It smelled like chocolate heaven. "Sodas are in the fridge."

"Thanks," they said in unison. Each grabbed a cookie.

Simon watched her depart. "That should be it for a while." He pulled a keyboard tray from under the coffee table, pressed some keys, and the enormous screen switched from Mario to a computer. "Dammit."

Blake stared at the screen. "You didn't want your mom to know you're buying tickets to a play?"

"Not a play, the hottest musical on Broadway."

"Oh, Simon, sorry, I didn't know…"

"Cut it out, you idiot. I'm not gay."

"No, it's fine."

"I'm not buying them for me. I'm buying them to resell, but those jerks in India keep beating me. Instead of brilliant algorithms, they use a hundred-thousand homeless kids on computers."

"India's homeless kids have computers?"

"You know what I mean." He pushed away the keyboard. "They're even beating us at white-collar crime now."

So he hadn't gone completely straight. "I need to do one more job. For my daughter."

"Ah, Jessica. She's an awesome kid. Erica's going to let you be part of her life?"

"She will if I help Jessica pass a test."

"So she *is* your daughter."

"Jerk." Blake explained about the entrance exam. "We need to steal a copy of the test so she can look up the answers."

"Why not just steal the answers?"

"Because she needs to earn this. I don't want her thinking Daddy's gonna fix everything all her life."

Simon laughed. "So what school is it?" He had his hands on the keyboard ready to type.

"Maryland Christian Academy."

Simon's head cocked like a retriever's. Blake remembered the look. It meant trouble. Fun, but trouble.

"Are you serious?" asked Simon.

Blake nodded.

Simon seemed to debate something, then went back to his keyboard and entered the test's initials. "The exam comes from a company in Washington, DC."

"Not Maryland?"

"Just across Rock Creek." Simon grinned like the boy he had been. "It'll be like old times."

"Like old times."

Blake and Simon had earned money stealing and selling exams during Blake's extra years of twelfth grade. Simon used his portion to fund community college. Blake's had eventually gone to help Erica.

"I'll take a few days off," Simon said.

"You have a job?"

"Course I do."

"Where?"

"Here." Simon's eyes never left the screen. The cursor flew too fast to follow. "I work freelance. When someone needs information, or a certain... item, they pay me to find it."

"So like a librarian?"

Simon glanced at Blake, a smirk on his face. "Yeah, a world-wide webrarian and a personal shopper all rolled into one."

Simon had gotten weird. Or weirder.

"Have you stolen a big exam like this before?" Blake asked.

"Not this particular one, but I did steal the Law School Admissions Test a while back. That bought my computer and an awesome trip to Comic Con. The one for Med School has always been a goal."

"So a private school entrance exam should be simpler, right?"

"Most definitely."

They worked through the night, mostly Simon on his computer. Twice, the light blinked in the corner of the screen with the warning beep, and Blake grabbed up the controller and pretended to play Mario

Brothers when the game appeared. Mrs. Slocum brought sandwiches once. The other time, she informed Simon she was going to bed. "Maybe you can get Blake a job with the bank, too."

"Sure, Mom," Simon said. When she'd closed the door, he said, "She thinks I work for a global bank."

On the exam producer's company website, Simon pulled up a directory. "How about we find someone for you to meet?" In the old days, Blake's role was distractor. He flirted with the teachers, or told them a sob story, while Simon broke into their office for the exam. If there was only one copy, he took pictures of each page with a Polaroid camera.

A window popped up with photos of people and a box that read, 'Myspace.com, a place for friends.'

"It's a social networking site," Simon said.

Clueless, Blake nodded. He'd been released from prison on a different planet.

"It's like an online phone directory, except you can add whatever information you want to your listing. Speaking of which, we need to get you a cell phone."

"You know I don't like talking on the phone. My charm is in person."

That earned a sideways glance. "You really should have taken a prison class in computers, or real life, or something useful."

Not Simon, too. Blake wasn't a school kinda guy. Never had been. Three years of twelfth grade finally convinced his mom, though prison probably wasn't what she had in mind.

"Here's one," Simon said, as a young woman's face appeared on the screen. She had long dark hair and a bright smile, showing straight white teeth. And they were all there, no holes.

Blake had all his, too. His mama gave him a mouth guard to wear "most any time you're out of your cell." And he'd done it.

"She might be a little young," Simon said. "And she's engaged."

Blake went to the refrigerator for another Sprite.

Simon went back to the company directory. "How about Ms. Susan Hornbeam? Graduated from American University in DC in '02. Current position is administrative assistant. Single. No kids. Has a golden retriever named Spot."

"What kinda name is Spot for a golden retriever?"

"Just checking whether you're paying attention. Her name is Acadia."

The scrolling images froze on a photo of Ms. Hornbeam holding up a fancy cocktail. Her shiny eyes suggested it was not her first of the evening. Her face was round and pretty, not gorgeous, which was good. "Look here," Simon said. "She has plans tomorrow night, at a bar right around the corner from the testing center office." Some text on the screen turned yellow as the cursor flew by.

There it was, her plans for the evening, right there online for all to see. Well, all who knew how to operate a computer anyway.

"So, I need to get some clothes," Blake said.

Simon looked him over. "That you do, my man. That, you most definitely do."

Blake crashed on Simon's couch for a few hours, showered, enjoyed a hearty breakfast, then hit the mall. Simon insisted on paying. "I still owe you, man. I'll take care of this little mission."

Simon owed him nothing. Friends take care of friends. Blake was screwed, caught with stolen office keys and exams from every high school in the county. There was no reason to take Simon down with him. But at the moment, Blake's focus was on his daughter. He'd reimburse Simon later.

They rode the train from Baltimore to Union Station in DC and then the subway to within a block of the bar. Blake spotted her first, as she entered the bar in a dress that hugged her curvy form in all the right places. Ten years was a long time without women, not that he'd been all that experienced at twenty. In prison, he'd avoided TV and magazines and most books. He did get better at reading, but stuck to old novels, before they became graphic. Why torture himself with something he couldn't have? Ms. Hornbeam looked amazing.

"Eye on the prize, Romeo," Simon said, eyeing Blake.

"I got this," Blake said. "No problem."

In the old days, Blake grifted alone, but this wasn't the old days—in so many ways. They entered the bar together, moments after Susan. She stood at a corner high-top, greeting two other women as only women do, with smiles and hugs and way more physical contact than necessary.

From nearby barstools, Blake listened intently to her drink order. Some kind of margarita. Even drink names had changed in his absence. Moments later, the bartender served her a bright pink beverage with salt on the rim. "So what makes that a pickled bear margarita?" he asked Simon.

The bartender laughed out loud. "Pickled bear?" He kept laughing, louder than necessary. "Did you hear that? Pickled bear margarita," he said to pretty much everyone in the bar.

Ms. Hornbeam—Susan, he reminded himself—turned. If she approached now, her drink would clash with Blake's face. And then, she did. She lifted the neon drink toward him in salute from barely a foot away. "Prickly pear," she said in a sweet, seductive voice. Well, female anyway.

Blake laughed at himself and returned the salute with his beer. "Enjoy," he said.

He and Simon nursed their drinks and talked quietly. Twenty minutes later, as Susan drained her glass, Blake ordered two prickly pear margaritas and made his approach. He offered one to her. "You convinced me to try it."

She smiled uncertainly, then accepted the drink. "I tried it on vacation last summer, and now it's my go-to first drink. But I can make an exception tonight."

Blake took a sip—the salty beginning, the sweet middle, and the alcohol ending. "Wow, it's good."

Very good.

"Really? You like it? Most men won't get near a fruity drink."

"Most men don't know what they're missing."

She smiled again, without caution this time. A beautiful smile.

He almost slipped. "So Su—ppose we introduce ourselves." She didn't seem to notice. They talked for several minutes, maybe longer, until her friends said good-bye, and he suggested dinner.

"What about your friend?" she asked, nodding to the bar where Simon still sat.

"He has other plans." Blake stepped away to talk with him. They arranged a place to meet, and Simon slipped him some cash.

"Where would you like to go?" she asked, as they stepped outside.

He wrapped his coat around her shivering shoulders. "I'm new in town. You pick." He knew it was dangerous. She might choose a restaurant beyond his means. Heck, a Happy Meal was beyond his means, and he had no idea how much cash Simon had given him. The first two restaurants they considered had cloth napkins and candles. Gratefully, they also had lines out the door.

As they passed a deli, Susan said, "I'm tipsy, and I'm starving. Do you mind if we get something here?"

"I was thinking the same thing." Which was even true. He was back in the groove.

They ordered sandwiches and beer at the counter. He paid cash with plenty to spare. Simon must be doing okay. They chose a table for two in the back, far from the door and its intermittent cold breeze.

"Tell me about yourself," she said.

"Ladies first."

Even her close-mouthed grin was attractive.

"I'm an administrative assistant."

"That sounds interesting." So, maybe he wasn't back in the groove.

"It's not," she said. Her grin flattening.

"What would you rather be doing?"

She swallowed a sip of her beer. "Writing. I want to write mystery novels."

"So, why don't you?"

"I do, in my spare time. There just isn't enough."

"Why not write full-time?"

"Oh, a little thing called cash flow. Few writers can afford to just write, but it's my dream, after I get good enough, and get published."

"But how will you do that, if you don't have time to write?"

"And therein lies the rub."

"'Ay, there's the rub,'" Blake said.

"What?"

"Sorry, Hamlet. It's always misquoted."

"You read Shakespeare?" Her eyes shone wet and sparkly in the overhead lights.

Blake chuckled. It wasn't often he was mistaken for intelligent. "For a while, I had a lot of time to read, but not a lot of books to choose from."

"You're... different."

The way she said it, it didn't sound bad.

"Your turn. What do you do?" she said.

Blake glanced at the time. First contact required careful orchestration. This had gone on too long already. "How about next time?"

Her face fell, until she checked her own watch. "Oh my. Early staff meeting tomorrow."

"That doesn't sound fun." He stood and helped her on with her coat.

"It's not." She swayed, and he put an arm around her waist. "Got a deadline."

"That doesn't sound fun, either."

"No. But tomorrow night at eight, we're done. Then it will be time for fun." Her slurred words were somewhere between sad and comical. "Fun for me, but not for the poor kids who have to take that test."

"Kids are taking a test at night?"

She slapped him playfully on the arm, nearly losing her balance. "No, silly. They go to the printer at eight."

Tomorrow at eight. Not much time.

He walked her to her apartment building, gave her a peck on the cheek, and watched until she disappeared into the foyer.

Simon appeared from the shadows. He'd spent the evening checking out the office building. They shared information on the ride back to his mother's house and came up with a plan.

* * * *

Back in DC the next morning, Blake dropped in at Susan's office, a triangular brick and glass structure wedged in a forty-five-degree corner northwest of the Capitol. Unable to find an office directory, he asked the friendly receptionist.

"Ms. Hornbeam is in Testing Services," she said. "Fourth floor." She pointed toward a bank of elevators.

Simon wanted to know about stairwells, so Blake hiked up, pausing on the final landing to catch his breath. He entered the brightly lit hallway and found the Testing Services office without difficulty—it took up half the floor. They must make tests for more than just Maryland elementary schools, Blake thought. He glanced through the glass entry, but didn't see Susan. Inside, a receptionist directed him to her cubicle.

"Blake, what a surprise," she said.

She looked great.

"I was in the neighborhood and thought I'd see how you were doing."

"Fine. I'm fine. Sorry about last night. I must have been a bore."

"No, not at all." Their eyes met, and he hesitated. "You can make it up to me over lunch."

She looked at her watch.

"It can be quick," he said. "You have to eat."

She seemed about to decline, then said, "Sure. I can take half an hour."

"I saw a Mexican restaurant on the other side of the building."

"Yeah, it's good." She stood and pulled on her coat. "Let's go out the back."

He followed her through a cubicle farm, maybe a hundred backs hunched toward screens.

No exams lay conveniently in the open. He looked for a place they might be stored, but came up empty.

Susan pushed open a door under a red EXIT sign. "Hope you don't mind stairs."

The door clanged shut. "And if I did?"

She gave a small laugh and gazed at him. Were those 'kiss me' eyes? He was so out of practice. Instead, he took the lead down the stairs.

Four flights later, the landing had two doors. One marked Fire Exit Only. He opened the other into an enormous garage, just as Simon had predicted.

"This way." Susan opened the other door. No alarm sounded. She hooked her arm in his as they walked along the sidewalk.

"How's your day going? You mentioned a deadline last night."

"It's going. Eight o'clock can't come soon enough."

They waited for a taxi to pass, then crossed the street. As they stepped up on the other curb, a skateboarder side-swiped them. Blake caught Susan before she hit the ground, but her purse flew from her arm, with a little help from Blake. The contents scattered across the sidewalk.

"Sorry," the skateboarder yelled over his shoulder, but he didn't slow down.

Once Susan had her balance, Blake dropped to his knees and collected her belongings.

No keys. Where are they?

Heart racing, he placed her Tic Tacs into the purse and felt for her keys. With relief he palmed them tightly together and continued gathering items from the sidewalk.

She knelt beside him.

"Are you sure you're okay?" he asked.

She nodded.

"That kid is going to hurt someone." He helped her up.

"That was no kid."

Observant. He would have to be careful.

At the restaurant, he pulled the door open for her, then waited to let another couple enter ahead of him. Meanwhile, Simon came up behind him and slipped the keys from his hand, just like old times.

Over a lunch that felt more like an interview, Blake invented a personal history to complement hers. One of his many, rarely useful, talents. He made a mental note to write down the story. It was really quite good.

By the time Simon finally texted, 'Bushes,' Susan had her purse in her lap. "My keys. They're not here."

"I don't remember picking them up." Blake stood. "I'll go look."

He found them under a bush near where she'd fallen.

"Oh, thank heaven," she said.

He accompanied her to the back stairwell, where they said another chaste goodbye. He watched which key opened the door.

* * * *

The men regrouped at the same bar where they'd met Susan the night before. "They're still on for eight tonight," Blake said. "Did you figure out where they're printing the test?"

"In the basement," Simon said.

"How do you know one of those keys will get you in?"

"It won't. I'm not going into the basement. You are going into the loading bay."

Light-headed, stars flashed in Blake's peripheral vision. He was the grifter, never the thief. Simon explained the rest of the plan. Blake felt no better.

* * * *

At midnight, Blake approached the back door. It was different at night—lonely, threatening. He'd been in prison and didn't want to go back. He thought of his daughter. Did she need private school more than she needed her dad? Then he thought of Erica. She was the gatekeeper. He had to do this.

He willed his trembling hand to still, and he unlocked the door. Eyes squeezed tightly shut, he pulled open the door and held his breath. Nothing, no alarm. He relaxed, slightly. He slipped into the dimly lit stairwell and closed the door behind him.

Deep breath.

He turned the knob for the loading bay door, almost hoping it would be locked. It wasn't. Inside was total darkness. With the press of a button, his new cell phone glowed, illuminating a small area. He explored briefly, tripping frequently, and selected a hiding spot as near the door as possible, but well hidden behind crates. He sat and typed a note to Simon, 'In.'

A response followed soon after. 'Good. Rest.'

Too terrified to sleep, Blake imagined his capture, and a return to prison. Would he get the same cell? Maybe he would take classes this time and learn about computers—much more useful than Shakespeare.

Arms wrapped tightly around his chest, Blake leaned back against the crates, certain sleep would never come.

He startled awake to a sound, and bright lights, followed by voices. It was seven on the dot. A punctual crew. Blake peered from his hiding place. Men in blue uniforms rolled dollies from a huge elevator, piling boxes near the loading area.

His phone vibrated. A text from Simon. 'Status report.'

'About to shoot.' Blake whispered the steps to himself—touch the camera icon, aim at the men, touch the round button. A bright light nearly blinded him. The flash. He'd forgotten the flash.

'Don't forget the flash,' Simon texted.

Blake closed his eyes and shrank behind the crates. Before they caught him, he would text the photo, so Simon knew what uniform to wear. He hit send, and waited. No one approached. His phone vibrated. 'You took a picture of yourself, you idiot. And TURN OFF THE FLASH.'

Blake peeked again, two men leaned against the boxes, talking and holding coffee cups. The elevator doors were closed. With trembling fingers, Blake tapped icons: Flash off. Lens reversed.

The elevator dinged. He knelt, aimed the camera, ensured the image on the screen was of the uniformed men, and clicked. No flash. He texted the image to Simon, then sat down to wait.

'Got it,' came the response. 'Have the uniform. On my way.'

Sometime later, ten minutes or a hundred, Blake couldn't tell, the overhead doors rumbled, and cool air flooded the room, chilling the sweat on his back.

Footsteps approached. Blake's pulse accelerated. Above the pounding in his ears, he heard Simon say, "Make it quick," as a box landed on its side nearby. Tamper-proof tape secured the top and bottom. Blake opened the switch-blade he wasn't allowed to carry, slit the box near the bottom, and reached in. He barely noticed the cardboard scrape his hand as he withdrew a single paper packet. 'MCAT' was written in large black letters across the front. He'd done it.

'Got it,' he texted.

"What's going on over there?" a male voice yelled from a distance.

Blake's heart seized. His throat seized. He feared his brain might seize.

"Oops, wrong pile," Simon said loudly. "Sorry about that."

He grunted as he lifted the box and disappeared from view.

When the first truck pulled out, Blake took the opportunity to sneak back into the stairwell and out into the cool morning. Simon caught up near the Metro stop, a blue uniform crumpled in his hand. They sat in the back of a nearly empty car. Simon asked to see the exam and then took photos of each and every page. It took nearly the entire trip. Blake didn't ask why. Simon had come through for him. He was entitled to a keepsake.

When they parted, Blake thanked his friend, then rode on, up to Baltimore, to see the daughter he'd never met.

He found the address, an apartment building far nicer than he could afford. On the front steps sat a young girl studying something. She pushed hair from her face, and Blake's breath caught. She looked like her mother, and Blake's mother. Beautiful.

"Jessica?" he said.

She clutched her backpack to her chest and leaned away from him. "Who are you?"

"Ummm." He couldn't do it. He couldn't give her stolen goods the day they met. She wouldn't want a thief for a father. He returned the envelope to his jacket pocket and smiled at her. "I'm Blake."

"My dad's name is Blake."

Tears pricked his eyes.

Erica told her?

"But he's in prison."

"Not anymore," he said.

She looked at him, less wary now, her brown eyes narrowed, her head cocked to the left. It reminded him of her mother's expression when she thought he was lying, which was most of the time. Then, the little girl's face brightened. "Perfect timing." She released her backpack and patted the step next to her. "You can help me with this." The booklet she held read, 'Maryland Christian Academy Entrance Exam Study Guide.'

Not MCAT.

"I have to get a hundred, or I can't go to this school, and my life will be crap."

Blake cleared his throat, in part to hide a smile. Good parents don't smile at swear words, even little kid ones. "I beg your pardon?"

"Sorry, but that's what momma says—'crap.' So I have to get a hundred."

He'd stolen the wrong test. He couldn't help her.

His phone vibrated. Then it vibrated again, and again.

"Someone's texting you," Jessica said.

He pulled out the phone and blinked several times to focus on the small screen. It was Simon. First was a picture of the test they'd stolen that morning. Then, 'You can afford private school now.' Last was an image zoomed in on the exam's title—MCAT: Medical College Admission Test.

Tammy Euliano writes medical thrillers inspired by her day job as a physician, researcher, and medical educator. A tenured professor at University of Florida, she's been honored with numerous teaching awards, 75,000 views of her YouTube teaching videos, and was featured in a calendar of (fully-clothed) women inventors. Her short fiction has been recognized by Glimmer Train, Crime Bake, and the Faulkner Society, and her novel *The Cure* was a finalist for RWA's Daphne Award. Unlike most doctors, she dispenses free medical advice—for fictional patients—at teuliano.wordpress.com, because nothing ruins a scene quite like a character on a ventilator carrying on a conversation.

EXIT INTERVIEW

BETH GREEN

"You don't pick up a balloon when you need a bazooka. And you don't shove your feet into flip-flops when the weather calls for snowshoes."

Sweets leaned her elbows on the piss-colored plastic table in the Agency's shittiest conference room. She lowered her voice for emphasis, knowing exactly how menacing she sounded, even when wearing a ripped satin ball gown. And even when the woman across the table didn't know she had the Agency's regulation pistol in the hidden pocket of her red leather jacket.

"I'm telling you, you don't send an assassin to do a thief's job. But that's what you asked for. And that's where you messed up."

Ms. Moffat, that priss from H.R., wrinkled her thin little nose like she'd just taken a drag of a vinegar-flavored vape. "I still don't understand what went wrong last night, Amelia—sorry, *Sweets*. Tell it from the beginning." She pulled Sweets' contract out of the dog-eared pile of paperwork on the table. "I'm going to be checking your story against your contractually obligated duties to calculate your compensation, if any actually applies after such a failure, and the proper conclusion to your engagement with our agency as a…" Her voice trailed off where it should have said *hit woman*. "A problem solver," she finally substituted.

Sweets had never understood how Moffat could be so ill at ease with their line of work and stay with the Agency. But now wasn't the time to tease her about it, as Sweets normally would have. So, she nodded, eyes on the contract.

Despite having come straight from the job with zero hours of sleep and wearing a bridesmaid's dress, Sweets had entered the room as she habitually entered any room in her agency—as bold as a bull snake. But now, the adrenaline of a completed mission ebbing from her nervous system, the paper version of her job security suddenly struck her as flimsy. Very flimsy indeed. *Keep it together*, she told herself. *You're gonna ace this interview.*

One of Moffat's bony fingers indicated the ever-present eye-in-the-sky camera in the corner of the room. "Your consent is immaterial, but just so you know, we're recording this interview."

Sweets bared her teeth. "Don't worry. I'm good on camera. Where do you want me to begin?"

"Just tell it. I'd like to be done by lunch." Moffat glanced at her narrow purple leather wristband. Its thin face displayed the time and the photo of the person who had last sent her a message. Even looking at it upside down, Sweets gathered he was handsome. *Interesting*.

* * * *

The objective was clear, Sweets explained to Moffat—"but you already knew that"—waltz right into the grand opening of their client's competition and steal the golden statuette of a block of cheese that had been commissioned for the event. The objective wasn't necessarily for the value of the topaz-encrusted object d'art, but rather for the psychological implications of its theft. Take the competition down a notch because they were getting too big for their britches.

For one evening only, the life-sized cheese statue would be taken out of its bullet-proof Plexiglas housing and displayed in the middle of a glitzy ballroom, full of the city's most influential—and most paranoid—residents. As with any gathering these days, everyone who was anyone would have a bodyguard there, all on the lookout for Sweets or another of the city's licensed 'problem solvers.'

But unlike most operations, where she could concentrate on one task and one task only, with a team of tactical agents behind her, in this one Sweets was supposed to do it all: arrange a distraction, swipe the cheese, and get the hell out.

* * * *

One of Moffat's overplucked eyebrows raised. "So, you did understand the venture. Sweets, you've spent years with our agency. You know how to run an op. But now, the news is telling me there are six dead bodies? And you show up without the statuette? Colossal mess. Why didn't you refuse the job if you couldn't do it properly?"

"I didn't feel like I could say no, considering how many people you've laid off recently." Sweets pulled a packet of cinnamon gum from her jacket pocket, unwrapped a piece, and put it in her mouth. The assignment had been handed out late, only hours before the event. Agency staff was thin on the ground. A rash of recent firings had put their boss on a tear and sent everyone with vacation days running for the farthest beach resort they could book. Sweets took the assignment from Moffat herself, with instructions to come up with a foolproof plan—team or no team.

After thirty seconds of silence broken by Sweets smacking her gum, Moffat's poker face faded into a scowl. "Go on."

Sweets grinned. "I realized I've never worked without a crew before. So, I called on my besties."

Moffat rattled the contract paper like she was about to unhinge her jaw and strike. "That's part of the problem. The Agency relies on you to show better judgment. You should have pulled from our pool of professional contractors." She took a red pencil from a tiny mesh bag and made a note on a legal pad. The red lead scritched on the paper. Under her jacket, Sweets felt the weight of her pistol nestle against her breast.

"No one else was around. You fired all the people I could trust. Besides, Moffat, unlike most of us—what'd you call us?—*problem solvers*, I'm a local. I got plenty of people to back me up."

Moffat spluttered something from the latest marketing department talking points about the Agency's impeccable track record and copious resources.

Sweets talked right over Moffat. "That's horse shit, and you know it. Now, where was I?"

* * * *

The first thing Sweets had to take care of was transport. So, she found her favorite mechanic.

Pandora was in before Sweets had even explained it. But she wasn't without questions. "Dude, you know I'm not a pro driver, right? Don't you need someone with a superfast car?" They were sitting in the bicycle repair shop where Pandora worked as lead grease monkey.

"Yeah," Sweets said. "The Agency told me to steal a sports car from the event. But I think that's dumb. The cops'll be on the lookout for a muscle car after the gig. It's better if you drive us in your '90s sedan."

They agreed to meet in the back of the shop when Pandora closed up at 5:30 p.m., so Sweets could lay down the plan.

As the shop door tinkled shut behind Sweets, Pandora called after her, "Wait, who else is in? Whatever you do, don't call Lara."

Sweets waggled her fingers at Pandora and smiled, so Pandy would think she didn't hear her. That door glass looked thick.

Now Sweets had a driver, but she still needed at least one more crew member. Someone to handle the distraction. If she didn't call Lara, the one other person she considered a "bestie," then who else? A former surveillance expert at the Agency, Lara had been caught snoozing on a thirty-six-hour shift and now ran security down at the local grocery store.

When Sweets arrived at her little cubbyhole office, Lara was giving a stern lecture to two teenagers who'd been trying to shoplift ice cream.

"First things first, assholes," Lara was shouting. "You don't shove the ice cream in your hoodie pocket and then go look at the magazine aisle! Warm day like today, I could track you through the store by the sticky trail you left." She shoved a hand in the pocket of her jeans and handed them each some cash. "Now, use this to pay for the Rocky Road you stole and come back next week and try again."

"Thanks, Aunt Lara," they mumbled as they walked out the door.

Sweets grinned and flopped down on the threadbare couch. "You running a school for petty theft now?"

"Nah, I don't really know how to steal. Just trying to help out my sister's kids."

"Well, how about we run a little master class for you this evening?"

Lara looked around the cluttered enclosure and at the rows of black-and-white screens displaying aisles of zombified shoppers swaying over their purchases.

"Hell, no one will miss me. Let's go right now."

Before Lara locked up the door, she passed Sweets a tub of half-melted Rocky Road and a broken plastic spoon. They went to a park nearby to share the ice cream while Sweets explained the gig to Lara.

When Sweets was done, and the ice cream was a mere film of chocolate on the waxed paper tub, Lara guffawed.

"You think we're going to walk right in and swipe that gaudy piece of junk and get back out? With no backup? Girl, you're a hit woman. I'm a mall cop. Who else we got on this?"

"Pandy."

Lara dropped the spoon in the tub and lobbed the whole thing into a trash can three feet away. It was a nice shot. "She know I'm coming?"

"Sure, Lara. Other than this being super quick, everything's above board."

* * * *

Moffat interrupted again, her chin jutting like a bulldog's as she scanned a printout in front of her. "Wait up. What about this other woman. This Amy?"

Sweets slapped the flat of her hand on the table in mock exasperation. "Moffat. I'm telling a story here. Have some respect."

"Don't get cute, Sweets. I'm reviewing your contract as we speak. Things are tough in this city. Are you sure you want to gamble with unemployment? The city has plenty of other problem solvers who'd just die to take your place."

Sweets snapped the gum between her teeth and considered. From where she was sitting, the cold eye of the camera in the corner told her nothing. But someone in the building was watching. She hoped.

"I was going to tell you about a couple of phone calls I made and the supplies I got, but sure, sure, let me get to Amy."

* * * *

By the time they'd provisioned and walked to Pandora's bike shop, it was already 5:30. Sweets took Lara through the alley in the back and knocked three times on the service door.

A woman Sweets didn't recognize flung the door open with such alacrity Sweets reached for her pistol. The new woman had bouncy brown hair and magazine-glossy skin and wore yoga pants and a stretchy tunic that said "Nama-Slay."

Before Sweets could even ask for Pandora, the woman began chirping. "Oh my god, you guys must be here about the job! Pandora told me all about it. I'm so thrilled!"

Sweets' heart sank. Pandy and Lara's ongoing feud she could deal with. But who the—

"Sweets! You're right on time, the pizza just got here," Pandy shouted as they entered. "This is my cousin Amy. She moved to town last week and needs work. I said she could help."

Sweets sucked in her breath. "Well, I thought Lara—"

"Yeah, like last ti—?"

Lara didn't even let Pandy get to the *me* in 'time.' "Your engagement party fistfight wasn't my fault. How was I supposed to know your grandma was a raging alcoholic?"

"Because you should have paid attention to the briefing!"

Only Pandy would call her bridesmaids' group text a "briefing." Sweets cleared her throat to get their attention. "Look, guys, we can rehash the wedding plans later. But right now, we've got a gig to plan, and it's really important to my job we do it right."

* * * *

Moffat grunted and checked her watch. "You're taking too long. Hurry up, so I can get to lunch."

Sweets settled back in her chair. If her legs were a tad longer, she would have swung them up on the table to show Moffat just how relaxed she was. Or wanted to be. "I'm just telling you what you asked for."

Moffat's eyes narrowed. "Why are you so cavalier about this? You made a huge tactical error here. People are dead—"

"Kind of my specialty."

"But not what this job called for," Moffat said sternly.

Sweets shrugged. "The situation manifested, and I went with it."

* * * *

The crew tucked into some meat-lovers supreme pizza (except for Amy, who said she was lactose intolerant and a vegan this week anyway, so she only ate the crust, piling the toppings on the greasy cardboard box: a "total waste," Lara hissed to Sweets) and discussed the plan.

Pandy would drive them to and from the grand opening's opulent venue and monitor their comm lines. Lara would cause a distraction at the front door by pretending to steal a potted plant—"I know how *not* to steal, thanks to watching my dimwit niece and nephew"—and Amy, well, Amy was going to be around to make sure nothing went wrong.

"How is she going to know if something *is* wrong?" Lara asked. Amy was doing some deep breathing exercises because she'd had a little anxiety attack thinking about all the excitement to come.

"Give her a break, okay. She needs a job," Pandora whispered. "She just relocated. It's hard in this city if you're not a local like Sweets and you or attached to an agency."

"So get her a job at an agency," Lara sulked.

"What the hell do you think I'm trying to do?" Pandy said. "Now she's got Sweets as a reference."

* * * *

Sweets jumped, startling Moffat. "That reminds me!"

She half stood and extracted a folded piece of paper from her jacket pocket and held it out.

"What's that?"

"Amy's resume."

Moffat glared at her. "You think we'd hire her after all this?"

"Look, I said I'd hand over the resume. I promised. Now you do what you like with it—circular file, whatever."

Moffat snatched the paper out of Sweets' hand and set it on the table without looking at it, then closed her eyes as if in a prayer for strength.

Sweets winked at the camera in the corner and resumed talking. "We got to the ballroom, and everything was great. Pandy's old-ass car was a bit crowded, since I brought my op bag just in case, and we'd all dressed up in party clothes. You like my bridesmaid's dress? I was hoping to wear it at Pandy's wedding, but I guess it got trashed tonight. Anyway, Amy had some sarong thing she turned into a really cute sundress—sorry, off track again. Say, Moffat, could I get a drink of water?"

Moffat groaned.

"You want anything?" Sweets left the conference room without waiting for a reply.

In the corridor, Sweets double-checked that her pistol had a bullet chambered—an old, comforting habit more than a necessity—and got two paper cups of water from the dingy cooler in the kitchenette.

She was right on time: The person she expected was waiting there to talk to her. Sweets returned to Moffat in the conference room with a zing in her step and a different kind of ammo in her jacket pocket.

She set the cups on the table and launched right back into her story. "Where was I? Oh, yeah. The bodies."

* * * *

Lara and Amy entered the ballroom first, and Sweets came in after them.

A quick scan of the room revealed no preliminary issues. Sweets was pretty sure no one had clocked her. Just another woman in a gaudy satin dress sidling up to the canapé table and swiping an extra glass of champagne.

They arrived several hours into the soirée, and the impeccably dressed crowd was visibly trashed. Empty bottles of wine and spirits cluttered most surfaces, and in at least two of the room's four corners, drunken arguments had broken out to the amusement of their onlookers. It was perfect timing.

From force of habit, Sweets scrutinized the faces in the inebriated crowd. She was used to looking for marks. Over by the cheese statuette in the center of the room, she recognized the gala's host and a couple of agency types, but nobody she had to worry about.

* * * *

"What do you mean, 'nobody you had to worry about?'" Moffat demanded.

"They were cool. Nobody who was going to stop me."

"How could you make that risk evaluation on the spot?"

Sweets squared her shoulders. "I don't know how to explain it to you, Moffat. These are people I've known for a while. I'm a local, right? I know who's who. Geez, I thought you wanted me to finish early."

"I've missed lunch already," Moffat muttered. But she waved for Sweets to continue.

* * * *

"There's a ton of hot guys here," Amy breathed in her ear, startling Sweets so bad she spilled some of her drink on her left boob.

"Hey, watch it! Now I have to get this dress cleaned before Pandy's wedding."

"Sorry, sorry. Are we ready?" Amy looked as scared-slash-thrilled as a preschooler at her first sleepover.

"We've already started. Pay attention." Sweets nodded in the direction of the doorway, where Lara was nosing around the royal palms like a puppy looking for a fire hydrant to tinkle on.

"Watch her and give me the signal when she's ready." Sweets swished her skirt and walked further into the interior of the ballroom. She stopped once to refresh her raspberry lipstick using a gilt-framed mirror hanging on the wall. While she was at it, she checked Lara's progress in the reflection.

Good, the distraction had begun. Lara had picked up the smallest of the potted palms and was edging toward the exterior door, in plain view of the liveried waiters and bellhops. Though smaller than its cousins, this palm was only a few inches shorter than Lara herself, with a pot the size and approximate weight of a bowling ball. Even at this distance, Sweets could see Lara's arm muscles knotting under her satin dress sleeves.

Sweets turned from the mirror and stepped confidently toward the cheese statue. By now, half of the room was watching Lara. Even in this crazy town, you don't often see a woman in a fancy full-skirted dress and spike heels carrying around a potted plant. Lara still had five yards to go before she reached the outside doors. The pot sagged in her arms, the plant's fronds dancing frenetically above her chignon.

Sweets reached the statue, but her eyes remained on her friend. Lara's face was bright red. She was making smaller and smaller steps, and her arms bowed further toward the floor, as if the plant was sinking her like a ship.

Pandy's voice came through Sweets' earpiece, crackling and small. "We good to go? I've got a situation here."

Sweets pressed the button on her wristband to activate her comm and whispered back, "Amy, you on it?"

No response.

Sweets counted to ten and evaluated the situation.

It looked good: No one around her was looking at her. None of the security goons were looking at the statuette.

Everyone was still watching Lara's snail-like progress toward the sliding glass doors. The waiters and door guys stared, snickering. A group of men with financier's haircuts had started to laugh. A trio of ladies in furs watched, sipping their drinks and enjoying the spectacle.

Sweets tried the comm again. "Amy?"

No response.

One man from the financier-looking group, way past his first round of drinks, staggered toward Lara.

Sweets tensed. If this was a hit, it would be the perfect time. But a theft?

"Amy?!" she hissed into the comm. She looked down at her bosom. A wet mark on the satin bodice showed the problem: spilled champagne had landed right on top of her microphone. She could hear the team, but they couldn't hear her.

The financier guy reached Lara and held out his hands. Like the downbeat of a pop song, a sudden hush fell across the ballroom, and his words were audible even above the thin whine of the violin Muzak playing: "Need help?"

Before Lara could respond, another in the financier group shouted, "Let's help her!" and Sweets felt the tempo of the room speed back up. Laughing like jackals, four guys from the group ran to the closest cluster of potted plants and picked them up. Suit jackets straining across their muscles as they balanced the weight, they started moving to the exit along with Lara. One guy, clearly overestimating his own strength, staggered into the path of another, who in turn toppled into the fur-clad ladies and the whole bunch ended up in a heap on the floor, covered in potting soil, palm fronds, and spilled champagne.

With or without Amy, this was her chance, Sweets figured. She snatched the fist-sized cheese statuette and moved it into the pocket of her dress.

* * * *

Moffat held up a hand. "Wait a minute. I thought you didn't get the block of cheese."

"I got it. But I don't have it anymore. I told you, you don't—"

"Yeah, yeah, you don't send an assass—a problem solver—to steal something. I'm starting to get it." Moffat jabbed the contract in front of her with the tip of her red pencil.

Moffat's thin features were bland in the fluorescent lighting; only her eyes betrayed inner emotion. Excitement? Vindictiveness? Indigestion? Sweets couldn't begin to guess.

"Sweets, look. To be completely transparent, I don't think the Agency can continue to employ you. I've tracked sixteen different violations of this agreement so far. We're going to have to let you go."

And there it was. The sentence Sweets had known was coming. The threat made real: lose her income, her reputation as a hit woman, her top-dog status with the agency youngsters who looked up to her.

Sweets couldn't hide the scowl the news triggered, but she did force herself to loosen her posture. Her clothing relaxed with her shoulder muscles, and the weight of the pistol at her side reassured her. That, and the contents of her right jacket pocket.

"Okay, Moffat. Sure, it wasn't as tidy as we all like. But, for the sake of your interview, your data, whatever, don't you want the rest of the story?"

But Moffat had already stood and was sorting the mound of paperwork back into her briefcase. She left Amy's resume where it was. "I don't see the point. I'll send my colleague to collect your op bag and—"

Sweets took a chance. "What if I still had the cheese?"

"I'd have to report you."

"To the *cops*?" This was low, even for Moffat.

"You're no longer an employee, Sweets. We can no longer protect you."

Sweets smacked her gum. "But you're curious."

"What?"

"You're curious. You want to know what happened. I can see it in your ears. The tips are pink."

"You're none of my business anymore, Sweets. This interview is over."

"Not so fast."

"Excuse me?"

"I said, we're not done here."

Moffat laughed, a thin little whinny. "Sweets, it's hard to take, I know, but you had plenty of warning. You lost your job and—"

Moffat's eyes got big. The darker emotion boiling up in Sweets must have been showing on her face. "Did… did you remember to turn in your piece before this interview?"

Sweets slowly shook her head.

Moffat gulped, eyes flitting to Sweets' jacket, where the tailored leather completely concealed the weapon.

"Sit back down, Moffat," Sweets instructed.

Moffat did as she was told, her ears turning from pink to burgundy. "We're on camera. You won't get away with—"

"Shut up."

"What do you want?"

"You were sure in a big hurry to get to lunch earlier, Moffat. Meeting someone?"

"I'm not going to answer that. What do you want?"

"You should answer it. When I came in, I saw the message on your smartwatch. Real handsome guy in the profile pic."

"Some guy from a dating app."

"Is that so? That's sure funny."

"I don't know what you're talking about."

"I'm not a great thief, Moffat, but I've been in this business for a long time. I pay attention to faces. And I am a hundred percent sure I saw your date—or whoever that guy in the picture is—at that gala last night."

"So what if you did? He's a businessman." Moffat shifted in her chair.

"Remember when I said Amy noticed a bunch of hot guys at the gala? Well, she noticed them because they were noticing us. Like, on the lookout for our agency.

"Amy intercepted your guy, pretended she was drunk, started showing off her yoga headstands. That made her sarong fall down around her panties, and he got so flustered I could pick his pockets as easy as picking flowers in the springtime."

Sweets laced her fingers together and looked at Moffat coyly. "You know what I found?"

No response.

"A written list of instructions for the evening. The same list you gave me, down to the typo on page two." Sweets *tsked*. "Seriously, Moffat, spell check your shit first.

"Later, after we left the gala, Lara hacked into the hotel CCTV system and traced the movements of this Mr. Handsome, the very same guy who showed up on your watch. I've got a picture of you and this super-sexy mystery guy meeting at the hotel a whole two hours before the party."

Moffat broke; or at least, she replied. "Where are you going with this? My contract states I can date outside the company."

"Sure. That's not the problem."

Moffat pulled a *so-what* face, but her fingers curled white on the handle of her valise. "He must have stolen the paper when we met for coffee yesterday. Can't you see, he must have targeted me?"

"That's what we—and by *we*, I mean the Agency—hoped."

"How did—"

"I called the boss, Moffat." Sweets grinned. "I believe that's in clause three of my contract, if you care to check. 'When the allegiance or moral rectitude of an operative of the company is in doubt, it is the employee's responsibility to notify top management.' Did I quote it right?"

Moffat sat as still as a paperweight.

Sweets continued. "After I got the go-ahead from the big cheese, me and my besties weren't so interested in the little cheese statue. And we changed up our tactics a bit."

Moffat's jaw worked.

Sweets continued. "We took care of Mr. Handsome—sorry if you were hoping to have lunch with him, he was certainly cute—and a couple of his goons. But genteel-like. No bloodshed in the ballroom." Sweets gave a self-deprecating laugh. "That's what you call a pro 'problem solver' like me for, isn't it?"

Moffat cleared her throat like she might vomit. "I don't believe any of this. He's not dead. He messaged me about lunch two hours ago."

Sweets' brow creased. "How little you think of me, Moffat! Of course, I took his watch and phone after the hit. You've been texting with Lara's nephew this whole time."

Moffat didn't have any response to that.

Sweets continued. "I found Amy, and she hid the cheese statue in her sarong and took it out to the car. Pandy's situation was that the valet recognized her from the bike shop and wanted her to leave the parking lot for her own safety. Strangely, they'd had a tip someone was going to steal a fancy supercar. You know, like you told me to do? Well, Pandy got him talking about mountain bikes instead, and pretty soon he calmed down, and we were able to leave as planned. I handed the cheese over to the client before I came in for this interview. He was pleased, and we agreed to tell you I'd botched the job." Sweets paused. "Still want to fire me?"

A teardrop trembled on Moffat's pointy chin "Now what? You're not going to kill me, are you?"

Sweets smiled and let the question hang in the air for a beat. This was more like it: Sweets, back in charge.

"Wouldn't that be fun? Sadly, though, our boss has asked me to make sure we get your full statement on camera. We need your full co-operation." She waved at the eye-in-the-sky in the corner. Somewhere in this building, in a better conference room, the boss was watching. Like always.

Moffat's shoulders relaxed. "Okay, Sweets. I'll say whatever you need." She giggled, shrill and nervous. "I mean, I guess you've basically learned it all, that guy who stole the list from me is dead, and the client's happy, so we're good now, right? I'll be careful to screen my next dates. This won't happen again."

"No, it won't," Sweets agreed.

She let the smile in her heart warm her cheeks.

"But, of course, there's the fact that while we've been in here having this nice little interview, my besties and Lara's niece and nephew searched your house and your desk. They found a real interesting chat string about all the agents you've fired over the last couple of months."

Sweets extracted the paper Lara had handed her by the water cooler and slapped it on the table. "Seems like you've been working from the inside to get rid of the Agency's best talent."

Moffat leaned toward her, not even bothering to deny the evidence. "Look, Sweets, I'm not the one in charge. I'm just a pawn in this. This agency has big enemies. I've got all the info. I can help you guys—"

In one fluid motion, Sweets stood up, unholstered the pistol, and shot her, right under that thinly plucked brow. Moffat looked even more surprised when dead.

Yeah, the boss said not to kill her.

But you don't send an assassin to do a negotiator's job either.

Beth Green grew up on a sailboat but these days is most often found ashore—currently in Prague, Czech Republic. Beth is a former reporter, English teacher and travel blogger; she is now a full-time freelance writer. When not writing for clients or plotting international crimes to take place in her fiction, Beth enjoys reading, scuba diving, and the art of slow travel. Connect with her at www.bethgreenauthor.com.

THE DARK UNDERGROUND

STEVE SHROTT

I had just squeezed my last book onto the shelf as Lionel Krebbs, my fellow library worker, ran up to me, pale, out of breath and holding his chest. "What's wrong, Lionel?"

"Emergency."

"What? Is it your heart? Do you need me to call someone?"

He shook his head, still gasping for air. "Worse..."

"What?"

"It's my..."

"What? What?"

"My... library book... It's... overdue."

I stared at him, not believing this. "You're a jerk. You know that, Lionel?"

"I need your help, Karen."

I probably should have rolled my book cart right out of there.

I first found out about Lionel's jerkiness two years ago when we were both hired by the Westport Library in downtown Harrisburg.

That first day, he said he needed my help too, claiming his cat, Mr. Boggles, was missing. I'm an animal lover, so the two of us began searching for him.

We had no luck, so we went back to his cracker-box-size of an apartment with the many disturbing pictures of Lionel up on his wall flexing—believe me that's not something you want to see on a full stomach—and we found Mr. Boggles sitting on his couch, watching Dr. Phil.

I found out later that Lionel had rented the cat for one day, just so he could spend time with me, looking for the cat that had never left his apartment. Since then, by my calculations, Lionel has expressed his undying love for me, oh, about twenty-seven million times, rounding off.

In a way, the whole Lionel thing is kind of a pity. With his blue eyes and blond hair, he would actually be handsome if he weren't so darn... jerky.

"Please, Karen, just this once."

"Sorry, Lionel, you're on your own."

Tears began to flow down Lionel's cheek. Of course, knowing his past history, I wondered if he had just squeezed some onion into his eyes when I wasn't looking. I wouldn't put it past him.

He wiped his fake tears. "The thing is I have an interview with Miss Kingman for a promotion tomorrow—Library Technician/Advisory Committee Member."

"I know. You've been telling me about it for weeks. Isn't this like your seventh attempt to get that job?"

"Seventh is the charm."

"What's this have to do with your overdue book?"

"You know how important that is. Before Miss Kingman promotes anyone, she looks at their entire borrowing history—lateness, book stains, wrinkled pages etc. If everything isn't perfect, adios amigo."

"And you think one overdue book is going to stop you from getting the job?"

"It may have had jelly stains on it, too."

"I don't think you have anything to worry about, Lionel. You'll get promoted on your merits." Of course, whether he had any merits was up for debate.

"Don't tell me you don't remember Derek Friedlander. He had a dollar fine that he never paid off. Kingman said that was like stealing. So she let him go, and he was never heard from again." Lionel whispered. "She disappeared him."

I blew out air. "Lionel, I seriously doubt Miss Kingman disappeared him. Plus the man was over eighty, and he couldn't move the book cart without falling over."

"That's what they want you to believe. The library is not what you think it is. It's a dark, dark place. A secret underground society of evil library lieutenants who work in the shadows. I wouldn't be surprised if they've disappeared lots of people. Think about it. What happened to Dickson, the security guard?"

"Retired."

"Billy from the Children's Department?"

"Retired."

"Alan in…"

"Retired."

"Sure they are." He raised his index finger. "Take it from me. Once Kingman gets you trapped in her sinewy web of horrors, you'll never get out. None of us is safe." He moved close to me. I moved back.

"You know, Kar, tonight could be my last meal. Wouldn't you like to help me through this trying time by joining me at the Burger Barn? Say, sixish. If we get there before seven, we get free mashed potatoes."

"I don't think so, Lionel."

I attempted to move my cart, but the wheels wouldn't budge, since Lionel had stuck his leg in front of it.

"Lionel, please remove your leg, or I may remove it for you, and it may not be attached afterwards."

"The thing is I'm in competition with Bob Acker. You know, the guy who bullied me for years."

My eyes snapped open. "Acker?"

He nodded.

"Acker won't get the job. Everyone hates him."

"Everyone but Kingman. He's dating her daughter."

"Oh."

"It would be terrible if they hired him, Kar. I heard him talk about policy changes, if he gets in. He wants to make us all work till nine, take away our breaks, and even…"

"He has no power to do any of that."

"He knows people at the top."

I thought about it for a moment, and then, against my better judgment, I said I'd help Lionel.

"Great. The planning meeting is tonight."

"Planning meeting?"

"Yes."

"Where?"

"The Burger Barn."

I stared at him. "Isn't that where you just asked me out for your last meal, but really a date?"

"Yes, but this is a professional planning meeting, very different than a date—unless you start kissing me a lot."

"That's not going to happen."

"Are you sure?"

"Yes, very."

"You know, sometimes unexpected things happen when you're around a sexy guy."

"Is Ryan Reynolds going to be there?"

"No."

"Then, it won't be happening. What time do you want to meet?"

"0400 hours."

"When is 0400 hours?"

"I don't really know. Let's make it five."

"So, after we've finished work for the night."

"Yes."

"You could have just said that."

* * * *

I bit into my Guadeloupe Burger as I sat at a back table at the Burger Barn. Lionel arrived a few moments later with a white sheet of paper and a cheese sandwich.

"I don't think they allow outside food here, Lionel."

Lionel shrugged. "How can they tell it's from outside?"

"Oh, I don't know. It's a cheese sandwich, and they only serve burgers here."

"You are one sharp lady. That's why I chose you." He winked, then placed the white paper on the table. I saw that he had drawn the upstairs of the library on it with stick figures representing me and Miss Kingman. For himself, he had pasted a photo of Robert Downey Junior.

"I have a simple plan, Karen. Eleven o'clock tonight, we climb up the side of the library, sneak into Kingman's office through the window, change the thingies in her computer, and then leave. That's it."

I nodded. "Yes, sounds extremely simple, Lionel. Good luck with that."

I stood up to leave.

"Where are you going?"

"I just remembered I have a root canal that I would suddenly love to get done right now. It would be less painful than this."

"Come on. Sit down. You have to help, Kar. I have no idea how to do any of that stuff."

I don't know what evil force compelled me to stay, but I did. "I don't know how to do that stuff, either, Lionel. We're librarian staff. We're not computer hackers, acrobats or Spiderman."

"You know computers…"

"Yeah, I kinda know a bit…"

"You took that programming course."

"I never did anything with…"

"And don't you know Miss Kingman's password?"

"Yes, there was that day when she was sick, and I had to check on her files. She's probably changed it since then, and…"

"Plus I heard you take a dance class."

I stared at him. "Why does that matter?"

"You're limber like me. It'll help when we climb up to the window. I'm quite the dancer myself, you know."

"Really?"

"You didn't think I got this graceful shelving books, did you?"

Lionel jumped out of his seat and started to move his body, as if he had suddenly been infested by war ants who were attacking one another. He ended up banging into the table and knocking over his cheese sandwich.

I stared at him, trying to use the force of my mind to make him forget this whole darn thing.

"And Kar, with all that dancing you do, you probably have an extra pair of leotards. It'll help us with aerodynamics. I need something manly, you know extra big in the front, if you get my meaning."

I didn't want to get his meaning.

"Questions?"

"Yes, I wondered…"

He looked everywhere except at me.

"Anyone?"

"Lionel, I'm right here."

"Maybe I'd see you, if you used the proper protocol." He indicated I should raise my hand.

I rolled my eyes, but I raised my hand.

"The planning committee recognizes Karen Witzen."

"Thanks. Shouldn't we do this during the day, Lionel? We just go up to the second floor, watch for her to leave her office, and then go in."

"We don't want anyone seeing us."

"We work in the library, Lionel. Everyone sees us."

He leaned close to me. "Do you want to be disappeared?"

"I don't think there's any chance of that happening."

"So naïve, Karen. So naïve. Meet me at the back of the library at eleven tonight."

* * * *

I got up from the table and left, deciding I wasn't going to take part in Lionel's wacky plan. I went home and tried to take my mind off everything. But as I watched some completely unbelievable sitcom about a loony woman helping her even loonier guy friend do some, well, loony things, my eyes noticed the lone greeting card sitting on top of the TV. I went over and picked it up.

It had been from Lionel.

He had sent it to me when I had to go into the hospital to have my appendix out. I was concerned about it, even though I knew loads of people had the very same operation. Lionel wrote, "Don't worry about anything, Kar. You know, I've always liked everything about you, except your nasty appendix, so I'm glad you're giving him the boot. Maybe after, we can get married. Love, Lionel."

I laughed and felt a tear roll down my cheek. Lionel was nuts, but he could be a sweet nut, at times. And right now, he was going to do something stupid. I don't know why, but I had to make sure he was okay. I looked at my watch and realized it was ten-thirty.

I drove to the library and saw Joe the security guard standing inside the door. He was a big man and could beat anyone to a pulp but he might have trouble telling you what fruit is in an apple pie.

As soon as he saw me, he opened the door.

"Hey, Joe, why are you still here?"

"There's been some crazy hooligan causing issues at night."

"Oh?" I said, knowing that tonight there was going to be a crazy hooligan causing some issues.

"Listen, I left something up in Miss Kingman's office. Could I go and get it?"

Joe thought a moment. That wasn't something he did often, and I worried he might strain something doing it.

"I don't know…"

"Don't worry. I have mace in my pocket."

"I guess it's okay, but be quick." He handed the key to me.

"Thanks!" I ran up the stairs to the second floor and headed over to Miss Kingman's office. I was about to open the door when I heard strange sounds from one of the storage rooms.

I should have just told Joe. But I took out my mace and headed toward the room, my body trembling.

I opened the door. And there it was—the monster.

Only this monster was nice. It was our short, chunky cleaner, Sal Deluca. He had his ear buds in and was doing what some people might call dancing. To me, it looked like a cross between the Tango and someone trying to do the Heimlich Maneuver on themselves. Sal was a great guy, but he was no Fred Astaire. That's okay. I don't think Fred was so fanatical about making all surfaces known to man, spic and span.

"Hey Miss Karen. Nice see you. Floor still wet. Careful."

"What are you doing here, Sal? You're usually don't clean on Tuesdays."

He shrugged. "They call, say messy."

"Oh."

"Why you here?"

"I forgot something."

He nodded, then said. "All finished, I go now." He rolled his cleaning cart out of the room.

I was alone, which would have been okay normally, except at that moment the window suddenly shattered.

My heart pounded.

I watched as a face poked into the room. I maced him.

He screamed.

I realized that his female scream sounded familiar. It was Lionel.

His face was red, and he was breathing like he had asthma. I helped him into the room. But as soon as he got there, he fell onto the ground. He lay there for a few minutes.

"You okay?"

"Yeah, but this isn't Kingman's office. My blueprint must have been backward."

I smiled at him. "Something's backward, Lionel. Are you going to get up today?"

"I can't. I'm not breathing properly. You have to give me mouth-to-mouth."

"I am not giving you mouth-to-mouth."

"Please, this could be the last heroic mission that I undertake."

I stared at him. "You call entering the window of a building that you're not supposed to be in at night, to alter something in your boss's computer, so that you will get unfair advantage over your competition, heroic?"

"Yes, and I do it for all of mankind."

I rolled my eyes and started to walk away when my foot slipped on the waxed floor. I started to teeter back and forth until I finally fell. Of course, I've never been that lucky, and this time was no exception. I fell on top of Lionel.

That wouldn't be such a big deal, normally, except this time my lips were inches away from his, and he had puckered up.

Strangely enough, in that moment, I felt drawn to Lionel. Maybe it was being so close to those sparkling blue eyes or soft blond hair. But most likely it was the smell of Sal's cleaning products that had somehow damaged the part of my brain that made good choices.

I moved closer to those lips.

But just as I was about to lay a big wet one on him, common sense prevailed, and I got to my feet. I looked down at Lionel. "You're supposedly on your last breath, and you're puckering up your lips?"

"My lips naturally form this position when I'm dying."

"You're not dying, Lionel. Get up."

As he lifted himself off the floor, I heard him whisper the words, 'so close' to himself.

We both left the room and hurried to Miss Kingman's office.

Lionel turned the door knob. "Hey it's locked. It's never locked."

I spoke to him as if he was nine. "That's because the library is closed. The door is open during the day because the library is open. Got how it works?" I pulled out the key Joe had given me for the door when Lionel yelled, "Hold it."

"What's wrong?"

"I have to make sure the room is safe for you. You don't have an appendix. Who knows what could happen. I will call for you when it's okay."

"Fine. Go ahead."

A moment later, I heard a scream and a loud bang.

I threw open the door and dashed inside the room.

I turned on the lights, and there I saw Lionel in his favorite position—lying on the ground again. This time, his eyes were closed. Which was probably a good thing, since he was lying next to a man's body with a knife in its chest. I forced myself to remain calm.

"You okay, Lionel?"

"Karen, is that you?"

"Yes, of course."

"Thank goodness. It's nice to feel your touch on your face. You have lovely soft hands. I knew if I was persistent, eventually you'd see that I was what you were missing. That I..."

"Can it, Lionel. That's not my hand on your face."

"Sure, it is."

"Turn your head to the left."

"Sure, I know you ladies love my profile."

Lionel turned, snapped his eyes open and saw the body. A look of horror filled his face. Then, he jumped up as if he had seen, well, a dead body.

I knelt down and turned the body over. It was Bob Acker.

Lionel began to scream. I put my hand over his mouth. When I removed it after he stuttered for a while, he said, "This is terrible."

"Death always is."

"No, they're going to think I killed him, because I wanted the job so desperately. They know I'd be just hard-nosed enough to do it."

"I'm not sure about that hard-nosed thing, Lionel. You went to the hospital the other day for a paper cut. We should get out of here."

"You gotta change the thing in the computer first."

"What?"

"Think about it. If I don't get the job, who knows who Kingman will put in that position? It could be worse than Acker."

"Fine."

I looked over at the computer and saw it had already been turned on and showed Acker's overdue books. "It looks like he had some fines he was trying to erase, too. But I guess he was killed before he could finish."

"But who killed him?"

I shrugged. "I don't know. But you know what's odd?"

"You didn't kiss me when we were on the ground in the storage room."

"No. The odd thing is that there's no blood. Not on his shirt. Not on the floor. There should have been blood everywhere."

"You're right."

I didn't think any more of that, as I got rid of Lionel's fine. Then, I was ready to go. Acker's dead body was creeping me out.

"Just one question, Kar."

"What now, Lionel?"

"How are we going to dispose of the body?"

"We're not."

"What are you talking about? We have to. My fingerprints are all over him. If the librarian lieutenants find Acker dead, they're going to figure out I did this and disappear me."

I let his words blow over me.

"So here's what we'll do, Kar. We'll load the body into a green garbage bag and then carry it down the side of the building. We put it into your backseat. I took the bus here, but I don't think that would work. When you bring something that big on, passengers get curious. Then we drive to an abandoned field, and bury the body."

At that moment, the building alarm went off.

Lionel started to shake.

I grabbed him, and the two of us flew down the stairs.

I gave Joe back his key. He said the alarm was due to someone noticing a smashed window. Said the police would be there soon. I decided it might not be a good idea to tell him about the body.

We raced to my car, and I drove a still shaking Lionel home.

* * * *

That night, I didn't sleep at all. The blood thing still bothered me. Why wasn't there any? At three o'clock in the morning, it hit me. I knew who had committed the crime.

I called the police in the morning and told them it was Sal Deluca. He's such a neat freak that, after he killed Acker, he must have cleaned up the blood. He can't stand to see a dirty room—even if there's a dead body there.

He was arrested the next day and confessed that he did it, because Acker had bullied him, too. When he saw him that night, he confronted him and got so mad he used his scraping knife to kill him.

The next day, everything went back to normal at the Westport Library.

Lionel still thinks there's a dark side to the place and believes that's the reason he didn't get the job, even though he was the only applicant. But that night did bond us together, and though I still think he's kind of jerky. I also think he's kinda cute.

But I'll never tell him.

Steve Shrott's mystery short stories have appeared in numerous publications such as *Over My Dead Body* and *Sherlock Holmes Mystery Magazine*. His work can be found in fourteen anthologies including Flame Tree Press's *Crime and Mystery* compilation, where Steve appears alongside Edgar Allen Poe and Sir Arthur Conan Doyle. Steve has had two humorous mystery novels published, *Audition For Death*, and *Dead Men Don't Get Married*, as well as a book on how to write humor. His comedy material has been used by well-known performers of stage and screen and some of his jokes are in The Smithsonian Institution.

THE TROUBLE WITH TROUBLE

LESLEY MANG

The night was cloudy and moonless, perfect for what we planned to do. My buddy Craig and I sat in my mom's old beater waiting for the lights in the surrounding houses to go out. We were parked on a quiet tree-lined street in Rose Park, an old district of the city filled with red-brick mansions. The house we had our eyes on was already dark. We waited in the car just beyond the end of its driveway, hidden by the high hedge that surrounded the corner lot.

When the last of the house lights flickered out, I activated the hacking device. Craig and I pulled on some latex gloves and exited the car, gently closing the doors. Then, we made a dash for the back door.

The owner of the home, Alexander Prichard, was one of the richest men in the city. He had inherited money from his family, but was also a shrewd entrepreneur, investing in high tech. I had followed business stories about his exploits online and in the magazines left in the waiting area of the service station where Craig and I worked. It was a bit of a thrill when he'd sometimes gas up at the station, and we'd have brief conversations about the weather or the Blue Jays.

One of the magazine stories that really interested me featured Mr. and Mrs. Prichard at a charity ball. She was wearing an heirloom set of jewels. The sapphire-and-diamond necklace and matching earrings and bracelet glowed almost as brightly as Mrs. Prichard's smile.

When I showed the story to Craig, he snorted and said, "I bet that jewelry is worth a fortune. And they already have so much money. It doesn't seem fair."

I scowled at my small, blond friend. "Well, it's not. I wonder all the time what I did to deserve my life. At least we have some work."

We had temporary work with a summer youth-employment program at one of the few non-self-serve service stations in the city. Between gassing the tanks, selling pop, chocolate, and chips, and clearing up the mess in the repair area—Ted, our boss, never put his own tools away, but expected us to do it—we rarely had a chance to talk about anything but work.

One morning when things were slow, we started talking about our plans for the fall.

"What are you going to do when the summer is over?" Craig asked.

"Go back to the employment center and see about welfare," I sighed. I partly blamed my mother for getting pregnant with me when she was in high school. I had never met my father, although my mother told me I looked like him, tall with dark hair and eyes. We lived with my grandparents until they died. Then, we moved into a basement apartment in south Scarborough. My mother juggled three jobs. Nights, she worked for Reliable Cleaners. Days, she divided between serving at Tasty Fish and Chips and cashing out customers at Walmart. No wonder she was so tired all the time. I was two years out of high school and had to work. What I really wanted to do was study electronic engineering. I read everything I could find about new electronic devices.

"I hear you, Matt," Craig said. In many ways, he was worse off than me. He and his mother lived in subsidized housing, because she had been diagnosed with manic depression and borderline personality disorder. She also received a monthly government disability allowance. They often ran out of food halfway through the month, because as soon as the money came in, Craig's mother would blow it, usually buying new clothes for herself. Craig himself was not very good at budgeting.

When I asked him what he did with his money, he shrugged and said, "Aside from my phone? Food, cigarettes, weed."

I'd give him bus fare to get home or drive him, sometimes, when I had my mother's car.

"Anyway," I asked, "would you be interested in getting ahold of that jewelry?"

Craig grabbed my arm. "O' course I would. But that's pretty impossible for guys like us."

"It might not be." I smiled. "I have an idea how we could do it. The other day when Prichard and his wife were here gassing up, I overheard a bit of their conversation. She wanted his SUV to take Bentley, their dog, to the vet because they're going away next week. The dog needs shots or something. Anyway, their house will be empty in a few days."

"But how will we get in?" Craig objected. "Everything will be locked up electronically."

We had read about Prichard's security system in one of the magazines. He had an app on his cell phone that automatically locked all the doors and turned on the security lights.

I replied, "I learned a few things in computer club at school and also online." I went on to tell him about my software-defined radio which was basically a computer that could transmit and receive radio signals. "I can program it to unlock the doors. We'll have to do a trial run before we try for the prize."

That night, the test was unnerving. I sat in the car, fiddling with the hacking device, while Craig stood at the back door, listening for the snick of the locks loosening. He pushed the door open and texted, "OK." Then, the dog barked, so he pulled the door shut and ran to the car. I quickly relocked the doors, and we took off.

* * * *

Now, here we stood in black jeans and hoodies at the back door, ready to enter the house together. I tentatively turned the knob. Success! It actually worked. The door opened easily, and we slipped inside.

From the vestibule near the back door, we stepped into a large kitchen with a marble island and granite counters.

"We need to find the safe," I said. "The jewelry is probably there. I bet it's in Prichard's office. Let's check the rooms on this floor first." I turned on a low wattage flashlight, which I kept at waist level, pointed at the floor. "I hope none of the neighbors is up."

We moved into a hall with rooms on either side. The dining room with its beautiful wood trim stood next to the kitchen. Beyond it was a gigantic living room, divided into several sitting areas. The place looked like the fancy decorator program my mom sometimes watched on TV— tall wooden bookcases along one whole wall, a wood-burning fireplace, and paintings of flowers and of people wearing old-fashioned clothes. I wondered if the Prichards had read all those books. The whole room shouted "Money!"

"You see anything that looks like a safe in here," I whispered, as we walked the length of one side and up the other. My t-shirt was soaked and my stomach felt hollow.

"No," Craig said in a normal tone. "Why are we whispering? Nobody's home." I heard him swallow hard.

"Let's check the rooms across the hall," I answered in a softer voice. "I feel safer talking quietly."

From the living room, we stepped into the spacious front entrance to the house. Beside the grand staircase that curved up to the second floor sat a small ornate table with an iron statuette of a man in breeches, a tailcoat, and a wig. The first room was just behind the staircase. Its oak door was slightly ajar. I pushed it open, stepped in, and shone my flashlight to the other side of the room. What I saw made me hastily step back, shoving Craig and pulling the door closed.

"What the—" Craig began.

"Sh, sh," I hissed. "It's a bedroom, and someone's in the bed. It looks like a girl." I didn't tell him she looked like an angel.

"Let's get out of here," Craig pulled on my sleeve.

"Listen a minute. If she doesn't wake up, we can do what we came for. Just be very quiet." I didn't think the girl looked dangerous. Besides, there were two of us. The sound of gentle snoring came from the room. "Let's check the next room."

This room proved to be an office, complete with a large wooden desk, a black swivel chair, and a safe in one wall.

"Are you sure you want to do this now?" Craig murmured. We both stopped and listened for movement. The house was perfectly still.

"I don't want to come back," I told him, as I moved toward the safe. I shone my flashlight on the dial. The manufacturer's name was imprinted on it. It was one I knew. In my research on getting into safes where you didn't know the combination, I found different manufacturers used a unique number of turns to the left and to the right.

"Let's hope this doesn't take too long." I twisted the dial several times to the left feeling for slight resistance and then counting back two numbers. "Write down 39," I instructed Craig. Then I twisted to the right and again to the left, following the same procedure. "Okay. I think we have the numbers," I said. I turned the dial to the left and the right. When I stopped, the safe popped open. I laughed as I high-fived Craig.

I held the door and lit the interior with my flashlight. Sitting on a shelf by itself was a black velvet box with rounded corners. I picked it up and gave the flashlight to Craig. As I opened the box, I held my breath. The necklace, bracelet, and earrings lay nestled in a white satin bed.

In a loud whisper, Craig shouted, "Yes!"

I closed the safe, and the two of us ran to the kitchen and out the back door. I closed the door, and once in the car, I hastily relocked the house. I shoved the box under the driver's seat and took off. We sped in silence to Craig's street.

"We'll talk after work today about the best place to sell the stuff," I said, as Craig jumped out.

* * * *

The next night, we decided to have supper at Fiddler's Tavern on the Danforth, a rare treat. The beers had just arrived at our table, when a face at the bar caught my attention. A lovely girl was sitting there, apparently alone, sipping her own. I put down my drink and looked some more.

"Craig," I whispered. "That's her. The girl who was at the house last night."

"Are you sure?" Craig was skeptical.

"Oh yeah." I'd know that angel anywhere.

"Do you want to leave?" Craig whispered back.

"No, no, she didn't see us. Let's find out who she is."

"Matt, are you kidding?"

"I'm not. You can go if you want to."

"I'll stay, but this is stupid."

I gulped the rest of my beer, walked up to the bar, and slid onto the stool beside the girl. She was small and slender with long blond hair, large blue eyes, and dimples in her cheeks. I was so smitten that I was tongue-tied.

I had come to Fiddler's Tavern often enough to know the bartender, Jason. I liked the man. He was well-muscled, so also acted as a bouncer to customers who became inebriated. He was gentle, but firm, rarely strong-arming anyone. I admired his technique. I also knew that he heard a lot of things. People talked about their business at the bar, not paying any attention to Jason, because he stayed in the background. I wondered if he had heard about Craig and me, although I couldn't think how.

"Hi, Jason. What's new?" I asked with a smile.

"You mean beer? Well, we've just brought in a new one from our main supplier. Want to give it a try?"

I nodded and turned to the girl beside me. "Is this your neighborhood pub?"

She laughed a little. "Sort of, most of the time. My mom and I live in a co-op not far from here, but I'm housesitting a little further west in Rose Park for a couple of weeks. I got bored sitting around the house. The owners don't mind, as long as I'm not gone too long."

"What's your name? What do you do all day?"

"I'm Emma. I'm taking a summer-school course, which happens in the mornings. In the afternoons, I do homework and take care of stuff around the house.

"Sounds pretty good. I hope they pay you all right."

"Well," Emma hesitated, "I do okay."

"Glad to hear it. How did you get a job like that?"

Emma laughed, "Oh connections. My mom works for Mr. Prichard, the owner of the house. What about you? What do you do?"

I picked up my beer and said, "Why don't you join my buddy and me? We have a table just over there."

I pulled out a chair for Emma and saw that she was comfortably seated before I introduced her to Craig. We talked about Emma's studies in nursing and my ambitions. Craig said almost nothing and looked around the room. Eventually, he went to the toilet. I took the opportunity to ask Emma for her phone number and gave her mine.

When Emma looked at her phone sometime later, she leaped to her feet and said, "I've got to go. It's been really nice talking with you. Let's do it again." She glanced at Craig and grinned at me.

Craig and I hardly spoke on the way home. My head and heart were filled with Emma. Such a smart, beautiful girl, and she seemed to like me too. But oh god! She was going to be in so much trouble when the Prichards got home and found the jewelry missing.

Right then, I decided what I had to do. I went home and very quietly let myself in, although Mom usually slept like a log. I grabbed my hacking machine, got back in the car, and headed for Rose Park. The Prichards' house was dark, but I waited half an hour before I began to work on the security lights and the locks. This time didn't take as long as the previous night.

Clutching the jewelry box, I crept through the kitchen and went directly to the office. The safe opened in a moment. I wiped the case with my shirt before I tucked it back in the safe. Then I wiped the combination dial after I shut the door. I stopped a moment, just outside the office door. The house was silent. Then I slipped outside, relieved that Emma had not caught me.

* * * *

"You did what?" Craig screeched. "No, you didn't. I really need that money, Matt. I told my mother I would help her out this month. You had no right. What am I going to do?" He began to cry. "I also need to pay Jeff." I knew the weed dealer could get really nasty, if he didn't get paid on time. I slowed the car to stop for a red light.

"Pay him a bit when you get paid this week," I advised.

"I also need new shoes," Craig held up one of his feet. The sole on the runner was coming away from the worn top.

I was quiet. Craig did need money just to live, but I needed money to get myself out of the terrible hole that was my life. I needed to go to school, but I couldn't abandon my mother.

Eventually, I said, "I have an idea. When the Prichards come home in a week or so, I could go back to the house and get the jewelry. It won't be safe. I'll have to be super careful. But then, Emma wouldn't be blamed for anything."

"I can come, too." Craig shouted.

"Okay, but I want you to wait in the car. It'll be easier for one of us to sneak in than for two of us."

We sat in our usual spot, just beyond the Prichards' driveway. Both of us were nervously munching hamburgers, while we waited for the street to fall asleep. Finally, the lights disappeared in the last of the nearby houses.

"Okay, let's do this," I said, as I shoved the remains of my burger into the pocket of my jacket and reached for my software-defined radio. I was quite fast now at hacking the security lights and the door locks. "If anything happens to me, Craig, please take the car back to my mom." I pulled latex gloves from the pocket in the door, slid out of the car, and gently closed the door.

I followed the familiar route through the kitchen, dining room, and living room into the hall. I wanted to listen for any sounds upstairs. A growl and a sharp bark stopped me. A giant bull mastiff crouched in the gloom. I froze, stepped back, and reached into my pocket.

"Here, Bentley," I whispered, as I whipped the remains of my burger along the floor just beyond the dog. Then, I lunged for the iron statuette on the little table beside the stairs. As the dog bent to wolf down the food, I conked it on the head.

I listened a minute for sounds upstairs. I heard laughter, both male and female, then silence. I guessed the dog's bark wasn't enough to interrupt whatever they were doing. I scurried to the office. My hands shook, as I turned the dial on the safe. It took three tries to get it open. I shone my light inside.

The jewelry box was gone.

I was stunned. I couldn't believe my eyes. Then, I hastily closed the safe and ran. I was scared of a trap.

When I reported the missing box to Craig, he sneered, "What did you do with it? Hide it somewhere in the yard for future pickup without me?"

I was flummoxed. I was doing this as much for him as me. "No. Don't be an idiot. If I was going to double cross you, I wouldn't have invited you to come along. I'm really upset. I need that money, too."

"Well, I hope Emma's worth it." Craig was bitter.

I smiled a little. "She just might be. If someone else took that jewelry, and it's not out for cleaning or something, I bet Prichard will offer a reward. If we can track down who took it, then we can get that money."

"How're we gonna to do that?" Craig was skeptical.

"We'll figure it out. Let's wait 'til we know if someone lifted it."

I relocked the house doors, and we drove home in uneasy silence.

* * * *

Two days later, a short item on the local news caught my attention. The anchor announced that Alex Prichard would give $10,000 to whoever gave information, leading to the recovery of family jewels that had been stolen.

"So, what do we do?" Craig grumbled.

"We ask around. You ask your weed guy if he's heard anything. I'm going to ask Jason over at Fiddler's Tavern. Bartenders hear a lot of stuff."

I didn't tell Craig that I was also meeting Emma there. We had seen each other several times a week in the evening and once for a glorious Saturday afternoon. We had gone for long walks and fairly often ended up at Fiddler's Tavern. Our time this evening would be short as Emma had to be up early the next morning to go to her practicum at the hospital. I saw her home before returning to the pub. The evening was still young.

I sat at the bar, slowly drinking my beer, thinking about Emma and our possible future. I wanted to catch Jason when he wasn't too busy, but customers kept coming in. This was looking like a late night. I checked my email and played games on my phone to entertain myself, as I sipped.

Long after midnight, Jason approached me and asked, "Matt, are you okay? You don't usually hang around this long."

"I've been waiting to talk to you." I hesitated, then said, "This is probably a weird question, but do you know anything about the robbery at the Prichards' house, like who could have done it?"

Jason pursed his lips. "Why do you want to know?"

"Oh, I was just interested. That girl I was with tonight was housesitting for them. I'm glad it didn't happen while she was there."

"Rumor has it that it was dudes from Montreal—Luc, the Duke and his friends."

"Yeah?"

"That's what they're saying."

"Do the cops know this?"

"I have no idea. I haven't talked to them, and I won't unless forced to."

"Prichard is offering ten grand for information." I leaned forward on the bar.

"My life is worth more than ten grand," Jason asserted. "Those guys from Montreal don't care who you are. If you betray them in any way, they knock you off. And you won't escape, because they always find out who told."

"You're saying that, if I tell the cops, we'll both be killed?" I spoke, slowly controlling the quaver in my voice.

"Yeah, it's very possible." Jason raised his eyebrows.

I went home and lay on my bed, thinking. I didn't like to admit that I had committed a crime. What I had done was cause trouble. The trouble with trouble, I concluded, is that it always hurts someone, even if it sometimes helps you. Did I regret taking the jewelry back, when I met Emma? No, I didn't. Emma was becoming an important friend. Did I want to take the chance and tell the cops about Luc the Duke? No, I didn't. I liked Jason, and I liked being alive. Did I let Craig down? Yes and no. We didn't have the money we needed, but we were safe from the law. Did I still need money to do what I wanted to do? Yes I did.

Then, I had a brainwave. I could invent an unhackable electronic security system and market it. I already knew quite a bit about how they worked. It would take some time and some research, but the idea excited me.

And I had an even more delicious thought. Maybe Alex Prichard would invest in it. I could show him how it would personally benefit him. Luc the Duke must have some serious hacking talent.

And I even had a connection. I was sure Emma would introduce us.

"This is my friend, Matt. He's an expert on electronic security systems." I smiled to myself.

A former English teacher, textbook editor, and author, Lesley writes fiction in retirement. She's had two short stories appear in the anthologies, *The Whole She-Bang 1* and *The Whole She-Bang 2*, published by Sisters in Crime, Toronto Chapter. Lesley recently stepped down as president of the Toronto Chapter of Sisters in Crime.

IT TASTES LIKE CARDBOARD

JOAN LEOTTA

"It tastes like cardboard!" said the T-shirt clad older man as he chewed. He curled his lip. Before he could cast further aspersions on my creation, or try to spit it into a napkin, I smiled.

In my sweetest voice, I replied, "Well, of course! If it tasted good, you would eat too much and gain weight. Our Fibe-Fit Byte Bars fight fat by filling you up, while helping you to slim down." I waved toward a picture of an article showing several national-brand weight loss cookies.

"You can read the article. It says people gobbled up so many of those low-cal treats that many actually gained weight."

My prospective client swallowed and looked at the display. He picked up a six-pack of Fibe-Fit bars. "How much are these?"

"Six for ten dollars or a baker's dozen for twenty. That's thirteen. We advocate half a bar a day, so the cost is really quite low." I smiled again. My mark, aka client, handed over a twenty-dollar bill. I gave him our Baker's Dozen pack.

For the rest of the afternoon, business was very good. People want to lose weight. They don't look for an FDA approval label on homemade goods sold by a smiling young woman. I was staffing the booth myself that day, as usual. My partner Ellie was occupied with promotion.

That usually meant she was schmoozing with her newest boyfriend. No worries. Her skills were mostly behind the scenes. I did the baking and selling. Ellie set us up with fake documents, inspection certificates, and the like. I was quite happy with our fifty-fifty profit split.

At the end of each day, we usually cleared $200 each. Not bad for a small con. Ellie always added, "Not bad while we wait for something bigger to come along." I was content with things as they were.

Our ingredients hardly cost anything. We lifted them from the local wood-chip pile at the tree removal company a few doors down from our apartment. A bit of oatmeal, some water, and flour pasted it all together. Dollar-store flavorings and chocolates made the bars smell good. They were chewable. Not very tasty.

I had scored the permanent booth in the North Myrtle Beach flea market for us at no cost by offering to be the morning manager—open up the place, unlock, etc.

I got the idea for this scam while doing time for selling luxury vacations that sent folks to bargain-basement motels. I pocketed the difference between the hotel costs and what people paid me. I met Ellie in the prison library. She was in the last few months of her sentence for scamming men into getting engaged to her. Once they gave her the ring, she moved in, cleared out their bank accounts, and then, left them. Until she was caught.

I met her while I was searching new recipes to use in my work in the prison kitchen. I found a collection of old Depression and WWII-era cookbooks. These gave me the idea that eventually became Fibe-Fit. The books specialized in fakes, recipes that showed how to substitute low-cost ingredients for high-cost goodies to make the treats people loved, in spite of hard times. I learned how to make an apple pie from Ritz crackers, among other things.

I began to experiment. A consumer magazine article clued me in to the rampant inclusion of wood fiber in processed foods, and well, it was time to perfect my bars.

Ellie also took art classes in prison. Sometimes, she hid in the stacks with a pile of art books, using the blank back pages of same to copy art pictures, and later, to make fake documents for some of her friends.

I told her about my idea for a bar that was almost all wood fiber— sooo cheap to make and then easy to sell at a premium price. People could eat it without harm. Ellie agreed to partner with me. And so, it began. She designed our labels and created all the inspection certificates we needed. By selling directly in a market, we avoided mail-order-product scrutiny by the government. After a few weeks, I found I began to really enjoy the routine—baking, wrapping, and selling.

We even developed regular customers. I'm a short, plain, brunette with large, trustworthy brown eyes. No one realized I was an ex-con. People trusted me. Nice. Several of our customers were lawmen—a local sheriff bought the bars as a dietary counter-attack on daily donuts. Two FBI agents, both young and fit, came by, tried the bars, and came back for more. They told me they were training for a marathon, while they were on a short-term assignment to the local area office. Even took a selfie in front of the booth.

No one questioned the taste or ingredients. My skill at masking cheap ingredients with the addition of cheap cinnamon, chocolate, and sugar was improving with each new flavor I developed. When an inspector actually visited us onsite, I called Ellie. She would come by, and in short order, we were cleared. It seems men just could not resist her combination of green eyes, blond hair, and a va-va-voom gorgeous figure. If the inspector was a woman, I did the verbal shuffling, and Ellie provided any necessary changes to written certificates. We were a good team.

Ellie seemed happy to plug along in our harmless little scam, but then again, every time I handed her the money, she added that little phrase about how it was good "until something better came along."

About a month ago, Ellie went to an art exhibit and came back with an idea about art forgery. However, although her skills were good, there was no passion in her brush—and it showed. She realized it, too. Then, two weeks later, she came home with a new boyfriend and another idea.

"Hold on to your hat, Hattie! We'll soon be swilling champagne and moving into a great apartment." She told me her new boyfriend, John, was going to put us up in his elegant condo in a better part of town. I would be able to come along, because Ellie had in mind a prime role for me in the new scam.

After we established that my favors were not part of her agreement (Ellie laughed at that idea), I became enthusiastic about having a bigger oven and safer address. She kept quiet about our new work, but told me our days with Fibe-Fit were near an end. I wasn't sure how I felt about that, but then again…

Moving day came. As I entered the glossy, white-and-gold-decorated, big-window-view condo, I breathed a sigh of appreciation. "Wow! Such a nice kitchen."

Ellie laughed. "You'll like John, too. He and his friends are into a real moneymaking thing. It's a con similar to ours, but theirs pays big bucks, may even get into the millions. Your flavor-imitating skills will be put to good use."

"That's some uptick in income. What's the game?"

Ellie lowered her voice. "Okay, I'll tell you now. Vaccines."

"John makes vaccines?"

Ellie laughed.

"John doesn't make the vaccines. He remakes them."

"Huh?"

"John has a legit job for the big drug and trucking companies, finding hijacked shipments. Stealing and reselling drugs is big dough. What they don't realize is John is often the one who does the hijacking. He grabs truckloads of vaccines destined for overseas. Then, he finds the trucks with stolen vaccines and returns them for a fee—with another twist."

"A twist?"

"Yep. While he has control of the vaccines, he sets half of the vials aside. Then, he takes the rest and repackages them at half strength, often just diluted with water. He had a pretty good guy making new seals and labels, but I'm better. The diluted vaccines go back to the shipper, and then, on their original destinations. John then sells the ones that are one-hundred-percent real vaccine to people in some of those same places. But his customers can pay big bucks to be sure the vaccines they get are real and full-strength."

"What kinds of vaccines?"

"What does it matter? Everything from polio to influenza," Ellie replied.

I tried to smile, but inside my head, little bells of alarm were going off. Diluting meds? The idea of someone taking a child for a polio vaccine, thinking the child was protected, only the child had really received water and just a tiny bit of real vaccine, was entirely different than someone eating just a bit more wood cellulose than the big companies used—okay, a lot more, but still.

"What would I be doing?"

"I told John all about your skill with flavorings. He wants you to experiment with how to make low-strength serums, and even cube and powder meds, look and smell more like the regular full-strength ones. He's hoping to make his fakes in even lower strengths to rake in even more money. I came up with a dynamite new seal design, much harder to detect as fake than the one they were using before."

The challenge of creating new flavors did interest me, but mental pictures of children in hospitals, when vaccine that would keep them out of hospitals had been diluted... those pictures assaulted my brain and my heart.

Before I could express any dismay to Ellie, the door swung open. A tallish man stood in the doorway dressed in black jeans with a tight black T-shirt. The hall light created an aura of sickly green around him. He was carrying a suitcase. He dropped it in the doorway and announced, "I am moving in now! Wife is gone for good."

Ellie greeted him with lavish hugs and kisses and introduced me. First names only. Even though he had never met me before, my status as part of the group was set. I was definitely a serf. John motioned for me to take his suitcase into what had been Ellie's room. I took a look at his slicked-back red hair and the zillion tattoos curling up his muscular arms and neck and decided to keep my second thoughts about the new scam to myself. Wife gone for good? What did he mean by that?

I dragged his leather bag from the doorway into the master bedroom. Remarkably heavy. As I set it down, I noticed a brass nameplate—Ivan Lorovich. John was Ivan. Russian.

I made dinner for the three of us that night. John talked non-stop, telling tales of his exploits in business, beating out one competitor after another, often with the help of well-placed friends. A wink, wink to Ellie often followed his mention of friends. Ellie responded with adoring glances and noises. I thought it might be best to at least smile and nod approvingly, as each tale opened up the overall story of his success to the possibility of the friends being very unsavory connections—mob?

* * * *

Next morning, before the lovebirds were awake, I headed back to the booth with a supply of Fibe-Fit. I tried to put the whole ugly, new business out of my mind and was successful, until a family with a young boy in a wheelchair came by.

Mom was worried about her weight. Dad asked, "Some doctors have recommended more fiber in our boy's diet? Would these work for him too?"

"Uh, we only recommend them for adults. Too powerful for children under eighteen."

The little boy, probably nine or ten, smiled at me.

I smiled back.

"I've had polio," the boy volunteered. "In case you were wondering why I use a chair."

Since polio has been pretty much eradicated in the USA, I must have looked puzzled by the boy's statement. Mom filled me in.

"We were missionaries in India when he was born. Because of a shortage of vaccine there, he was not vaccinated early enough. He contracted polio. We came back to the US for treatment. We were lucky. I saw lines, such long lines, at the Indian clinic treating polio."

My heart constricted. I felt tears. So, without vaccine, or even worse, with a vaccine that parents thought kept them safe but would not—this is what would happen. I began to feel dizzy. A few minutes after the parents left, with a free pack of bars, and strong admonishment not to serve them to their child, I closed up the booth. It was early, so I asked someone else to lock up for me.

When I got back to the condo, Ellie was lying on the white couch in a white silk something or other watching television. She looked like a large cat.

"John's with some friends, working on the deal. Make something nice for us for dinner tonight, will ya, Hattie? I went out and bought some steaks. And beets. John likes beets. Do you know how to make beet soup? He says he likes that a lot."

Okay, so I am not really bright, but even a moron could not miss all of these signs. Ellie had gotten us involved in a scheme run by, or in some way connected to, the Russian mob. During one of Ivan/John's numerous table talks, I learned one of his so-called friends owned a chain of beach junk stores. These stores were long rumored to be a front for the Russian mob to launder money. Foreign students, many from Russia, came in every year to work there. I wondered how many of those young eyes and clever fingers were put to work at repackaging vaccines as well.

Now I was afraid about my work hurting people. But I was also very worried about getting hurt myself, or even killed, if I either failed at my task or tried to do anything to bring about an end to the lucrative vaccine business. After I developed new formulas for them, they could easily deem me no longer useful, and I would be gone like John's wife. Serfs are easy to find.

That night, I told Ellie and John I wanted to keep Fibe-Fit, at least for a while. I said I would use my downtime at the booth to think up new recipes to add to the vaccines. They agreed.

* * * *

Each day, in the booth, away from the vials and tubes that now filled the counters in our kitchen, I plotted, planned, and finally had an idea. Local law help was not a possibility. I decided to contact the FBI. I thought my two FBI customers had probably left the area and was trying to work up the courage to make a call when they sauntered up to the booth. However, they were not returning as customers. Badges in hand, guns showing but not drawn, they give me an ultimatum: "We saw the wood chips in your bars. We think those certificates behind you are probably forged. If you don't cease and desist, we'll call this in to local law enforcement and have you arrested."

Normally, in such circumstances, I would argue that they were wrong, and my product was good. I would show them our brilliantly faked inspection certificates, bluster my way through it all, find a way to leave, and just never return.

However, this time, I said, "Well, guys, you may be on to something here, but in return for going easy on me, you might want to digest some info I have on a case that could make your careers."

From their ID's, I now knew them to be Ron and Dave. They were interested but wary.

I made a shrewd guess. "Ron, Dave, your temporary assignment here is about Russian money-laundering, right? Maybe those beach stores?"

They tried not to look surprised. I continued. "What do you know about an even bigger scam, the trade in diluted vaccines?"

We danced around a bit, and I offered to show them some info the next day. It was easy to make a few printouts from John's computer, since he foolishly, and with great arrogance in regard to my abilities, left it on the counter each night, while he and Ellie retired for a little private dessert party in their room.

The next day, I showed the pages to Ron and Dave, who were both impressed and horrified.

"I can offer it all to you. As of today, I have not done anything but experiment for them, so you won't need me to testify. Even if you burst in with a warrant, claiming you got the initial tip from an anonymous informant, I will be toast. John or Ivan or whatever his name really is—well, he is no idiot—careless, arrogant, but no idiot. So first things first—how are you going to help me get away?"

They said the best strategy would be to arrest all of us on an anonymous tip, separate us later, and then claim I escaped. I didn't like that plan. Witness protection would be my fate. No, the mob was too smart for that. The only escape for me was to be dead. I countered with a plan to use my culinary skills to botch up the dinner on the night they planned to raid—as in some low-level poison. I would give John and Ellie a dose, and I would take just a bit, but would pretend to be even worse off than they were.

"So, when you come in to arrest us, you will have to take us all to a hospital, where they will recover, and I will conveniently die. How's that?"

Ron made noises about needing me to testify. I again pointed out I was not necessary. Dave said there was still the little matter of my illegal Fibe-Fit bar operation.

They finally agreed to my terms. The local FBI office in Columbia, South Carolina, worked with them, and we set a date. The wheels of bureaucracy turn slowly, so I was able to skim a grand from the mall receipts before we arranged a firm date and time. I admit I was already working on usable formulas for the Russians by that time, but I did not reveal this to my FBI friends.

* * * *

On the arranged night, I put the poison, an arsenic mix, into the beet soup. About halfway into gulping down her portion, Ellie began to complain of an upset stomach. John too. I yelled loudest of all with my imaginary stomach pains. The sound of my screams was the signal. Ron and Dave and the others broke in, swept the room, and took us all to the hospital.

At the hospital, I choked out to Ron and Dave that I had accidentally ingested more of the stuff with the poison than I had planned and was afraid of really dying. Stomach pumps all around. Then, Ellie, John, and I were put in separate, guarded, hospital rooms.

I suspected Ron and Dave were not really going to let me go free. Maybe, if I was lucky, I'd get a change of ID, but still, I was more worried about mob reprisals than doing another stint in prison.

That night, since I really had not taken any of the soup at all, I palmed the medication the nurse gave me. Around midnight, I slipped out onto the fire escape, down to the next floor, back in, and helped myself to the street clothes of the person in that room. Then, I sauntered out (carefully) and went back to the condo. I ducked under the DO NOT ENTER crime-scene tape, got my hidden stash of cash, grabbed Ellie's art kit, and headed for the bus station, where a cash ticket can get you pretty far with no passenger listing required.

I lived off-grid, in and out of homeless shelters, for a couple of months, moving west as fast as I could. While I was on the move, *USA Today* broke the story about vaccine smuggling and the Russian Mob. It felt good to know I had helped. When I got to Chicago, I enrolled in a public art-training program and soon learned enough to craft myself a new set of identity papers. Not as good as Ellie's would have been, but good enough to pass in the small Indiana college town where I planned to settle. My cousin, the good one in the family, had gone to school in Indiana, and I had visited her there, years ago.

* * * *

The place was still as idyllic as ever. I snagged a job in a local coffee and smoothie store. After a few months, I cheerfully suggested some additions to the menu. It was not long before I had developed a following for my new smoothies. I loved the atmosphere of the place. Students. Professors. Talk about poetry.

"Mmmm, this new cinnamon smoothie is great! Is it lo-cal too?" a svelte young woman asked one afternoon.

"Of course," I replied. Well, sugar doesn't have many calories, I rationalized. Anyway, she had nothing to worry about. Just fending off guys probably used up all the extra calories she got in the smoothie.

One afternoon, I offered to make health cookies to sell alongside the drinks. I managed to do it with low-cost ingredients, so the cost to the owner was a lot less than it had been with the national brand. My expenses were even lower. I'd found another free source for wood chips. I was making a bit of money, and it all went into an emergency fund.

Most folks liked the cookies, especially when I explained they might help people lose weight. When somebody complained to the manager that they tasted odd, my cookie/smoothie-fan friends rallied.

One of these fans was Miss Svelte, who turned out to be the President of Tri-Chi, a prominent sorority on campus. When she heard someone complain, she offered to help, and last week, she brought her entire sorority into the store. Each girl dutifully ordered Miss Svelte's fave smoothie (cinnamon) and a cookie. There were so many girls, some had to sit outside on the lawn. After making the smoothies, I put together a plate of extra cookies (told the boss I would pay) and went around to the tables offering second helpings to the girls to thank them for their support. Of course, I started with Miss Svelte herself. As I passed the tray around her table, I listened in to the conversation. They were chatting about the school's language department. Miss Svelte's Tri Chi friends were as smart as they were beautiful, several engineering majors and five or six dual-language majors at that table alone.

"Did you see the new professor?"

"The one they brought in for the new language offerings?"

"That's him! Cute, in a doesn't-know-much-about-clothes way."

Miss Svelte, herself a dual major in Italian and Chinese, spoke up. "Well. You can't expect a native Russian to dress as well as my Italian professor, who hails from Milan and has all his suits hand made in London."

I gulped. Native Russian speakers coming to campus? Would they have ties that went beyond teaching basic phrases? And what about their friends and relatives? You could never tell who might show up in this little academic paradise as the native-speaker professor or friend of same. I almost tripped in my sudden anxiety.

Then, I recovered my mental equilibrium. I took a deep breath. "You can go anywhere with your new forging skills and recipes. The cookies or bars will always make money for you," I told myself silently. After all, people will eat anything to lose weight, even if it tastes like cardboard.

Joan Leotta plays with words on stage and page. Her short stories, poems, essays, and magazine and newspaper articles are in or forthcoming in overmydeadbody. com, *Betty Fedora*, *Clubhouse*, *Lakes*, *Peacock Journal*, and others. Her blog, "What Editors Want You to Know," is a series of interviews with magazine editors designed to give insight beyond the guidelines. Visit and sign up at www. joanleotta.wordpress.com so as not to miss any. When Joan is not writing or performing, you can find her looking for shells on the beach.

THE HOLLERITH EFFECT

ANDREW MACRAE

Tourists rarely visited the Hotel Fredrico, a swayback wood structure that rose three shaky stories above a sleepy street a few blocks off Hidalgo's commercial district. In the early afternoon, harsh sunlight baked the sidewalk outside, and pedestrians clung to meager shadows.

An oasis from the heat, the hotel's bamboo-walled saloon was protected from the sun in the rear of the hotel. Leather belts snaked under a tin-stamp ceiling, turning wide-bladed fans and powered by a softly hiccupping hit-and-miss engine behind the back wall. A leather-clad door with a massive polished-brass doorknob served as portal from the Fredrico's lobby.

The congregation daily assembled in Freddie's, as the saloon was known by the expat community, was comprised mostly of Americans and Europeans, travelers who had taken up residence in Hidalgo, far from their native climes. Freddie's provided respite and refuge for retirees, remittance men, and more than a few rogues and rascals.

The curious gaze of all of Freddie's patrons, save one, was drawn when a stranger entered.

He was a middle-aged man, florid of face and broad of build. He wore a panama hat and a checkered sports coat, suggestive of Moose Lodges in the American Midwest. To outward appearances, he was letting his eyes adjust to the cool gloom of the room, though a keen observer would note the way his eyes scanned the tables until, apparently, spotting his quarry—a slim, angular man nursing a drink at a small table against the back wall—the sole person who had shown no interest in his arrival.

The man at the table looked to be in his early sixties, with close-cropped gray hair. He wore a pink, open-neck shirt, khaki trousers, and deck shoes. A white seersucker jacket hung on a hook in the wall next to him. In brief, the uniform of an expat in the tropics. Although appearing not to have noticed the other's arrival, our keen observer would have seen the man's eyes track the newcomer's progress toward him.

"Hey, buddy. Care if I join you?"

"Be my guest." The expat moved his drink a token inch toward himself.

"Thanks." The newcomer lowered himself with a sigh. He loosened his tie and undid his collar. "This sure is one hell of a hot place."

"You get used to it after a few years. But then, I'm not the one wearing a wool coat in a tropical country."

"Heh. Good point. I guess you can tell that I'm right off the plane." He slipped off his jacket, exposing a dress shirt with short sleeves. Sweat darkened his chest and underarms. "Yeah, that's much better." He hung his coat on the back of his chair, then tilted back his hat and studied his tablemate. "Actually, you're the reason I'm in Hidalgo."

The expat's eyebrows rose.

"My name is Richardson. I'm from Medville, Minnesota," he said, as if that explained everything.

A smile flickered across the expat's face. "Oh, dear, my beloved home town. Am I in trouble?"

Richardson gave a tight smile in return, one that neither confirmed nor denied. "Let me buy you a drink and tell you a story. I think you'll be interested in it." He waved, until a hostess deigned to leave her stool at the bar and take their orders.

Richardson asked for a popular American beer. He received a bored shake of the head in return. He asked for another and received the same response. He turned to the expat for assistance.

The expat shook his head. "Sorry, only regional brews are available here. I suggest you try the Belikin. A truckload from Belize arrived yesterday."

"Thanks. You heard him, honey?"

An equally bored nod confirmed his order.

The expat ordered a glass of sherry. "That's what my time is worth these days, one glass of good sherry. But I warn you, when I finish my drink, I shall also be finished with you."

"Right, then, I'll get to it. A few years ago, back in Medville, a man named Leon Brask worked at a local bank. He was a Brit. Say, you're a Brit, too, aren't you? I can tell by your accent."

The other man raised his sherry. "Very astute, sir. Pray, continue."

He pretended to listen as Richardson told his story. He didn't need to listen. It was his story.

* * * *

Seven years earlier, an intriguing idea came to Leon Brask, a transplant from England, lured by significantly higher wages for those with skills such as his. Despite living and working in America's heartland for over a decade, he still clung to his clipped, Oxbridge accent and never forgot that his place of origin would always rank above that of certain uncouth upstarts.

Leon was not normally given to larcenous schemes. He had spent his career as a high-level systems programmer, helping to protect computers against such. But the idea that came to him would only require the insertion of one line of computer code, a line so innocuous that it would go unnoticed, unless specifically sought.

Leon spent months studying his idea from every angle, carefully running and re-running what-if scenarios. They all returned the same result. The Hollerith Effect, as he christened it, would work.

The darkening sky was clear and cold on a February evening when Leon pretended to leave with the rest of the staff. He slipped unnoticed into a restroom and remained for several hours, emerging only when he was certain he was alone. He used a contractor's badge instead of his own to regain entry to the IT offices.

Leon took care to cover his digital tracks as well, by using the department administrator's computer. Leon viewed Mrs. Peabody, when he noticed her at all, as an efficient but utterly forgettable woman, whose timid, tentative nature and short stature, reminded him of a dormouse.

Leon knew that Mrs. Peabody kept her password on a square of paper stuck to the bottom of her keyboard. In less than a minute, he used her computer to log into the bank's main computer. He found the target file buried deep within the system and inserted his patch:

sleep(5)

A single, simple line of code. That was all it would take for Leon to make a great deal of money.

* * * *

Richardson paused and wet his throat with some beer.

"Hope I'm not boring you, buddy."

The other man started, as if lost in thought.

"Sorry. I was caught up in your story, so to speak." His teeth showed as two parallel lines of white when he smiled. "Please, do continue."

Richardson did.

* * * *

It was autumn, with rain sheeting against his bedroom windows, when Leon first conceived his idea. He was reading a book about the early history of computers and had arrived at a chapter about Herman Hollerith, the inventor of the punched card and founder of the company that became IBM.

Herman Hollerith was born on February 29th, 1860. An irony in that date caught Leon's attention. Hollerith was a leap-year baby, which meant that his birthday came only once every four years.

Leap year and leap day caused headaches for anyone maintaining computer calendar software. There was more code written to handle Herman Hollerith's birthday than the rest of the year combined. And it was out of mulling over that odd irony that Leon's idea was born and took shape.

The simple line of code Leon injected into the bank's primary system would provide him with a brief window into the future. Three years hence, at the start of February 29th, midnight of leap day, the bank's main computer would pause for five seconds before adjusting the date—and during those precious few seconds the computer would believe that the date was March 1st.

Leon intended to make good use of those five seconds.

* * * *

The clock ticked closer to midnight as Leon Brask sat at Mrs. Peabody's desk on the fourth floor of the First Bank and Trust of Medville. He was alone. The only sounds were the whisper of the heating system and the muted howl of the frigid winter winds outside the windows. Leon kept the office lights off, working only by the light of the monitor.

Leon had worked stealthily, skillfully, and successfully during the three years that had passed between the genesis of the Hollerith Effect and the next leap day. Step by careful step, he had built a backdoor into the bank's account management system. It allowed him to manipulate any account in the bank without leaving a trace.

A garden-variety embezzler would have immediately helped themselves to a few million dollars. But Leon was a cautious man and forestalled touching any of the accounts. He knew that embezzlers are uncovered, inevitably, because a firm's books must always balance. "A" minus "B" must equal zero. That was a fundamental formula in bookkeeping.

Leon was going to secretly change that equation, via the Hollerith Effect. He would add a third value, "C". Its value was enough cash for Leon to retire comfortably in a place without extradition treaties. A place such as Hidalgo.

* * * *

"Beautiful, hot Hidalgo," remarked the expat. "Quite a change from a Minnesotan winter."

Richardson mopped his face with a napkin. "Sure is. How about another round?"

The expat drained the last runnels of sherry and set the glass down.

"Thank you, except I believe I'll have tea this time around." He gave a tight smile. "I want to keep my head clear."

Richardson shrugged, signaled the waitress, and then continued his story.

* * * *

Leon had crafted a linked set of auto-transaction computer scripts on Mrs. Peabody's computer. He had made a point of using only her computer for his clandestine work. He kept all his notes and plans on that computer, disguising them as system files, so as not to arouse suspicion.

Each script was timed for precise execution, down to the millisecond. Now he could only wait. His clock, skillfully synchronized to the bank's main computer, counted down the seconds until midnight. The system date displayed February 28th.

Eleven fifty-five. Leon licked his lips and wished he had brought a bottle of water. The wind howled outside.

Leon found himself distracted by a slide show in an electronic frame on Mrs. Peabody's desk. Each photograph displayed for a few seconds, and then, was replaced by another, in an apparently random order. Many of the images featured a young man from a decade or two before. In some, he wore a soldier's uniform. He was the late Mr. Peabody. Other photos were of puppies and kittens and such, all offensively cute. Leon was tempted to turn the frame face down, but he resisted. He might forget to right it when he was done, and it was important that he leave no trace of his presence.

Eleven fifty-nine. Doubt flooded Leon's thoughts. Perhaps there was a mistake in one of the scripts. A single errant letter or an extra space or period would wreck everything. Leon willed himself not to open the files and check them again.

Midnight. One second past. The system date changed to March 1st.

Mrs. Peabody's monitor flickered as dozens of fund transfer requests and subsequent confirmations scrolled by, each recording the movement of cash out of First Bank and Trust of Medville accounts and into a bank account in the Cayman Islands. Most importantly, each transfer was date-stamped by the bank's computer as occurring on March 1st.

The last script executed moments before the fourth second passed. Done.

Five seconds past. The system date changed to February 29th.

A second set of auto-transaction scripts started running, and transfer requests and confirmations again scrolled past. This time they reported the same funds being moved back into their original accounts—but these transactions were date-stamped the 29th. In only a few seconds, the balance in each of the targeted accounts doubled, or so the bank's poor, befuddled computer thought. Then, a third script ran that moved the excess money out again to the Cayman Islands. From there the money was moved to an eCoin exchange, where tracing it would be impossible. Next, a script closed the Cayman Islands account.

The last thing Leon did was to execute a special program on Mrs. Peabody's computer that removed all trace of his work. He was done.

The bank's books would stay balanced. The only upset would come twenty-four hours later, on March 1st, when the bank's computer would try to transfer the funds again. It would fail, due to the receiving account being closed. Since no transfer could take place, the matter would not be awarded a high priority. Leon's abrupt departure a full day before would not be seen as connected.

Leon left the office and drove through dark streets, ice-covered, and lined with snowdrifts, out to the interstate and to the airport. He took a flight at dawn to Dallas and from there, to Hidalgo.

* * * *

His story complete, Richardson took a long pull from his glass and fanned himself with his hat, exposing a pate of thinning red hair.

The peak of the afternoon had passed as he talked. The shadows were longer, the frequency of glasses clinking at the bar had increased, as had the hum and thrum of conversation as Freddie's woke from its daily siesta.

The expat spoke after a long while. "That's quite a story. You are correct, of course. No point in denying it. I am Leon Brask. I wonder, though, why you even bothered to find me. After all, you can't arrest me. No extradition treaty, remember?"

"Arrest you? That's a good one. I'm no cop."

"Then, who are you?"

"I'm the guy they hired to replace you after you walked out. One of my assignments was to figure out why the bank's computer tried to transfer a few million dollars to a closed account in the Cayman Islands."

Leon frowned and lowered his glass to the table. "I still don't understand how you figured it out."

Richardson waved his hand. "It wasn't too hard. Naturally, the first thing I did was to search all of the office computers. I found your notes and scripts on Mrs. Peabody's computer. Heck, I even found your travel itinerary. How else do you think I tracked you here?"

"That's impossible, quite impossible. I erased them. I made double and triple certain all my work was gone."

"Of course, you did. But Mrs. Peabody didn't trust her own IT department to keep her files safe." He smiled. "That photo frame on her desk was actually a backup drive in disguise."

Leon mulled over the notion that a mousy little department administrator had confounded his expertise.

"You must have been quite the hero, sussing me out like that."

"But I didn't. I made up a story full of techno-babble about a database hiccup. The bank's board was satisfied." Richardson leaned back and gave a broad grin. "Leap day was yesterday, you know."

"And…"

"And let's just say that the Board of Directors of the First Bank and Trust of Medville, Minnesota, is once again scratching their collective heads, wondering what happened."

Leon raised his glass to Richardson. "Welcome to Hidalgo, my friend."

Richardson matched his gesture, as they toasted one another.

"I have to admit to being impressed at how you put it together. It was almost as though you had known me for years."

"That's because I had help from someone who did." He looked up as the door opened. "And there she is."

More than a few heads turned in admiration of the smartly coiffed and tailored woman who swept into the room. Light from the lobby streamed through the door behind her, giving her a soft glow. She twirled, showing off her matching, and beautifully crafted, skirt and blouse.

Her entrance complete, she covered the distance to where Richardson and Brask sat.

"You're as pretty as a picture," declared Richardson.

"Thank you, dear. I think you'll like the other outfits I bought, too. The store is delivering them to our suite." She fingered his wool sports coat. "Now it's your turn for some shopping."

She gave Brask a sidelong glance and flashed a catty smile.

Leon couldn't keep his teacup from rattling against the saucer as he set it down.

"Mrs. Peabody?"

Andrew MacRae is a misplaced Midwesterner who rolled downhill to California several decades ago and where he has lived ever since. He is the author of two novels, *Murder Misdirected* and *Murder Miscalculated,* both about a pickpocket who can't help getting into trouble. He has also edited numerous anthologies for Darkhouse Books, including the recently released, *Shhhh... Murder!,* a collection of crime stories set in and around libraries.

THE FORK, THE SPOON, AND THE KNIFE

T.G. WOLFF

Part I: The Fork

Charley Danger stepped out the door, his hand going to the knot at his throat. Nothing suffocated him like ties and courtrooms, and he'd just spent the better part of the day in both. He had stood behind the client charged with second-degree murder, his hand on her shoulder, as the jury read the verdict. Not Guilty. The prosecutor was an idiot for bringing charges in the first place.

"Danger, I want to talk to you."

Speaking of which. "Nothing to talk about, Rafferty."

"Bullshit. Everything that happened in there was bullshit." Rafferty crowded Danger, bumping him with this barrel chest. "You set it up. You're the reason a man is dead, and that woman is walking free."

"The man is dead, because he liked to beat women. The woman is free, because she didn't make him dead. The case was a loser from the start. You need a refresher in Lawyer 101. Motive. Opportunity. Evidence." Danger glanced at his watch. Court ran longer than he'd hoped, cutting into a day he'd been planning for a month. "Call my office, and schedule an appointment. I'll give you the civil servant discount." As he turned to walk away, a hand gripped his arm.

"You think you've got everyone snowed," Rafferty said in a voice meant just for them. "Saint Charley Danger, defender of the downtrodden. Just remember, I know exactly what you are."

"You think?" Danger reached in his empty pocket for the cigarettes he'd given up.

Rafferty squeezed his hand in warning. "I don't think. I know."

"I don't think you know, either. For once, we're in agreement." Danger pulled his arm free, pointing with his chin, as salvation hurried up the court house stairs. "Better put on your professional face, Rafferty. The press is here."

* * * *

Thirty minutes later, Danger stepped over the short fence separating the park from the parking lot, hands full with a box of ice cream sundaes and a hot cup of coffee. The path led toward a man hovering above a stage and the small crowd of children below whose mouths hung open like goldfish at feeding time. Danger knew how the illusion worked and still was amazed how his friend appeared to float above the stage, balanced on a pole too small for his weight.

Little eyes were wide, and mouths hung open in perfect Os. Hands clapped, and someone whistled when the magician's feet were back firmly on the earth. "Now for my final trick," he waved his hands and then pointed to Danger. "Ice cream!" The kids spun around then hurried to the picnic table where Danger got busy.

"Charley Danger. My favorite mistake." The children's hospital doc, who was doubling as a chaperone, came up behind him as he handed out the last treat.

"Nothing that good can be called a mistake. I have something for you. Abracadabra." He waved his hands over the very visible cup. "Two cream, one sugar."

"Some things never change." Her eyes laughed, as she accepted the drink.

"Things can change. Take you and me for example—uh oh. Looks like I'm in trouble." The star of the show stalked towards them, his smile bordering on maniacal.

"Like I said, some things never change." She brushed a hand over his arm. "Don't be a stranger, Charley." He was appreciating the shape beneath the white lab coat when a less appealing face popped in front of his.

"You're late."

"I'm on time. Looks like another great show, Mylo."

"Mysterio. You know the rule. When the cape is on, I'm Mysterio, Master of Shadows. And you're late. I had to stall for over twenty minutes."

"What can I say? The wheels of justice move at a glacial speed. Let's get packed up. We're behind schedule."

Danger had a small office in a high-end suburb where indiscretions kept his checking account full. A Mercedes-Benz sedan was parked in his space. A familiar pair of legs stretched out from under it. Danger pounded on the hood as he walked past it. "Nap time's over."

A loud bang answered, followed by some creative swearing. The legs rolled out, followed by a T-shirt advertising motor oil and a face with five o-clock shadow and a red strawberry on the forehead. "Dang it, Danger. I should skin you alive. You 'bout took ten years off my life."

Danger pulled Fast Willie Wushinske to his feet and into a one-armed hug. Willie was the progeny of an accountant and a middle school teacher, both of whom lived in the suburb where they stood. His accent was a blend of NASCAR, satellite radio's country music stations, and the Andy Griffith Show.

Willie eyed Mylo. "You still wearing a cape?"

Mylo flicked his hand toward the stained shirt. "You still wearing grease?"

Then, the two hugged with both arms. "Glad you're home, Willie. Two years is too long."

"It ain't just me, bro. Last time I was 'round, you was on the TV instead of at the dining room table."

"Let's get down to business. We're cutting it close as it is," Danger said. Inside, they sat at the table crowded with fast food and a map of a mansion. "This is the home of the international banker, Hugh Williams. Tonight, he is hosting an art exhibition and auction as a fund raiser for his pet charity, *Save the West African Black Rhinos*. The charity is a scheme run by Alastair Swagger."

Willie raised a finger in the air. "Why you so sure it's dirty, Danger?"

"West African Black Rhino was listed as extinct in 2011."

"You never know. Circumstances change."

Mylo threw a paper cup, bouncing it off Willie's head. "Do you know what extinct means?"

"Guys, focus. Our target tonight," Danger said over the brothers, "is a nineteenth-century dagger." He laid a photo on the table.

"I still can't believe it's real," Mylo said. "I thought she'd made up all those stories."

"We all did." They had grown up together in a neighborhood where both parents worked, with Danger's great-aunt Nan starring as their Mary Poppins. Every day after school, she would have some dish from her native England waiting for the three of them. They suffered through the horrendous meals for the crazy outings and outrageous stories. In an accent undimmed by decades in the States, she painted pictures of battles and treachery, of broadswords and bloodshed. "If you remember, this dagger was made by Nan's grandfather, Angus Dangerfield, as an engagement present for the famous American knife-thrower Kitty Cactus. Before he could give it to her, a Swagger stole the knife. He challenged Swagger to a duel but lost the blade, the girl and his right arm."

Willie double pumped, then threw the cup back at his brother. "Nan said he lost a bit of his mind, too. Didn't he end up broke?"

"Nearly. It forced him into an arranged marriage with the daughter of a successful businessman who wanted a title. Nan said her grandmother had inherited her father's looks and talent for filling the coffers. Dangerfield Building and Trade, known now as DBT, is a global building and investment company headed by my third cousin, twice removed." Danger tapped the image with his index finger. "Tonight, this same knife will be on display, on loan from Alastair Swagger, fifth generation douchebag. The Swaggers stole the blade out from under my family's nose. We are going to return the favor."

"Now you see it," Mylo said, holding a coin between his index finger and thumb, "Now you don't." With a flick of his wrist, his hand was empty.

"Nan would be all over this. I can hear her plain as day." Willie switched from Southern to British. "Mind the details, boys, lest they nip ya in the arse."

* * * *

An hour later, the three were in the Mercedes, dressed for the evening. Danger rode shotgun, wearing the tuxedo he claimed as a business expense in 1999. Willie wore tails, putting the top hat in the back seat. Why he thought a head valet wore tails was beyond Danger. Mylo, in the character of Mysterio, sat in the back seat, a classic picture of a vampire sans fangs.

Willie shifted, Jack-be-nimbling through the amateur vehicles, as though he was playing a video game. Suddenly, he stood on the brakes, the next in a long line of stopped cars. Danger drummed his fingers on the armrest as the minutes ticked by. He sneered when a bicyclist sped past them. He swore when a three-legged dog ran laps around them. When a grandma on a motorized scooter blew him a kiss, his temper snapped like a rubber band.

"Damn it, Willie! We don't have time for this. Get us moving. Now."

"Your wish is my command. Hang on, boys. There's a fork in the road just up ahead."

Calling the dirt stretch a road was like calling a Chihuahua a beast. Technically, the term was correct, but it grossly overstated the merits thereof. The Mercedes charged forward, heedless of hills, dales, ruts, and holes.

"Willie, I don't think this car was made for this. It's too rough." Danger held onto the Jesus bar, trying to keep his butt above the seat that kept slapping him.

"I modified her myself. Don't let her pretty lines trick you. She's all muscle. Stop worryin'. I scoped the entire route out on the Google Earth just in case of an emergency. We're golden."

Danger pointed ahead. "What is that?"

"Deer!" Willie broke hard, pulling the wheel left, while the white tail leaped to the right. The Mercedes fish-tailed, getting close and personal with a different kind of animal.

"That was a Deere. As in John Deere. We're off-roading on a farm in a Mercedes." Danger planted his feet on the floor, stepping on a brake he didn't have.

Mysterio was buckled in, both feet braced under his brother's seat. Still, he got tossed like a salad. "You got us lost. Damn it, Willie!"

"I know exactly where we are. The fancy house is just on the other side of the creek. We just have to cross the next bridge."

Danger braced himself. "Bridge? Willie... there is NO BRIDGE."

The land angled up sharply, the approach for where a bridge would be... next year. The engine rumbled, and the Mercedes's tail kicked up, as it sailed over the creek. The wheels slapped down, dirt kicking out from tires eager to get going. The suspension leveled out when the tires grabbed honest-to-goodness asphalt. A few hundred feet and a right turn put them at the security box of an ornate gate.

Willie pushed the button and then announced, "Mr. Charles Danger and Mysterio have arrived."

* * * *

Part II: The Spoon

"Hello, boys. Nice of you to drop by." A ravishing six-foot tall beauty in feathers and sequins was draped against the doorframe of the servant's entrance. "I was beginning to think I'd been stood up."

"If you ever come to a fork in the road, don't take it." Danger rounded the front of the car. "You look perfect, Spoon."

"Of course, I do." The artist currently known as Spoon was formerly known as Betty Tyler Moore, and still known as Joseph Littleton to her mother. Danger's first paying client had blossomed into an artistic force of nature, a good friend, and an occasional accomplice.

Mysterio took Spoon's hand and gave her a twirl. "You ready to dazzle them, Angel?"

"Always. We have time for a drink and to mingle. I need to find the man lucky enough to take me home tonight."

"Not tonight," Danger said, laying down the line. "You're on the clock."

"Charley, Charley, Charley. All work and no play makes Spoon a sad girl." Her satin red lower lip jutted out. "You don't want Spoon to be sad, do you, Charley?"

He lifted her chin with his index finger. "Work first. Got it?"

She took his finger in her mouth and sucked. "Only for you, Charley."

"Everyone to your positions." Danger issued the order before getting to work himself. He had his own job to do, and it began in the dining room, where the table for sixteen had been replaced with white table-clothed stations, offering a menu inspired by artists. As Danger verified all security measures were in place, he had a moment to be glad he'd eaten at the office.

"There you are, Charley. I've been looking for you. Everything in order?" Hugh Williams had the ruddy complexion of a man who worked with his hands, despite spending his days in meetings. "Have you tried the van Gogh bean salad? It looks just like *Wheatfield with Crows*."

Danger expected that described the taste, too. "My team is in position. You can enjoy yourself, knowing the art work is secure."

"I never worry when you're on the job, Danger." His employer stayed with him into the ballroom. The high ceilings, deep green walls, and parquet flooring created the vast feeling of being out in a wild forest, if the forest had two crystal chandeliers and golden sconces adorning the trees. The curator had selected this room for the Swagger art collection because "the room reflected the rugged, almost primitive nature of the art." There was an oxymoron somewhere in there.

"They are beauties, aren't they, Danger?" On the far side of the room, five daggers were displayed on clear polymer stands, points down. From a distance, each appeared to float in an ethereal light, as if God himself had commissioned their creation. "Ah, let me introduce you to Alastair Swagger. He finally arrived a few hours ago. Some blasted mix-up with his travel documents. Alastair!" Hugh beckoned to a man resembling a scarecrow hiding a basketball under his belt. "Let me introduce the man responsible for the display and security. Charley Danger."

"Now there you go, Hugh, overhyping my stock. I took care of security, hired a talented curator for the fancy stuff, and then did my damnedest to stay out of her way." Danger wore a mask of professionalism, as he extended his hand. "Good to meet you."

Swagger accepted the offering. "I'm sure it is. It's good to know it's the same on both sides of the pond. I once had a French curator who nearly henpecked me to death. The woman was inexhaustible."

"Did you fire her?" Hugh asked.

"I married her." He elbowed Hugh. "I've never met a man who didn't enjoy an energetic woman."

With that image burned into his brain, Danger made his escape. "Gentlemen, if you'll excuse me, I need to do one more walk-through before the performance begins." Two men and two women were paid to blend with the crowd. Danger communicated with them through pre-set gestures, assured all was in place. The library in the rear of the home acted as security headquarters. Two more operatives kept eyes constantly roaming over the video displays showing every door and each piece of art.

Finally, it was time. Danger returned to the ballroom and sought out Hugh. "The performers are ready. Let's get your guests in their seats."

"Thank you, Danger. Can't stomach a show that doesn't start on time. Must be the banker in me." Hugh moved into the heart of the crowd, raising his voice over the murmur. "Ladies and gentlemen, if I can have your attention. Thank you so much for coming." He put his hand to his heart and sighed. "Raising funds and awareness for the plight of the West African Black Rhinoceros has become my passion. I was on safari when my guide, Jambo, told the sad story of the little rhino that couldn't. Working with the Swagger Foundation, it has been my privilege to be the voice of the Black Rhinoceros, an elusive treasure, here in the States. Tonight, you are going to be treated to two very different treasures. All around you are seldom-seen works from the private collection of the Swagger family, brought to you through the generosity of my friend and business acquaintance, Alastair Swagger." Hugh began the round of applause, keeping it going when Swagger stepped into the limelight and took a bow.

"It is my pleasure to share the artistry my family has been collecting for hundreds of years. Each one has its own story, often mired in intrigue and violence." The audience oohed and aahed on cue. "One worth noting is this delicate beauty." Swagger removed a dagger from its perch. "The Swagger Dagger was hand crafted by my great-great-grandfather to win the heart of an American woman. She was one of your cowboys. The night he proposed, he was challenged to a duel for the woman and the blade by his greatest rival, a filthy cur by the name Dangerfield. Though his love begged him not to, he accepted the challenge. Needless to say, the blade and the woman remained his, while his opponent was a hand shy."

Danger stilled, careful to keep his face a mask, as he wondered why Swagger had singled out the blade. Had he recognized the British Dangerfield was the American Danger?

"Now, if you will all take your seats. There will be plenty of champagne and Picasso pâté waiting for you." Hugh waved his hand to indicate rows of chairs set on the parquet floor. Danger took the end seat, front row, where he would be recorded by a security camera. Swagger sat down next to him. Danger couldn't have planned it any better. Hugh watched as the crowd filed into the rows. "Wonderful. You are all in for a treat. She has been called the new face of American dance and recently completed a trans-Atlantic tour, including performances in Amsterdam, Paris, London, Miami, New York and Toronto. It is my pleasure to present to you... Spoon." Hugh took a step toward his seat, but then abruptly stopped. "Performing with her tonight is the Mysterious Magician."

The white lights extinguished. The grin Danger couldn't suppress was hidden in darkness. For a moment, the room was night. Then, a light show started, bringing the magic of fireworks into the forest room. The lights flashed and swirled, ebbed and flowed, until they coalesced onto a single, feminine form curled on the floor. Silence hung. A single drum began to beat, a spark of life. Spoon pulsed with it, her stature growing with the rhythm, a flower unfurling. The sequined bodice hugged her curves revealing the woman without exposing skin. Great, curling feathers in a rainbow of colors draped near to the floor, providing glimpses of shapely leg.

Seven minutes and fifteen seconds into the performance came Mysterio's cue. He entered the scene, night to Spoon's day in his billowing black pants, black shirt, and cape. While Spoon danced, Mysterio did a series of tricks. He began with sleight of hand, but when Spoon failed to notice, his tricks became more daring. A man wooing a woman. Then, his shirt was gone. His muscled chest gleamed under the lights while he dazzled his partner and the audience, pulling brilliant colored scarves from thin air. Still, he was invisible to her. Frantic, Mysterio moved behind the daggers, pantomiming the desperate need for her attention.

The music came to a dramatic pause. Mysterio grinned wickedly. With flowing movements, he swept up the five daggers and began juggling. Under the piercing white of the LEDs, they became flashes of light and streaks of color. He caught one, two, three behind his back, four over his left shoulder, five over his right. He selected the shortest blade, held it between his index finger and thumb, opened his mouth, and swallowed the blade. When the audience responded, the target of his affection noticed. He withdrew the blade, set it back in its stand, then selected the next shortest blade and swallowed it. Spoon edged closer, the jeweled hand pressing to her throat. He reseated the second blade, only to swallow a third, this one notably longer.

As he positioned the fourth blade, the *Dangerfield* Dagger, Spoon protested. Mysterio bowed, offering her the blade. She accepted demurely, tilted her head back, and swallowed to the hilt. The audience applauded uproariously. The music darkened, as a jealous Mysterio came behind the curtsying Spoon. He raised the fifth dagger high, holding it with both hands. The cry of a crow ripped through the room, as Mysterio plunged the knife into Spoon's unprotected breast. The lights flashed with the betrayal, the music weeping at the loss. Then, the world was dark and silent. An instant later, a thin beam of pure light cast down upon two huddled bodies. Spoon mourned her deceitful love. Draped across him in a white version of her previous costume, she appeared to glow. Mysterio laid beneath her, his cape spread across the floor, a dagger impaled in his bare chest.

"Where's the fifth dagger? Stop the show!" Swagger stood between the audience and the players. "Stop it this instant."

* * * *

Part III: The Knife

"I want my bloody dagger, and I want it now!" The audience, robbed of the chance to savor the performance, chided Swagger with murmurs of discontent.

Danger left his seat and stood over the prone body. "Mysterio, give the man his knife back."

Mysterio climbed to his feet, the hilt still protruding from his chest, and an ovation rose with him. He wrapped his cape around his torso, spun three times, and came to a halt holding both the missing dagger and the one formerly embedded in his chest. His skin once more immaculate.

Swagger snatched the daggers and approached the pedestals. "These aren't in the same order." He collected the knives, examining each one before returning it to the assigned pedestal. His body stiffened, Dangerfield dagger in hand. A lion stalking his prey, he closed on Mysterio. "Where. Is. It?"

Danger stepped between the men. "Is there a problem?"

"This… this… street hustler has stolen my dagger." The audience gasped at the accusation, heads bobbing to get a better view of the unfolding drama. "I will dismantle you to get back what is mine."

"Stand down, Swagger. I'm in charge, and I'll get to the root of this. House lights." Full light filled the room, as if anticipating Danger's order. He took the weapon from Swagger and examined it. Steel blade, gold and silver hilt, delicate engravings.

"It's a forgery," Swagger charged, pointing at a clouded stone. "Not even a good one."

Hugh Williams joined the tête-à-tête. "Now calm down, Alastair. It has to be here somewhere. No one has left the house."

Danger called over a tall man in a well-cut tuxedo. "Clear the room. No one leaves without being searched. If they don't consent, we'll call the police."

"I'm sure we don't have to go to that extreme, Danger. I'll talk to them, explain the situation. I am sure everyone will be happy to agree." Hugh herded his sheep into the opposite wing of the house.

With the civilians in the dining room, Danger called his staff together. "Swagger handled the dagger just before the performance. Did any of you see anyone approach the pedestals, touch any of the daggers prior to the performance?" Six heads shook 'no'. "Did any audience member leave their seat?"

"Two did," one of his men said. "Both stepped into the center hall to use the bathroom. They both went directly to and from."

"It was obviously one of these two." Swagger sneered, as he waved his hand between Spoon and Mysterio. "Search them."

"Oh, me first." Spoon cried with delight, jumping into Swagger's personal space. "I've never gone Brit before. Be gentle. Wait. Forget I said that."

Swagger leapt back, uttering curses not fit to print. He looked Spoon head to toe, the elaborate costume revealing more than he wanted to see. "Him, then," he said, pointing to Mysterio, "Search him."

Mysterio took a fistful of pant in each hand and ripped it from his body. He threw the pooled material at Swagger, standing in only black boxers, black socks and shoes, and still, his cape.

"Oh, fun," Spoon said. She pointed at Swagger. "You do him, then he'll do me, then I'll do you. We all get a turn!"

Swagger's air of ignoring Spoon was spoiled by his face turning tomato red. With disciplined focus, he squeezed and turned Mysterio's pants.

"Anything hard in there?" Danger asked.

"Hel-lo!" Spoon sang out. "Right here!"

"Get these two out of here," Swagger said, throwing the pants at Mysterio.

"Spoon, Mysterio, you're clear." Danger turned back to his staff. "I want this entire house searched. You two, get back to the library, and replay the video. I want to know who came within two feet of the dagger. You two, search the downstairs rooms. Start in here and leave no stone unturned. You two, start upstairs. Every bedroom, every bathroom."

"How incompetent are you? Wasting time looking where it clearly isn't."

"There is only one place your precious dagger is supposed to be, and it's not there. Every place is fair game. Thieves figure out where security won't look. So, we look everywhere." He paused, making sure Swagger was with him. "We look at everything. I'm very good at catching thieves, liars, cheats." He peeled off his coat and rolled up his shirt sleeves. "Let's begin by examining the remaining daggers to ensure they are intact. Hugh, did I see Anthony Davidson, the jewelry appraiser, in attendance? Can you ask him to join us, please?"

Swagger stepped between Danger and his collection. "No. I mean, it's not necessary. Let me see that dagger." He took the impostor blade to a wide spot of light. "It seems, I have, uh, made a mistake. This certainly is my dagger. I would know it anywhere."

"Maybe the light played tricks on your eyes," Danger offered.

"Yes, it must have been the lights. I had never noticed how much shine the century-old metal could have under white light." Swagger clenched his jaw. "Call your men off. We're through."

The theft was sold as part of the act, which delighted most of the audience. After the last guest was gone, Danger sipped scotch while Hugh Williams wrote out the check. "You earned every dime of this tonight. I never expected Alastair Swagger to be so melodramatic. He's British, not European."

"You never know how breeding is going to affect a man." Danger offered his hand. "Thanks for a memorable night, Hugh." He stepped out the front door, where the Mercedes waited at the base of the steps.

* * * *

"That was the most fun I've had in years." Spoon leaned a hip on Danger's desk, fingering the ruby on the Dangerfield Dagger.

"Good to know you enjoy your work." Danger pulled a sealed envelope from his desk and passed it to her. "You dazzled them."

"Honey, that's what I do." Spoon batted her fake eyelashes, her hand covering her share.

"Hey, what about me?" Mylo feigned insult, tugging on Spoon's hair. "I had the hard part, and the audience loved it."

"I hate to break it to you, Mysterious Magician, but all eyes were on *moi*. No one even knew you were on stage."

"Which was the plan." Danger took the dagger, hilt in hand, appreciating the balance. "Mylo, that was the fastest, slickest version of the three-card monte I have ever seen. The camera couldn't tell the difference between the real and the duplicate knife. I knew you were making the switch and didn't catch it. Then, the hand off to Spoon. Flawless. Spoon, I'll admit, I was worried when Swagger wanted to search you—"

"I wasn't. He wasn't man enough to take me."

"Few are," Danger said, replacing the blade in the cradle Willie had built. "The camera caught Willie opening your car door for you, but no more. Swagger and an army of cops can review the tape and see nothing but a performer and her partner leaving a gig. Last, but not least, Willie. That box you installed under the Mercedes's chassis worked like a charm. Not a scratch on the dagger."

Willie frowned with insult. "I tol' you I'm a professional. How did you know Swagger would back off?"

"The art arrived over a week ago, and I examined every piece. Nearly half were high-end fakes. I tugged a few connections and learned Swagger has money troubles. Six months ago, two medieval daggers went up for sale on the dark web matching ones owned by Swagger. Last thing he would want is someone looking too closely at him."

"What are you going to do with the pretty knife?" Spoon stroked the hilt as she would a cat. "Seems a shame to lock it away where it can't be appreciated."

"The dagger never mattered. Taking it was about Nan and everything she did for the three of us. The money Dangerfield is paying will produce Mylo's next cable TV special, buy Willie into a real race car, and keep you in sequins for a year."

Spoon slipped the fat envelope into her bag. "What about you, Charley? What are you getting out of this?"

He leaned back in his chair, the thought of the detail he had the jeweler add brought a satisfied smile on his face. "Winning the game is its own reward."

* * * *

Alone in the borrowed suite of Hugh William's home, Alastair Swagger fitted a jeweler's glass to his eye and examined his favorite family heirloom. His hands shook as he stared at the tiny coat of arms cast just under the hilt. He bounded to his feet, throwing the dagger across the room and roaring like an animal. "Dangerfield!"

T.G. Wolff writes thrillers and mysteries that play within the gray area between good and bad, right and wrong. *Exacting Justice*, the first De La Cruz Case File, is currently available. *Widow's Run*, a Diamond mystery, will be available summer 2019. T.G. Wolff holds a Master's Degree in Civil Engineering and is a member of Mystery Writers of America and Sisters in Crime. Visit www. tgwolff.com.

THE FUNERAL HOME HEIST

MARYALICE MELI

Margery squinted at her sister.

The plump woman across the table kept shifting cards from one end to the other of the fan they formed in her hand.

"You waitin' for those cards to change color?" Her gravelly voice deepened by a two-pack-a-day smoking habit, she said, "Bid already, Brenda."

A high-pitched mechanical squeal seared the air outside the dining-room windows followed by a loud, rumbling, throat-clearing roar of a garage door rising at the funeral home next door.

Three of the four card players pressed their cards against their chests and looked toward the window. Two of them half-rose. Margery motioned for them to ignore the noise and continue playing.

"This goes on all the time," she said. "Come on, Brenda."

"Pass." Brenda's rosy face beamed, as though she'd just successfully played a Nelo bid in the 500 game. She gazed around at the other players. No one even blinked.

"Not even an inkle, Brenda?" Margery underscored her disgust with a noisy exhale. "How am I supposed to bid when my partner gives me no clue?"

Brenda shrugged. "No clue is still a clue." She had been playing cards with Margery for forty years, starting at ages six and eight with Old Maid and Fish.

"Give her a break, Marge." The next player sounded sweetly sympathetic, until she pressed her lips together to hide a grin. Her tousled blond hair needed a root rescue. "I'll inkle the joker." She smiled across the table at her partner.

"I don't know where you guys heard it's okay to inkle the joker," Margery complained. "No other group does this." Then, she bid with a note of triumph, "Seven hearts."

"Nine no trump, and that's only because I'm feeling sorry for ya," said the blonde's partner.

"You've got to be kidding, Shirley," Margery squawked.

"I never kid with cards, you whiner," said Shirley in a voice that could've cracked ice. She knuckle-slammed a three of spades on the table. "Let's see that joker, Rosemary."

Brenda followed, playing the ace of spades, and the blonde plonked down the joker to match Shirley's slamming three. Margery, out of spades, threw on a five of clubs.

Shirley opened her hand to reveal the rest of her cards. "No need to play this out, ladies. I've got them all." She had a run of spades that was impossible to beat.

"Damn kids," Margery growled. "It's impossible to shuffle enough after my boys play solitaire with the deck." She swept the cards together and began a violent shuffling.

The sound of squealing brakes under the dining room window startled the women. All but Margery rose and headed for the window.

"I'm telling you, this goes on all the time," Margery complained to the cards she shuffled. "When it happens in the middle of the night, it jolts me awake, no matter how deeply I'm out. Doesn't bother Ed. He sleeps like a corpse, no pun intended. I've called the police, but they don't do anything about it." She imitated the official voice, "It's the man's livelihood, lady. Whaddaya want we should do?"

"You know, he has a point," said Brenda's soft voice. "After all, people don't die from nine to five."

"The problem isn't with dead people," blasted Shirley. "Who the hell expects noise from a funeral home after hours and, especially, not in the middle of the night?"

"Sorry, ladies, pause the bidding. I took a water pill today, and you know what that means." Rosemary rose quickly and ran down the hall to the powder room.

"Have you heard the rumor?" Brenda said and folded her cards.

Shirley and Margery looked at each other, both puzzling over what Brenda, of all people, could have heard.

"You heard a rumor about the funeral home?" Margery asked in a voice like velvet-covered gravel.

Brenda nodded.

"You gonna keep it to yourself?" said Shirley in a hands-on-her-hips voice. "Spill."

"Well, you know Walter..."

"Come on, Brenda, we went all through school together. Of course, we know Walter." Margery placed the deck near Shirley for her to cut.

"Right. Well, some of the teachers were saying, maybe Walter's crematorium is used for more than, you know, ah, bodies," said Brenda, in the careful voice she used to explain important matters to her kindergarten students.

"Like what?" said Shirley.

"Whatever people don't want to keep around," Brenda whispered. "Remember how greedy and what a little thief Walter was, even in third grade?" The other women nodded.

Rosemary rejoined them in time to hear Brenda's last comment.

"He stole my lunch in fifth grade," Rosemary said.

"They say he'll burn anything for the right price," Brenda said.

"Are there any windows that we could..." Shirley started.

"Forget it, Shirley," Margery said. "Your last scheme got us all arrested. Our husbands had to bail us out. I'm still trying to explain that to my boys."

"Me, too," Rosemary said. "But it was kinda fun, and my sons were impressed we had our fingerprints taken with the new digital reader."

"But, what if..." Brenda took a breath.

"You've been spending too much time with your five-year-olds, Brenda," Margery said. "You think you could sneak around a crematory without being caught?"

"Aside from getting grossed out over being in the area where they do the embalming," Rosemary said.

"What do you know about that?" Margery said.

"Well, back when Walter stole my lunch and I found out, he begged me not to tell. He said his father would beat his ass, which might have worn off a few inches. He was chubby, even then. So, I made him show me where the dead bodies are, uh, prepared, so to speak."

"That's gross," Margery said.

"Yeah, it was," Rosemary said, "but not as bad as the way I'd imagined it, like a Frankenstein movie."

"So, if we could get in, we might be able to find out what was going to be burned?" Shirley asked.

"Provided the *something* waiting to go into the flames was shady and might give me ammunition to halt his night activity," Margery said.

"But, Shirley, how would you do it?" Brenda was back to whispering.

"Bren, there's nobody around but us," said Margery. "You don't have to whisper.

"We go in mid-afternoon..." Shirley started.

"Who's this 'we,' *Kemo Sabe*?" Margery said.

"It's all of us, or none of us," Shirley pronounced. "We'll make up some excuse that'll sound right for all of us to be wherever it is they catch us, if they catch us—but they won't catch us."

"So, tell us your plan," whispered Brenda. "It must be marvelous to include all of us."

Margery groaned and clasped her head in both hands.

* * * *

"So, how did you know my grandfather?" The sweet-faced young woman looked up at Rosemary, who towered over her at five feet ten inches, plus four-inch heels.

"I didn't exactly know him," she said, "but I've heard so much about him through the years."

The woman sighed and shook her head. "I'm sorry about that. He had a terrible reputation, always drinking and fighting with the town supervisors."

"Oh, well, as to that," Rosemary gave a chuckle and waved away his past, as though she knew the dead man well and agreed that old guys will be old guys. "Your family has my sympathy," she added, silently cursing Shirley for not providing them with thumbnail sketches of the two bodies currently on display at Ringer's Funeral Home and Crematory.

She looked around at the mourners, mostly senior citizens dressed in casual attire, while she was still in her bank manager's navy pinstripe with smooth, navy, Italian-leather shoes. Brenda talked with an ancient couple across the room, possibly relatives of the feisty, dead piss pot. Her rose-colored, cowl-neck top matched her baggy jogging pants, suitable for floor-sitting with her students at story time.

Rosemary took in the usual funeral home décor, with walls and carpeting in muted, rich colors and elegant chairs, sturdy enough to handle the grief-stricken. She waited as Brenda slowly worked her way through the crowd toward her.

Together, they stepped into the hall and edged into the second viewing room. Shirley, in the smartly tailored green coveralls she wore in her florist shop, was pretending to have known the county's deceased recycling director. Margery was acquainted with him. She had interviewed him and written a story on the new recycling bins for her newspaper. She wore her usual jeans, sweater, and boots.

Shirley checked her watch, patted the arm of whoever was trying to remember who she was, and came toward them. Margery also followed.

"Okay, now, just as we planned." Shirley looked both ways to check that no one was watching them. "Rosemary, since you were there before, you go first and make sure nobody's down there. If we don't see you after three minutes, we'll come down, too."

"Or we'll run," Margery said, then shrugged. "Just kidding."

Rosemary silently strode along the thickly carpeted hall toward the ladies' room and hesitated, but didn't go in. At the last second, she pushed open a door just before that of the ladies' room and disappeared. They could hear her shoes clacking down the wooden steps. Then, silence. They eyed their watches, as the second hands crawled by three times.

"Okay, ladies' room, anybody?" Shirley murmured, and they all hurried toward the restroom. Brenda pretended to push open the restroom door, but the three women continued through the door Rosemary had used. They stopped on the first step. In the clog of bodies and darkness, nothing was visible.

"Where's the light switch? There should be one up here," Shirley fumbled along the wall on the left side, and Margery brushed her fingers along the other side, flipping a switch that lighted the steps and the pale face of Rosemary below.

"I thought the light switch was down here, but I couldn't find it, even with my phone light," Rosemary whispered. "I was really spooked."

"Let's check this place fast and get the hell out," Margery said. "I'm getting the creeps."

"Look at that big cardboard carton in front of what looks like a big pizza oven," said Brenda.

"That's probably the crematorium. I saw one on YouTube. That red light above the door may mean it's warming up to take care of whoever is in the box," Margery said.

"We've gotta work fast," Shirley said, elbowing her way to the long, deep box and lifting the lid.

Brenda grabbed her arm. "You're not going to look inside."

"Unless you've developed X-ray eyes, I don't know how else we're going to find out what he's cremating. Besides, I think I know who it is. Zampelia Cascatto's obit was in the paper a few days ago. That ancient beautician did hair and makeup for all the funeral homes in town. My grandmother used to go to her shop on North Avenue. It was gossip central."

Shirley pushed up the lid.

"Jesus, what happened to her?" Margery said. "Or is it the ghastly makeup job?"

"I heard Yolanda Flaminio took over doing all the funeral homes, once Zampelia got sick," Shirley said. "Yoyo hated Zampy's guts for cutting her out of doing funerals for all those years."

"Look at that knobby nose. Yoyo sure got her revenge," Brenda said.

"We don't know what we're looking for but, if there is anything, it's probably under Zampy." Shirley grabbed the burlap pad under Zampelia and motioned for Brenda to take the other end.

"Sorry, Zampy," Brenda breathed, and they rolled the body over to reveal a body bag underneath.

"Margery, Rosy, grab that bag and lift it out quick."

No sooner had they pulled the bag clear of the box than the red light on the crematorium switched to green, and the large box began a slow progress toward the crematorium's rising door. Shirley slammed the box lid shut and pushed away from the heat coming from within. The four women pulled the bag with them out of the narrow chamber and into the garage where the hearse was parked.

"I thought you said they burned paper receipts and financial records," Rosemary said, grunting. "This bag feels heavy enough to hold all the telephone books in town.

They continued pulling the lumpy bag toward the mandoor next to the overhead garage door, as voices came from the top of the stairs. One voice called out, "I'll check it, Mr. Ringer."

The women dragged the bag as fast as they could across the yards to Margery's garage door. Margery punched in the code, and the door lifted. As they pulled the bag inside, they heard a voice call, "Hey, who's there? Come back, you kids."

"He obviously didn't see us," Margery said.

"Mar, you can't keep this bag here," Brenda said. "This is the first place the police will look, if Walter calls in the cops. Let's put the bag in the back of your van and haul it over to my place. My girls never go in the garage. Spiders, y'know? And Hank always parks out front."

"Great idea, Bren. Thanks."

The women tugged and heaved the bag into the van's wayback.

"Climb in, ladies," Margery said. "Brenda has a full box of wine she hasn't opened yet."

"PARTY!" Rosemary shouted, "YES!"

Within minutes, the van rocketed off the gravel driveway and three blocks down the road to Brenda's house.

"Pull around the back, Margery. We'll take the bag into the garage."

A ropey cough started in the wayback and grew so intense that the spasms shook the car.

"What in fucking sweet hell is that?" Margery said. "I hope that's you, Rosemary."

Brenda clamped her hand over her mouth to keep her scream inside.

Rosemary turned to look at the shaking bag. A green-faced Shirley held her stomach.

"I think your bag of evidence is coughing its lungs out," Rosemary said, "and I have to pee."

"Dear God, just seconds before old Zampy went into the fire, we saved this person from being burned alive," Brenda said, wiping tears away. She and Rosemary jumped out of the van, Rosemary to run to the powder room and Brenda to the back of the van.

"Release the hatch door," she called to Margery. Together, the sisters pulled the bag to the edge of the rear hatch. They unzipped the bag to reveal a man—a naked man.

* * * *

Tim Ford, now dressed in Brenda's doctor husband's scrubs, slowly chewed dry toast and sipped decaffeinated tea. Hank examined Tim and said he was fine for someone who'd been drugged and starved for several days. Afterward, Hank stayed upstairs to keep the children from coming down, and the women, with a third less chardonnay in the box, listened to Tim's story.

"I'd been investigating Ringer's operation, talking with other funeral directors, and I guess he or his boss heard about it. The fact that you found me with no clothes or ID means they know I'm FBI." Tim paused, as the women gasped, drank, and refilled.

Margery said, "Keep going. This is better than *48 Hours*."

"How I wound up in a body bag heading for an ash heap, I don't know. I was unconscious, until somebody yelled 'Party!'"

"Walter has always been a louse, but it's hard to believe he would be so callous as to burn a man alive," Shirley went to the box for another refill.

"Think what's at stake and the kind of prison time he could face," Tim said. "If the man I suspect is behind this decided to blame the killings and disposals all on Ringer, he'd be on death row. The man we suspect is behind this is from Erie and operates in the U.S. and Canada. You don't ever want to meet him or for him to know of you. Don't bring in your local police. Leave it to us and the state police."

"You've got me scared," Rosemary said.

"Isn't there anything else we can do to help?" Brenda said. "This man should be stopped."

"I'd say you'd already done plenty in literally pulling my fat from the fire. You can help with information. For example, how often does Ringer use the crematorium?" Tim asked.

"His is the sole crematory in the county so far, so he takes bodies from funeral directors all over the area," Margery said. "He runs it almost every day."

"We need to crack Walter to talk about the man in Erie. But he's so terrified of Vince Bailey that he's denied all knowledge of the man or his operation. Tell me, who is a well-regarded figure in this county whose death would bring a crowd to his funeral?" Tim eyed the women, while they focused on their personal contact lists.

"An educator from this area wouldn't be well-known enough county-wide," Brenda said. "Nor would a minister or priest."

"A politician? Doctor?" Shirley said.

"I know someone well-known to everyone. His family has owned my newspaper for over 100 years," Margery said. "People either love or hate my publisher, but enough know him to draw a crowd."

The women raised their glasses. "To Wendell Jerome."

* * * *

As soon as Margery entered the lobby of the news building, the secretary pointed at the ceiling. Margery looked up to see her publisher smiling down at her from his office window, nodding, as if to say, "This is another fine mess you've gotten me into." She mounted the stairs to the second floor. Wendell's office, narrow and L-shaped, had windows that also looked down over the newsroom and the press area.

"Margery, you get your wish. You'll finally see my obit in tonight's paper." He grinned. "My wife doesn't think it's funny. She left for state college to be with our daughters to shield them from local nosy reporters. Their absence will be reported as 'under doctor's care.'"

"So, you're not going to give me a raise?" Margery said.

"Not this time, Margery," her news editor, Rafe Rondelli, said. "Wen's funeral is Friday from Ringer's. Special agent Tim Ford said we'd get the exclusive story and help to undo a serious criminal enterprise in our area. Has he told you any more than that?"

Margery shook her head. "Haven't talked to him in a while." That wasn't a lie depending on the definition of "a while."

"You'll do the story, since I understand you saved the FBI the loss of a fine agent," Rondelli said, handing her a folder outlining Ford's investigation. "This is for our eyes only. No copies. Read it here and take notes. Only we three, Wen's wife, the feds, and state police know of this plan. We need to crack Ringer to spill about the evil he's been helping to cover."

"The Staties have already put a burned and wrecked car on I-68 that I supposedly died in, which will account for the closed coffin at the funeral home." Wendell said.

"How are you going to keep Ringer from checking to see that Wendell's ghastly remains really are in the coffin?" Margery said.

"The closed coffin will arrive at Ringer's just before the funeral at 1 p.m. from a funeral director who's worked with us before. He knows just enough to help but nothing more that could tip anyone off," Rondelli said. "This is to let Ringer feel assured that the closed coffin is at the family's request and that all he has to do is conduct the service and further cremate the remains."

"So, what's next?"

"You and I are going back to work in the newsroom," Rondelli said. "Plenty of folks are going to witness Wendell leaving early. At the end of the day, we'll supposedly get word of his death. He'll actually go over to Ohio for the night."

"I don't feel good about this," Margery said. "We're supposed to report the news, not make it or make it up. I can't go along with telling a room full of fellow reporters a batch of lies. How about printing what the State Police tell us as we do with other reports, no more, no less? No reports about what the paper is going to do. Give the usual dodge: more details later, blah, blah."

"What about your sister and the other two women?" Wendell asked. "Can you keep them out of it?"

"It would be easier for me to take out my own appendix," she said.

"Will they keep quiet about it?"

"If you weren't my boss, I'd have to smack you for that."

Wendell laughed. "Take the FBI report. Depending on what happens at the funeral, we'll have a story ready for Friday's afternoon edition. If nothing happens, my demise will be reported as mistaken identity, and I'll be back to work Monday. Go upstairs to the attic offices. I don't want anyone reading over your shoulder."

"How is the funeral supposed to break Walter's vow of silence about Vince Bailey? Do you two know more than you've told me?"

Wendell shrugged, grabbed his jacket and left, making sure to let as many people see him as possible in the press room, newsroom, and front lobby.

Rondelli said, "What I know, you know. We're just trying to cooperate to stop a bad guy. And I'd rather not say no to the FBI."

"You learn fast when you have to say no to four young boys every day," Margery said. "I could say no, if the feds asked me to do something unethical like lie to people I shouldn't lie to."

"Yeah, I'm glad you called me on that. It bothered me to lie to our colleagues and the readers. But would I have done it? I'm afraid to think too much about that."

"Maybe you should think about it, boss. Otherwise, why the hell are you here?"

Margery picked up the report, stuffed it in her bag with her laptop, and trudged up to the third floor.

She called a brief meeting of the card club that night. They met at Brenda's because her husband was on call at the hospital and not able to watch their daughters. Margery's Ed took their boys and Rosemary's two sons to a local haunted house, followed by their favorite fast food place. Shirley's kids were away at college.

"I wasn't allowed to make copies of the FBI report, but basically, it details how the murder scheme worked. Anyone who got in the way of Vince Bailey found himself dead and cremated, along with a regular customer of the Ringer Funeral Home. And Walter got $5,000 per body." Margery added, "You can't tell anyone you know this. All of us, plus kids and husbands, could find ourselves in Mr. Bailey's crosshairs, so please be careful."

"This is super heavy stuff," Shirley said.

The shriek of a screaming woman sounded clearly, but at a distance.

"Imagine living next to that," Margery said. "It's Walter's latest. Each time he fires up the crematorium, he triggers the screamer. Says it's for Halloween."

"What a sicko," Rosemary said, as she got up and went down the hall.

"I think I know another way to help," said Brenda, picking up her phone and climbing the stairs.

* * * *

On Friday, a crowd gathered from mid-morning, until a line extended outside the funeral home. The funeral was likely to be the biggest in town history, and few wanted to miss it, whether or not they knew Wendell Jerome or had just regularly read his newspaper. Walter Ringer stood at the door, as he often did before funerals, heavy-set but impressive in a black, silk suit. His receding, sandy-colored hair, graying at the temples, and his shiny, florid face reflected the look of a prosperous life.

Margery sat near the front of the large viewing room in a side section, clutching her reporter's notebook. She checked her watch and looked again at her group in the back row. Only two members present. She mouthed, "Where's Brenda?" Shrugs were Rosemary's and Shirley's only response. She couldn't have forgotten.

Recorded organ music played quietly in the background and a few people chatted softly. All voices stopped, as viewers watched a closed casket being wheeled carefully to the front, sole representative of the tragedy that allegedly had occurred.

Ringer entered at 1 p.m. and walked with gravity to the lectern in front of the casket. As he silently shuffled a few papers and pages in a slim book, two men in dark blue suits and ties stepped into the hall archway. Several state policemen took positions behind them. Ringer didn't seem to notice. He looked at those in the front row, where close family members usually sat, and intoned in an unctuous voice, "We honor today the memory of Wendell Jerome, a noted journalist and publisher, whose family has covered the news of our families and events for well over 100 years. Let us bow our heads."

At that, a startling, shattering scream came from the casket, along with a measured hammering on the underside of the lid. A male voice groaned, "Nooooo, noooo! Don't burn me. Nooooooooooooo."

The hammering, groaning, and screaming continued, as Ringer's florid skin paled to ash. His watery, blue eyes bugged out, and he began wheezing.

The screaming woman continued, "Whyyy are you doing this? Whyyyy? Let me out!"

The male continued too, "I'm burning, burning. Nooooooooooo."

"Andrew," Ringer called his assistant. He ripped off the top button of his shirt and tore off his tie. "Andrew."

No one moved. The men in the archway stood like figures in a tableau.

A man in the second row stood and shouted, "Open the damn casket, Walter." One of the blue suits pushed the man down by his shoulders.

Ringer grabbed the lectern, as though it were a life preserver and began mumbling, "I'm sorry. I'm sorry. I never meant to burn you. I don't know how you got into that bag alive. Usually, they're already dead. I'm so sorry."

The knocking and groaning continued. Ringer finally pushed off from the lectern and all but fell on the casket. He fumbled with the locks and lifted the lid. As though she was being lifted with the lid, Brenda screamed and sat up in the ugly marionette makeup worn by Zampelia. A dozen women and men also screamed.

Tim Ford then sat straight up, his long hair hanging in his face with a veil of smoke rising from it. He continued to groan. Ringer screamed and fainted. Two burly State Police officers hustled in and dragged Ringer out. The two blue suits smiled at Ford, as they helped him and Brenda out of the casket. When they left, Margery ran after them.

* * * *

As the sun went down that night on the last Friday before Halloween, the card club assembled around the table and chairs in Margery's dining room.

"Hey, Bren, you got any more of that chardonnay?" Rosemary asked.

"Heck, no. We finished that," said Brenda, setting an unopened box of pinot grigio on the table, along with a bottle of chianti. "I also have a crockpot of barbequed short ribs. Help yourself when you're hungry."

"Good. I'm hungry now," Rosemary said, as she set a tray of stemless wine glasses on the table and began filling them. "Why didn't you tell us you were going to make such a dramatic appearance?"

"I figured it would have a bigger effect on Walter if no one expected it, but it was Tim who put the final cap on it," Brenda said.

Setting down a bowl of potato chips and another one of pretzels, Shirley said, "Yeah, Tim. Whatever you put in your hair to make it look like it was smoking scared the shit out of me. No wonder Walter fainted."

"He started talking as soon as he came to," Tim said. "He's kept good records of each contract he accepted and the money he received. Agents now are arresting the kingpin behind it and his associates in Erie. But my co-star, Brenda, gets full credit for the dramatic action. She raised the suspense that broke Walter down."

"You surprised us all, Brenda," Shirley said. "Who'da thought you had it in you?"

Tim had been shuffling the cards, as they spoke and poured wine.

"Do you ladies play poker?"

"Poker?" Rosemary said, all wide-eyed and eager. "Is that a card game?"

"Maybe, if you tell us the rules nice and slow, we can try it," Shirley said, hesitantly.

"Do you play for money?" Brenda asked, her voice breathless and childlike.

Margery plunked a rack of poker chips on the table and said to Tim, "Deal, baby."

MaryAlice Meli lives in Steelers/Pirates/Penguins country: Pittsburgh, PA. She has written nonfiction in past careers in education and journalism. She earned a master's degree in writing popular fiction at Seton Hill University. She writes short and flash fiction, children's stories, middle-grade mysteries, and has begun reading all the books on her shelves designated *TBR when retired*. She placed third in Pennwriters' 2014 short fiction contest, had two short stories in Rehoboth Beach Reads anthologies and flash fiction online in *Every Day Fiction*, *InfectiveINk* and *Untied Shoelaces of the Mind*.

POWER OF ATTORNEY

JAMES M. JACKSON

David Colene focused the lobby-camera feed on the prospective clients seated on the couch. The male of the couple stared straight ahead with a dull, empty expression. His graying hair and full beard needed trimming, but underneath them, Colene sensed a long, lean face. Late fifties? Tendons showed on the guy's corded neck, which rose from a starched shirt whose collar was a couple of sizes too large. Completing the outfit was a crooked tie a decade out of style. He'd check the shoes when he saw the guy in person. They always provided insight to character, but so far, this individual looked diminished and rumpled.

Moving the camera's focus to the woman provided a shock. In Colene's experience, no one like her had ever crossed his law firm's oriental rugs. Young enough to be the man's daughter, purple spiked hair capped a face decorated with two eyebrow rings. A dragon tattoo curled from beneath her scoop-neck tee and twisted around her neck. Tattoos covered both arms. Her right thumb worked her cell phone. Her left hand—its wrist encircled by what sparkled like a diamond bracelet—rested on the man's thigh in a most undaughter-like manner.

Colene jotted a note to look into their relationship. Flicking off the monitor, he buzzed the receptionist. "Please escort Mr. McCree and his companion to my office." He stood to greet his guests, casting a quick glance at the man's wingtips—desperately needed polish. The suit made of fine wool hung limply off the too-thin man. "Mr. McCree? Ma'am?"

"Seamus, please." McCree mumbled without making eye contact.

Up close, the companion ("Call me Niki") looked like a hooker and smelled like fruit salad. Five gold hoops on her right wrist tinkled as she shook hands. She gawped at the hunting prints decorating the wall until Colene gestured toward the informal seating arrangement surrounding the burlwood coffee table. Niki led McCree past the wingback chairs to the loveseat and settled in tight to him.

Colene checked his notes: *Verify purpose. Determine competency. Determine relationship.* He cleared his throat. "Mr. McCree, I'd like—"

"Not Mr. McCree. Seamus!" Veins on his neck stood out, and he stared wide-eyed at Colene. "Do you know I played in the North American Soccer League? New York Cosmos. Played next to Franz Beckenbauer. Yes, I did." He deflated with a sigh. "Too many head balls. Too many."

Colene was taken aback by the anger. "Pardon me?"

Niki rubbed McCree's thigh and leaned into him, whispering something Colene couldn't hear.

McCree visibly relaxed. "I accept your apology."

Niki rolled her eyes. "He has headaches. And anger issues. Doctors think it's more likely chronic traumatic encephalopathy than Alzheimer's." She didn't seem to notice she butchered the pronunciation. "He got knocked out a bunch of times. Plus, heading soccer balls starting real young. He's only fifty-six. Course, they won't know for sure until he's—" her voice dropped to a whisper "—autopsied."

Colene put on his "good friend" smile, felt it pull against the side of his face. "Seamus, my assistant left me notes regarding what you want to discuss, but I'd like to hear directly from you."

Confusion plastered McCree's face. Niki spoke. "Seamus don't feel he can any longer do right by his finances. His son tried to help, and now they ain't talking to each other."

"I told you." Seamus spoke through tight lips. "I want you to do it."

"No, honey." She leaned in and pecked his cheek. "I do okay for myself, but I ain't got the smarts to handle your millions. I brung most of his financial statements. He's got foreign property I don't know nothing about. He can't tell me right, but there's papers in his safety deposit box. I got his power of attorney right here. And his will. He handwrote that. I get half when... well, when the time comes. Here."

Colene looked through the proffered documents. The power of attorney was dated six months earlier. McCree's signature looked strong. Notarized by one of Chicago's top firms. Niki Foster had legal authority. The statements showed mutual funds worth north of ten million.

"Why aren't you continuing with the firm that prepared your power of attorney?"

"They didn't treat me nice, and you was recommended by Mrs. Sibley. She has the apartment next to us in the independent living wing."

Working for Mrs. Sibley had generated one of his more robust legerdemains, as he thought of the arrangements that siphoned off a portion of his clients' assets into his offshore holding company. "She's a doll." He smiled warmly. "She's well, I hope." Time to check McCree's competency. "Seamus, you agree with Niki's assessment?"

Accompanied by the tinkling of the bracelets, she squeezed his thigh and gave him a smile to melt butter.

"Yes," he said. "Not nice."

"Seamus," Colene asked, "what year is it?"

McCree supplied the correct answer.

"And the month?"

"December. All I hear is Christmas music."

Wrong. Three points. "Could you remember this for me? Helen Smith lives at fifty-three Scrivener Place, Deerfield." Colene asked the remaining questions in the prescribed order to test dementia. Seamus missed the time question by an hour (three points). He nailed counting backwards from twenty but skipped July and June (four points) when he recited the months backward.

"Last question. Do you remember the name and address I asked you to remember?"

Seamus tucked a corner of his beard into his mouth and chewed. His eyes looked wild, frightened. "Helen? Helen." Headshakes. "Prime number. Fifty-three. But I don't... I'm sorry. Was it important?"

Sixteen points total. Not Competent. "Seamus, may Niki and I speak alone?"

Colene waited until the receptionist retrieved Seamus to ask, "How long has he been like this?"

"The headaches and anger, for years. But he's losing his smarts fast. What am I gonna do when he goes into the dementia side of that place? They'll throw me out 'cause I'm too young to live there alone. You seen the will. I get half when he dies, but..." She licked her lips and gave him a sideways look. "He runs an hour on his treadmill. Every day. He'll live for years. He talked about buying me an annuity. I ain't sure what it is, but it ain't happened. I can't wait thirty, forty years." She seemed to be appraising him. "Mrs. Sibley—now she's a nice woman who knows how to take care of herself—she said I needed the right lawyer to protect me." Her eyes seemed to grow in excitement. "Can you help me?"

"Help me understand your current arrangements with Mr. McCree."

She looked at the ceiling. "I get a thousand a week, plus room and board, and good health insurance. Of course, I'm also going to be losing my conjugal rights when he has to, you know, be locked up, so he don't wander off."

Conjugal rights? "You're married?"

She spun the diamond bracelet on her wrist. "Good as, except there ain't no paper says so."

He made a show of checking his Rolex. "I do believe we can help you. May I review this material and present you with a proposal describing how our firm can assist you and Mr. McCree in obtaining your goals?"

He offered an appointment a month hence, and with a lot of sighing and multiple checks of his calendar, he let her negotiate it down to Wednesday of the following week. Always make the pigeon anxious for the plucking.

* * * *

Colene found Niki Foster's phone right where her message suggested it might be, tucked down in the cushions of the office loveseat. Unease, maybe curiosity, at her relationship with McCree caused him to check her contacts list, which only contained McCree, his mother, his son, and a dozen other names. It was the first he had heard of a mother. That could complicate things.

He ran a detailed credit check on McCree, who had indeed played soccer on the US national team and the Cosmos before working on Wall Street. Quit early. Divorced. Moved from New Jersey to Ohio to Michigan. Son lives in Chicago, which probably explained the move to independent living in that city. Mother lives in Boston.

The financial data Niki had left showed McCree had within the last two years set up a trust fund for his mother, given his now five-year-old granddaughter a couple of square miles of property in the Upper Peninsula of Michigan. He recently changed his will to provide his son exactly one dollar and split his estate fifty-fifty between Ms. Niki Foster and various charities. Estate attorneys used the one-dollar provision to fend off suits challenging a will when a natural beneficiary is disinherited. No wonder there had been a split between father and son.

All those changes had occurred prior to the power of attorney. He had been a moderate trader until four months ago. Since then, several bonds had matured and hadn't been reinvested, leaving way too much in cash.

The guy was losing it.

Using various proprietary databases and a paid reverse-directory, Colene researched the other phone contacts. One guy had been arrested several times as a pimp. A couple had drug arrests. Cook County jail was one of the numbers, as was a home health service. A phone call to the home health agency brought the information that Niki had been fired for a failed drug test. Further digging revealed she had done time for hooking and check kiting. The booking picture was her, same spiked hair.

He leaned back in his leather chair, linked his fingers behind his head, and closed his eyes. What he had was a habitual offender with a legal power of attorney over twelve million dollars. He itched with the temptation to pad his offshore accounts.

The woman was as dumb as a stone, although probably a hellcat in the sack. The question was whether McCree still had sharp moments and could throw a spanner into the works. He'd personally return the phone and check on their domestic situation in that posh retirement community where they lived.

* * * *

Colene signed in at the reception desk and followed a floral-scented corridor in the independent living wing of the facility to its terminus containing suites occupied by McCree and Mrs. Sibley. Niki Foster responded to his knock. A Lycra bodysuit covered most of her tattoos and highlighted every one of her curves.

Her eyebrows rose. "Mr. Colene?"

"I found your phone where you thought it was." He handed her the instrument.

She stepped back to allow him to enter. "I woulda come down to get it."

The smell of fresh-brewed coffee came from the open kitchen straight ahead. To the left was a large living-dining room containing a Queen Anne cherry table with its leaves removed, two chairs at the table, and two against a wall. Paired leather recliners flanked a matching couch. An enormous, wide-screen TV dominated the opposite wall. English Premiere soccer was on, the sound muted. "I figured I'd stop in and see Mrs. Sibley. Is Mr. McCree around?"

"Unfortunately, Mrs. Sibley is in France. Seamus is in the study."

She led him to a large room with one wall sporting another huge TV, volume low, tuned to the same game. Facing the TV were a treadmill and an elliptical trainer. Pictures of McCree playing soccer decorated the other walls. Colene was captivated by a poster-sized black and white action photo. The photographer had caught the moment after McCree had headed the ball. Droplets of perspiration sprayed from his long, shaggy, brown hair. The ball showed a slight dent from the impact. Behind McCree's head was an out-of-focus goal post. A player with a different color jersey was about to slam into McCree.

Niki stood so close to Colene he could feel her heat. "That was just before one of his concussions."

Working at a standing glass desk, McCree ignored them. Colene looked over McCree's shoulder at the partially completed crossword puzzle. Clue 1A was "War President." L I _ _ _ L N. "Lincoln," Colene tapped the puzzle spot.

McCree ripped the puzzle from the magazine and tore it to pieces. "Out," he roared and threw the debris at Colene.

McCree's abrupt change to petulant anger shocked Colene. Given his size and strength, McCree could be a real danger if he attacked anyone. Colene retreated, and Niki pushed herself between them. She caught McCree's raised fists. "Shh, shh. It's all right, honey." She kissed him full on the mouth, and he relaxed into a rocking chair.

"He tries so hard," Niki said. She found a magazine, *Extreme Sudoku*, under the day's newspaper and flipped to a puzzle. "Try this." She handed him the mechanical pencil. McCree poked his tongue out the corner of his mouth and scribbled tiny notes in the boxes.

"I'm sorry, Mr. McCree—Seamus," Colene quickly corrected.

McCree looked up. "Do I know you? I'm sorry if I should. I just…. Do you know I played in the North American Soccer League? New York Cosmos. Played next to Franz Beckenbauer. Yes, I did." He deflated with a sigh. "Too many head balls. Too many."

Same words. "Seamus," he said. "Tell me about your investments."

McCree nodded sagely. "Best investment I made was buying Berkshire Hathaway in 1983 at a thousand bucks a share."

"Great buy!" Colene said, and meant it. "But I meant your current portfolio."

McCree's shoulders slumped, his head drooped, his knees flexed. It was like someone had stuck a needle in him and let the air out. "I don't know," he mumbled. "Niki?"

Niki gripped Colene's forearm and pulled him across the hall to a bedroom with a king-sized bed, which he tried hard to ignore after she closed the door behind them.

"That picture you was looking at?" She kept her voice low and glanced frequently at the door. "Seamus saved the goal, but the other guy cracked his head into the post. Seamus was out for ten minutes. Ten minutes! And played the rest of the game. Can you believe it? They asked him how many fingers he could see. He guessed two, because they always held up two fingers. Talk about stupid!" She gazed into Colene's eyes, lightly touched his arm, and licked her lips. "I'm sorry, it just makes me mad. I stopped by the safety deposit box on the way home." She removed a set of files hidden under sweaters in the bottom dresser drawer. "Here's everything I have." She leaned into him and kissed his cheek. "I think we need to hurry."

* * * *

Colene now was sure Niki had her hooks into a clueless McCree. It would almost be criminal if Colene didn't help himself while helping her. He needed to forget about the promise of her kiss—she was just the kind to hit him up with some trumped-up sexual harassment crap. He'd make sure not to be alone with her again. The safest approach was to get her to sign over the power of attorney.

She wasn't loyal to McCree—she didn't deserve his money, but he couldn't avoid that without her making a stink. He'd make sure McCree had fine care, even if he stayed in the memory unit for thirty years. Niki would be better taken care of than she ever dreamed. Even the charities McCree chose would eventually get something. The key to making this a win-win-win situation was pay off Niki up front and get her out of the picture.

The problem was most dementia units required monthly payments. Colene was sure he could negotiate payment for McCree's continued use of the apartment and eventual stay in the dementia unit using an overly generous annuity that included cost-of-living increases. If the institution saw a big enough profit, they'd go for it. Given the cost of care and McCree's young age, he guessed $5 million bucks would cover it. Colene's commission would be $1.5 million.

Niki was entitled to half of McCree's estate, so Colene could justify using $2.5 million to buy her a life annuity. She'd thank him each month when the money arrived—another $750,000 commission to him. *But, was it worth the risk?*

He'd draw up two plans—one strictly by the books, the other following his recent thinking—and see if McCree showed any spark.

* * * *

Niki arrived alone for the scheduled meeting with Colene. "Seamus wasn't doing good today, so I left him in the lock-down area."

Colene tried to determine whether she was wearing a bra underneath the blouse with its top three buttons undone. He forced his gaze up to her eyes. She smelled citrus fresh today but looked discouraged. "Lock-down?"

"To keep memory people from wandering away. Seamus got lost once, so I have to leave him there if I go out. He's slipping. This morning, he was calling me by his ex's name while we were… well, before we got out of bed. That's never happened."

Colene's face warmed as he remembered the promise of Niki's kiss, and he called his administrative assistant to join them at the conference table. Niki kicked off her shoes and tucked her legs underneath her. Her skirt rode up, showing so much leg he wondered if he might find out if her panties matched her bra, or lack thereof. She smoothed her hair behind her ears, displaying diamond earrings worth at least twenty grand. That girl had done well for herself, lining her nest at McCree's expense.

Colene pulled one pile of papers toward him, pushing the by-the-books set away. "I've drawn up a plan, but I had hoped Mr. McCree would be able to confirm that we've accounted for all his assets."

"He's too far gone for that. Far as I know everything is in them files." She reached past him, brushing his arm with her chest, to tap the files she had given him last week. "Now, whatcha got?"

"As you can imagine," Colene removed the fastener holding the red leather portfolio closed and placed the folder between them on the table, "this is a very complicated situation, what with domestic and foreign assets, Mr. McCree's potentially extremely long-term care needs, and your needs as well. How his care plays out could have a significant negative impact on your personal situation with ramifications for cash flow and asset growth." He watched her eyes glaze as words rolled off his tongue. The woman kept nodding, probably embarrassed to admit it was all gobbledygook to her.

She eventually interrupted his flow. "How about we cut to the chase and you tell me what this means for me… and for Seamus."

He put on his winningest smile, thought about touching her arm, but then remembered why he'd asked his AA to join them. "Now don't you worry. I'm sure you'll be pleased with the arrangements." He described how they could use an annuity to guarantee McCree's care in the facility.

"He'd always have a place there?" Her eyes shone with excitement.

"That guarantee costs five million dollars." At her expected gasp, he held up a finger to forestall her objections. "This way, we free up the remainder of his estate to provide for you."

She pulled her bottom lip up over her top lip. "I don't understand that."

"We'll trifurcate Mr. McCree's assets. Under the current will, half of his estate goes to you. By financing his long-term care needs up front, we satisfy your fiduciary responsibilities to manage Mr. McCree's assets to ensure his well-being. Rather than waiting until his actual death to allocate the remainder of his estate, we do that now. We are still unsure of the value of the foreign assets, but given a conservative accounting, we know Mr. McCree is worth over ten million. Setting aside the five million for his continuing lifetime care leaves five million, half of which is yours. My proposal is to immediately allocate your half to you." Making sure he had her full attention, he delivered the baited hook. "That's two and a half million for you. Today. Right?"

Her eyes widened. "Wow."

"You've already said you don't want to be managing millions, so we'll buy a similar annuity for you." He shifted through the pile of papers and pulled out the annuity quote he had obtained. "Your initial payment would be approximately twelve thousand dollars."

Her expression soured. "Seamus pays me way more than that now. Plus health insurance. And I don't have no living expenses."

The AA recognized Niki's misunderstanding before Colene. "Ms. Foster," she said. "What Mr. Colene means is that's twelve thousand *a month*."

"Oh?" A smile crept onto her face. "Oh!"

"We would have to pay for your medical insurance," Colene added. "And rent once Mr. McCree is fully institutionalized. But the annual total is almost a hundred and fifty thousand a year—before taxes, of course. And it goes up each year by three percent."

"You can do that? It's legal?"

He manufactured the brilliant smile again. "Now, with your power of attorney, you can do this all yourself. Or, if you want to make it easier, you'll sign the power of attorney over to me, and I'll take care of the details. I'll put everything in a trust for you and administer it, so you don't have to worry. We'll place Mr. McCree's residual assets in domestic and tax-advantaged offshore holding trusts."

"I wouldn't know nothing about that."

Well, duh. "That's why we'll handle those details for you as part of our annual retainer."

Confusion etched her face. "Retainer?"

"Tax laws change. Frequently." Blathering on about monitoring investments, accounting, tax filings, fixed costs, variable costs, he eventually retrieved another schedule and placed it in front of her. He tapped it. "It's all here."

She had the deer-in-the-headlights look. Per his plan. Now was the time for his final gamble. "I know there's a lot here. Perhaps you'd like to take it home? Read it to determine if you have any questions? Show it all to Mr. McCree if you think he'd be interested."

"I don't read so good. Just tell me in English what I'm signing."

"Sure. Sure." He could taste how close this was to working. "Once you sign this one, we can officially implement the plan. The cost to do all this work—" he riffled through the folder, letting the pages tick against each other, setting up a mini-breeze to illustrate how much effort this took "—is a flat fee of one hundred thousand dollars."

When she did not object, he continued. "We'll finalize the annuities for Mr. McCree and yourself and invest the remaining assets in appropriate trusts. We'll continually research and implement appropriate offshore tax-limiting opportunities to allow as much money as possible to flow to beneficiaries, not be wasted on taxes."

She licked her lips. Colene figured she, too, could taste the payoff. "All that," she said, "for only a hundred grand?"

"The upfront fee. As I mentioned, we'll incur ongoing fees to administer the trusts once they're set up."

She nodded, as if she remembered they had previously discussed the fees. "There's nothing illegal about these trusts? I don't want to get involved in nothing illegal." She leaned back, stretching the blouse tight across her chest. "Those days are past."

"It's all here." He shifted his bulk in the chair and counseled himself to silence.

"Where do I sign?"

He had marked each signature spot with a transparent "sign here" sticker. His AA witnessed the parts that needed to be notarized, and he sent Niki away with the suggestion she store her copies in her safe deposit box.

* * * *

Three weeks later, Colene let Niki and McCree into his office. McCree looked shabby and smelled like he hadn't bathed in a week. His eyes never left the rug. Niki all but ignored McCree, and Colene wondered if she'd take off, now that she had everything she could get from the poor guy. That might be a good thing.

He handed Niki the copy of her annuity and a checkbook and credit card to access her money. She leafed through the material, now patting McCree like he was a dog.

Even dogs have better memories.

Niki smiled. "Then we're done."

McCree rose and pointed a finger at Colene's heart. "Do you recall at our first meeting. you asked me to remember something?"

Colene felt paralyzed by the strength of McCree's blue-eyed stare. He wanted this loon out.

"Helen Smith," McCree said, "lives at fifty-three Scrivener Place, Deerfield. Ring a bell? I fed you that prime number nonsense, and I screwed up the time, date, and months of the year."

Before Colene could gather McCree's meaning, angry shouting penetrated his office walls. Niki flashed a badge at him. "FBI. I'm Agent Prescott. We have a federal warrant for your arrest."

She opened the door to two burly agents who yanked him to his feet and slapped old-fashioned cuffs on his wrists. Colene choked down bile searing his throat.

Niki read Colene the Miranda warning. "Enjoy your perp walk."

The first words Colene managed were, "I don't understand."

"Seamus?" She beamed at McCree.

"They have you on multiple counts of grand larceny and money laundering. I was delighted when the FBI asked me to participate in this sting. What I find most despicable is your abuse of fiduciary duty. You believed we," he pointed to himself and Niki, "were incompetent, simply sheep to be sheared. Niki, too stupid to understand your legal maneuvering. Me, mentally out of it.

"Those annuities you bought? Totally unsuitable, and you didn't disclose the millions you earned in commissions. You sold my index funds and bought front-end load funds, earning yourself more undisclosed commissions. At every opportunity, you lined your pockets at my expense. You thought Niki didn't know about my property in Spain, since it wasn't listed on any of the material she gave you, and you transferred it to an outfit you control in the Cayman Islands. Not to mention—"

"Who. Are. You?" Colene gasped for air like a flounder hauled from the water and dumped on the pier.

"One hell of a first-time actor, wouldn't you say? Just so you know, a judge approved me to follow every electronic move you made. The insurance company and mutual funds were happy to cooperate once we provided documentation of your chicanery. They set up bogus transactions to follow the money trail to your Cayman Island accounts. With that information, we can seek full restitution for Mrs. Sibley. She's the doll who alerted the FBI."

James M. Jackson authors the prize-winning Seamus McCree series consisting of six novels, one novella, and several short stories. Jim splits his time between the deep woods of Michigan's Upper Peninsula and Georgia's Lowcountry. He claims the moves between locations are weather-related, but others suggest they may have more to do with not overstaying his welcome. He is the past president of the 700+ member Guppy Chapter of Sisters in Crime. You can find information about Jim and his books at jamesmjackson.com.